ALSO BY GREG KEYES

The Infernal City: An Elder Scrolls Novel

LORD OF SOULS

An Elder Scrolls Novel

LORD
OF
SOULS

An Elder Scrolls Novel

GREG KEYES

TITAN BOOKS

Lord of Souls: An Elder Scrolls Novel
Print edition ISBN: 9780857680877
E-book edition ISBN: 9780857686589

Published by Titan Books
A division of Titan Publishing Group
144 Southwark Street
London
SE1 0UP

First edition September 2011

3 5 7 9 10 8 6 4 2

Lord of Souls: An Elder Scrolls Novel is a work of fiction. Names, places, and incidents
either are products of the author's imagination or are used fictitiously.

www.bethsoft.com
www.titanbooks.com

Book design by Liz Cosgrove

Did you enjoy this book? We love to hear from our readers. Please email us at reader-
feedback@titanemail.com or write to us at Reader Feedback at the above address.

To receive advance information, news, competitions, and exclusive offers online, please
sign up for the Titan newsletter on our website: www.titanbooks.com

A CIP catalogue record for this title is available from the British Library.

Printed and bound in Great Britain by CPI Group UK Ltd.

For Richard Curtis

ACKNOWLEDGMENTS

Thanks to Tricia Pasternak, my editor, and Mike Braff, her assistant. Thanks also to Peter Weissman for copyediting and Nancy Delia for production editing, Joe Scalora for marketing, David Moench for publicity, and Scott Shannon for publishing. Thanks to Paul Youll for the cover art and Dreu Pennington-McNeil for the cover design. Once again, thanks to Pete Hines, Kurt Kuhlmann, Bruce Nesmith, and Todd Howard for their input, advice, and a great playground to run around in.

PART I

PROLOGUE

Attrebus never saw the thing that cut open his belly and sent his guts spilling out into his arms. It happened in the dark, and the only things he remembered other than the agony was the stink of his bowels and something like rotting ginger—and Sul dragging him along, cursing in a language Attrebus didn't understand.

Now the pain—for so long the only thing real to him—was fading as his body finally understood it was done.

It was possible he was dead already—he wasn't sure what death was supposed to be like. He hadn't paid that much attention to such things when he should have.

He started, as from a dream of falling, and for a moment he thought he was falling, because all of his weight had vanished. With an effort he opened his eyes, but there wasn't much to see; the air was full of ash, a gray cloud that extended in every direction. He saw his companion Sul a few yards from him but steadily drifting off. Presently the dust would make him a shadow, and then nothing at all.

It was hard to breathe; the gray powder cloyed in his nostrils and mouth. After a few more breaths he realized that soon enough his lungs would fill up with the stuff and that would be that.

It was so hard to care. He was weak, tired, and even if he lived, the things he still had to do seemed impossible. No one could blame him if he quit, could they? Not now.

No one would even know.

And so he drifted, the ash caking his blood-soaked gambeson and hands, enclosing him like a shroud, preparing him almost gently for the moment his heart finally stopped.

In the darkness behind his eyes little sparks appeared and died, each dimmer than the last, until only one remained, fading. In it he saw the face of a young woman, tiny as with distance, and from somewhere heard a vast chorale of despair and terror that seemed to fill the universe. He saw his father on a burning throne, his face blank, as if he didn't realize what was happening to him. The wavering colors expanded, pushing the murk away, and the woman appeared again as his father faded. He knew her features, her curling black hair, but he couldn't remember her name. He noticed she was holding something up for him to see; a little doll that looked like him, but couldn't be him, because it was stronger, smarter, better than he was, made in the image of a man incapable of giving in or giving up.

She kissed the doll lightly on the head and then looked at him expectantly.

And so, beginning to weep, he cracked his dust-caked lips and summoned the air that remained in his lungs.

"Sul," he croaked.

The other man was hardly visible, a darker patch in the ash.

"Sul!" This time he managed to shout it, and pain lanced through him again.

"Sul!" Now it seemed to thunder in his ears, and everything spun. He thought he saw a sort of orange flash out in the gray, a sphere that appeared, expanded, passed through him, and then went on beyond his sight.

But it might have been the agony, taking him away.

Yet the light remained, the images continued. He saw the doll again, lying near this time, on a little gray bed. Its head was porcelain, and not unlike a hundred such likenesses of himself he'd seen over the years. The cloth of the torso was torn open, and the stuffing was coming out. As he watched, huge hands took up the doll and poked the stuffing back in, but there wasn't enough to fill it, so one of the hands vanished and returned with a wad of gray and shoved that in, too, before sewing up the doll with a needle and thread. When all the stitches were made and pulled tight, a knife came down to cut it.

He screamed, as air sucked into his lungs and a thousand pins seemed to sink into every inch of his flesh. He tried to vomit, but nothing came up, and he lay there sobbing, knowing nothing could ever be the same, that nothing would ever seem as bright or clean as it might have once. He cried like a baby, without coherent thought, without shame. A long time he did that, but in the end there remained something so hard and insoluble that it could never be made into tears and drained away. But he could feel the bitterness of it and make it anger, and in that he found at least a shadow of resolve, something he could nurse and make stronger in time.

He opened his eyes.

He lay inside a room like a gray box, with no discernable entrance or exit. Light seemed to filter through the walls themselves—he cast no shadow. The air had a stale, burnt taste, but he was no longer choking, and his chest rose and fell.

He sat up and his hands went reflexively to his belly. He realized then that he was naked, and he saw that a thick white scar ran from his crotch up to the base of his sternum.

"Divines," he gasped.

"I wouldn't invoke them here," a feminine voice warned.

He swung his head around and saw her. She was as naked as he, sitting with her knees drawn up to her chest. Her hair was rosy gold, her skin alabaster white, her eyes twin emeralds. She had the slender, pointed ears of an elf.

"Do you know where we are?" he asked.

"In Oblivion," she said. "In the realm of Malacath."

"Malacath," he murmured, touching his scar. It was still tender.

"That is what he calls himself," the woman said.

"My name is Attrebus," he said. "Whom do I have the honor of addressing?"

"You may call me Silhansa," she replied.

"How long have you been here, Silhansa?" he asked.

"Not much longer than you," she said. "At least I think not. It's hard to tell, with no sun or moon, only the endless gray."

"How did you end up here?"

She shrugged. "I'm not sure."

He paused, to give her a chance to ask something of him if she wished, but when she showed no sign of doing so, he pressed on.

"How do you know this is Malacath's realm? Have you seen him?"

"I heard a voice, and he said his name. That's all I know. But I'm frightened." She paused, and she looked as if she had forgotten something. "What about you? How did you get here?"

"It's a long story," he said.

"Please," Silhansa said. "Your voice calms me. What brought you to this terrible place?"

"I had a companion," Attrebus said. "A Dark Elf—a Dunmer—named Sul. Have you seen him?"

"Yours is the only face I have seen since coming here," she said. "Tell me your story, please."

Attrebus sighed. "Where are you from?" he asked.

"Balfiera," she replied.

He nodded. "So we're both from Tamriel—that helps. I'm from Cyrodiil, myself." He scratched his chin and found a beard. How much time had passed?

"Okay," he said. "I'll try to explain. Not long ago, a thing entered our world from Oblivion, an island that floats through the air, with a city upon it. Wherever the island flies, all those beneath it die and rise up again, undead. My companion and I were pursuing this island."

"Why?"

"To stop it, of course," he said, understanding how arrogant he sounded, how stupid. "Stop it before it destroyed all of Tamriel."

"You're a hero, then. A warrior."

"Not a very good one," he said. "But we tried as best we could. Before I met him, my companion Sul was trapped in

Oblivion for many years, and knows its ways. Umbriel—that's the name of the island—was too far away for us to reach in time—"

"In time for what?"

"I'll get to that in a moment," Attrebus said.

"I'm sorry. I didn't mean to interrupt, but this is a strange tale."

"No stranger than being imprisoned by a daedra prince."

"You have a point there," she allowed.

"To make it brief," he said, "Sul took us on a shortcut through Oblivion to get ahead of Umbriel."

"Did you stop it, then?"

"No," he said. "We didn't have a chance. The lord of Umbriel was too strong for us. He captured us and would have killed us, but Sul managed to escape into Oblivion, and brought me with him. But we were lost, far away from the paths Sul knew. We wandered through nightmare places. Just before coming here, we were in the realm of Prince Namira, or at least that's what Sul thought. Something there did this." He indicated the scar.

"I've been wondering how anyone could survive such a wound," Silhansa said.

"Me, too," Attrebus replied. "Sul must have gotten us out of Namira's realm. I remember floating in gray ash, choking to death. Then I woke here." He didn't want to think about his dream, much less talk about it.

"And so your quest is ended. I'm sorry."

"It's not ended," he insisted. "I'll find Sul, and we'll get out of here somehow."

"What makes you so determined?"

"It's my people at stake, my world. And there is—someone

counting on me, waiting for me. She might be safe, but if she isn't—"

"Ah," Silhansa said knowingly. "A woman. A lover."

"A woman, yes, but she isn't my lover—she's a friend, someone who depends on me."

"But you want her to be your lover."

"I . . . I haven't thought about it, and it's neither here nor there."

"And your friend Sul? He's driven by love as well?"

"Sul? He's driven by vengeance. He hates Vuhon, the master of Umbriel. I think he hates him more than I can imagine hating anything, and I've been expanding my capabilities in that sort of thing lately."

He found himself touching his scar again. Silhansa noticed.

"Do you think Malacath healed you?" she asked.

"Maybe—if this is his realm I suppose it is possible—but I've no idea why. Malacath isn't exactly known for his kindness."

"You know something about him?"

Attrebus nodded. "A little. My nurse used to tell me a story about him. It was one of my favorites."

"Really? Could you tell it? I know little about the daedra."

"I don't tell it as well as she did," he admitted, "but I remember the tale." He paused for a moment, remembering Helna's singsong voice. He closed his eyes and pictured his bed, and her sitting there, hands folded. For just an instant he felt the shadow of the comfort he'd known then, the innocence that had protected him from the world.

"In the bygone-by," he began, "there was a hero named Trinimac, the greatest knight of the Ehlnofey, champion of the

Dragon of Time. One fine day he betook himself to seek out Boethiah, the daedra prince, and chastise him for his misdeeds.

"But Boethiah knew Trinimac was coming, and he put on the appearance of an old woman and stood beside the trail.

" 'Good day, old woman,' Trinimac said when he came along. 'I'm in search of Prince Boethiah, to chastise him. Can you tell me where I might find the scoundrel?'

" 'I know not,' the old woman told him, 'but down the road is my younger brother, and he might know. I'll gladly tell you where he is, if you will but scratch my back.'

"Trinimac agreed, but when he saw her back, it was covered in loathsome boils. Nevertheless, having said he would, he scratched the noisome sores.

" 'Thank you,' she said. 'You'll find my brother on the road to your left at the next crossroads.'

"Trinimac went on his way. Boethiah scurried ahead by a shortcut and put on the appearance of an old man.

" 'Good day, old man,' Trinimac said, on meeting him. 'I saw your elder sister, and she said you might know the path to Prince Boethiah's house.'

" 'I do not,' the old man told him. 'But my little sister knows. I'll tell you where to find her if you will only wash my feet.'

"Trinimac agreed, but found the old man's feet even more disgusting and smelly than the old woman's back. Still, he had made a bargain. The old man told him where to find the younger sister, and again Trinimac went on—and again Boethiah went ahead, and put on the guise of a beautiful young woman.

"Now, Trinimac was dreading the meeting with the younger sister, fearing he would have to wash or scratch something even worse than he already had, but when he saw the beautiful girl, he felt better.

" 'I met your elder brother,' he said, 'and he told me you would know the way to the house of Prince Boethiah.'

" 'Indeed, I do,' she declared. 'And I will gladly tell you if you will but give me a kiss.'

" 'That I can do,' Trinimac said, but as he leaned forward to kiss her, her mouth opened wide—so wide that his whole head went in, and Boethiah swallowed him in a single gulp.

"Then Boethiah took on Trinimac's form, and made him burp and fart and say foolish things, until finally he squeezed out a great pile of dung, and that was what was left of Trinimac. The dung got up and slunk away in shame, a proud knight no longer. He became Prince Malacath, and all of those who loved him changed as well and became the orcs."

The woman's eyes had a peculiar look in them.

"That was your favorite story?" she said.

"When I was seven, yes."

She shook her head. "You people are always so literal-minded."

"What do you mean?" A thought occurred. "You're Altmer, yes? A High Elf? How is it you've never heard of Trinimac?"

"I have, of course, heard of Trinimac," Silhansa said, placing her right hand on the floor, palm up. It seemed to melt and flow into the surface.

"What are you—"

But Silhansa—still crouching—began to grow, and quickly. And as she grew, she changed; the colors of her eyes and hair faded to gray, her face broadened, became piglike, and tusks emerged. All signs of womanhood vanished, and as she stood, he felt the floor lurch beneath him, realizing that she held him in her palm and was lifting him. The walls of the prison dissolved, and the thing that had called itself Silhansa was now a hundred feet tall. The hand holding him brought him up to the monstrous face, and the other hand came up, too, presenting Sul, as naked as he and just as captive.

"Malacath," Attrebus gasped.

"So you call me," Malacath said, his voice like beams of wood rending, his breath a foul wind. His eyes seemed empty, but when Attrebus looked into them, crooked things shimmered into his mind and ate his thoughts.

Their surroundings had changed, too. Around them rose a garden of slender trees, and wound about the trunks were vines festooned with lilylike flowers. A multitude of spheres moved, deep in the colorless sky, as distant and pale as moons. He heard birds chirping, but it was a doleful sound, as if something with a vague memory of having been a bird was trying to reproduce sounds it no longer felt.

"Prince," Attrebus said, starting to shiver. "I did not mean to insult you. It was only a story I heard as a little boy. I don't presume—"

"Hush," Malacath said, and Attrebus choked as his mouth filled once again with ash. "I've heard enough from you. You don't interest me. But you, Sul . . . I remember you. You swore an oath by me once, against your own gods. You've slipped through my realm before, without visiting. I am offended."

"My apologies, Prince," Sul said. "I was in a hurry."

"And yet this time you demand my attention. In my own house."

"Yes, Prince."

The massive lids of Malacath's eyes lowered over his eldritch gaze. His nostrils widened.

"It's still there," the prince's voice ground out, almost below the level of hearing. "This place, this shadow of a garden, this echo of something that once was—you know such phantoms, Sul?"

"Yes," Sul husked.

"You loved a woman, and for her you destroyed your city, your nation, and your people."

"I did not mean to," Sul said. "I only meant to save her life. It was Vuhon—"

"Do not diminish yourself. Do not seek to lessen the beauty of the deed." Malacath opened his eyes and stared at them, and now Attrebus felt as if hot brass was being poured into his skull.

"I have healed your broken body, and that of your companion," he said. "What should I do with you now?"

"Release us," Sul said.

"To do what?"

"Destroy Umbriel."

"You tried. You failed."

"Because we did not have the sword," Attrebus managed to gasp through the cloying dust.

"What sword?" The air seemed to thicken, and all the hairs on Attrebus's arms stood out like quills.

"There is a sword named Umbra—" Attrebus began.

"I know it," Malacath said. "A tool of Prince Clavicus Vile, a stealer of souls."

"More than that," Attrebus replied. "The sword was prison

to a creature that also calls itself Umbra. This creature escaped the blade and stole much power from Clavicus Vile, and it is that power that motivates Umbriel, the city Sul and I seek to destroy. We believe that if we can find the sword, we can use it to reimprison this creature and defeat Umbriel."

Malacath just stared at him for a moment, and then the great head leaned toward one vast shoulder a bit. There was something oddly childlike about the motion.

"I have heard that Vile is weak, and that he searches for something. I have no love for him. Or any of the others." He glanced back at Sul, his vast brows caving into a frown. "How I laughed when you betrayed them, turned your homeland into no less an ash pit than my realm. The proud issue of the Velothi, humbled at last. By one of their own. And still there is the curse you made, unfulfilled."

"You can help him fulfill it," Attrebus blurted. He was shaking uncontrollably, but he tried to keep his voice steady.

"You knew who Sul was the minute you saw him," he went on. "You remember his curse after all these years. You healed us and interviewed me. In disguise. To see what we're up to. To assure yourself that the curse Sul made all those years ago is still walking with him. That he still craves vengeance."

Malacath's head shifted again, and behind him vines collapsed and formed into a cloud of black moths that swarmed about them.

"There are a few things I have a sort of love for," the daedra said. "What Sul carries with him is one of those things. So yes, I will help you further. The sword, Umbra—do you know where it is?"

Sul's mouth set in reluctant lines.

"How else will you go there if I do not send you?"

"Somewhere in Solstheim, I believe," Sul finally replied. "In the hands of someone who wears a signet ring with a draugr upon it."

Malacath nodded; to Attrebus it seemed a mountain was falling toward him.

"I can take you to Solstheim," the prince said. "Do not disappoint me."

Then both gigantic eyes focused on Attrebus. "And you—if I ever have use for you, you will know it."

"Yes, Prince," Attrebus replied.

The god grinned a mouthful of sharp teeth. Then he slapped his palms together.

———

"It's real," Mazgar gra Yagash breathed, staring, fighting the urge to draw her sword.

It wasn't often you saw a mountain fly.

She doffed her helmet for a better look. As it passed beyond the tallest birches, she saw how it hung in the sky—an inverted mountain, with the peak stabbing toward the land below.

Next, her gaze picked out the strange spires and glistening structures atop the thing, structures that could only have been made by some sort of hands. A forest clung to the upper rim as well, its boughs and branches dropping out and away from it.

"Why would you doubt it?" Brennus asked, his hands working fast with pen and paper, sketching the thing. "It's what we came to see."

"Because it's ridiculous," she said.

"I've never heard an orc use that word," he murmured. "I guess I thought you people believed in everything."

"I don't believe your nose would stand up to my fist," she replied.

"Fair enough," he said. "I don't believe that either. But since I outrank you, I also don't think you'll hit me." He pushed rusty bangs from his face and looked off at the thing. "Anyway—ridiculous or not, there it is. Aren't you supposed to be doing something?"

"Guarding you," she replied.

"I feel so safe."

She rolled her eyes. He was technically her superior, which galled, because he wasn't a soldier—or even a battlemage. Like most of the wizards in the expedition, his expertise was in learning things from a distance. His rank had been awarded by the Emperor, days before they'd left the Imperial City.

But he was probably right—as hard as it was not to stare at the thing, it was their immediate surroundings she ought to be taking in.

They were on a high, bare ridge, about thirty feet from the tree line in any direction. The air was clear and visibility good. Up ahead of her, four of Brennus's fellow sorcerers were doing their mysterious business: chanting, aiming odd devices at the upside-down flying mountain, conjuring invisible winged things she noticed only because they passed through smoke and were briefly outlined. Two others were surrounding their position with little candles that burnt with purple-black flames. They set those up every time they stopped; the candles were somehow supposed to keep all of this conjuring from being noticed by anyone—or anything.

Mazgar put her hand on the ivory grip of Sister—her sword—squinted, and licked her tusks. "I make it about six miles away. What do you reckon?"

"A little more than eight, according to Yaur's ranging charm," Brennus said.

"Bigger than I thought."

"Yah." He put the notebook down and unpacked something that looked like a spyglass but Mazgar figured wasn't. He peered through it, mumbled gobbledygook, turned a dial on the device, and looked again. He scratched his red hair, and his sallow Nibenese features fell in a frown.

"What's the matter?" she asked him.

"It's not there," he said.

"What do you mean?" she said. "I'm looking right at it."

"Right," he said. "Bit of a contradiction, I know. And I'm sure it *is* there, somehow. But all my glass sees is a bubble of Oblivion."

"A bubble of Oblivion?"

"Yah. You know, the nasty place where the daedra live? Beyond the world?"

"I know what Oblivion is," she gruffed. "My grandfather closed one of the gates Dagon opened between here and there, back when."

"Well, this is like a gate, but wrapped around itself. Pretty odd."

"Does that tell us how to fight it?"

He shrugged. "I can't think how it would," he said. "Anyway, the plan is to not fight it. We're just here to find out what we can and report back to the Emperor. It's still moving north into Morrowind. It may never threaten the Empire at all."

Mazgar looked at the island again. "How can that not be a threat?" she muttered. She felt the coarse hairs on the back of her neck standing and her heart quicken. Brennus was looking at her in apprehension, and she realized she'd been growling in the pit of her throat.

"Don't worry," he said.

"It sees us," she said.

"I doubt that," he replied.

"No," she snapped. "I can feel it, feel its eyes . . . "

"Is this supposed to be some sort of orcish sixth sense? The kind you get from not bathing?"

"I'm not joking, Brennus, something isn't right. I feel—"

But then the wind shifted, and she got the smell.

"Dead things," she snarled, clearing Sister from her sheath. Then she raised her voice. "Alarum!" she howled. She grabbed Brennus by the arm and hustled him toward the other sorcerers, where her fellow warriors were hastily trying to form a phalanx.

She wasn't quite there when they came out of the trees.

"So that's true, too," she said.

"Divines," Brennus breathed.

They looked as dead as they smelled. Many had been Argonians, obvious by their rotting snouts, decayed tails, sharp teeth set in worm-festered gums. Others looked to have been men or mer, and a few were just—things. They moved twitchily, as if uncertain how to use their limbs, but they came at a fast march.

And they *were* marching, organized, falling into ranks as

the landscape permitted. They were unevenly armed—some had swords, maces, or spears, but more than half had crude clubs or no weapons at all—but there were a lot of them, many times more than their thirty.

What surprised Mazgar most were their eyes. She had heard the rumors that an army of corpses walked beneath the flying city. She had imagined them as dumb, cattle-eyed beasts. What she saw as they drew near was something different, a glitter of malicious intelligence, a dark joy in the harm they promised.

"They're coming up from the south, too," someone shouted.

That was bad news. They'd left the horses and most of the supplies down there, not to mention their remaining six soldiers to guard them.

"Form up," Captain Falcus hollered. "We've got fighting to do."

"I thought they were supposed to be under the island," Mazgar said. "These are a long way from it."

"Well," Brennus replied, "there's the value of scouting, eh? Now we know something we didn't before. They can send their troops out. Way out."

"We can't let them trap us up here," Falcus said. "We're going to have to pick a direction and cut through."

"South takes us home, Captain," Merthun the Wall shouted.

"South it is," the captain said. "Re-form, now."

Mazgar moved to the back of the formation, along with Jarrow, Merthun, and Coals. She pulled her shield off her back and got ready, watching the rotting things approach.

"And you thought this wasn't going to be any fun," Brennus said, at her back.

Falcus shouted, and the phalanx started moving behind her. Mazgar and her line walked backward, slowly. The dead sped up, and when they were six yards away, they charged.

She howled, and Sister swung at something that had once been a two-legged lizard. The sword smashed into its head and it split open, spilling maggots and putrescence all around her. The body came on, and so she slashed at it, still retreating.

Just up the line she heard Jarrow curse and gurgle.

"Jarrow's down," Merthun shouted. "Close the gap."

They fell back, yard by yard, leaving a wake of rotting, twitching parts. She saw Jarrow's body, facedown, receding.

Then she saw him start to rise, surrounded by the things.

"Jarrow's still alive!" she bellowed.

"He's not," Merthun shouted back, his huge hammer rising and falling into the line of the enemy.

"But—" she began. Then she saw Jarrow's wound and the dark gleam in his eye, and knew it wasn't him anymore.

"Well, that's no good," Brennus opined.

"There's the south line," Falcus shouted. "Double time, soldiers. Rearguard, keep them off. We break through or die."

"I'm not dying here," Mazgar snarled, and let Sister do her work.

ONE

Wind opened Colin's eyes, but it was the unfastened window that sped his heart, and the utter lack of sound that sent his fingers to the knife under his mattress. A hand met his there and gripped his wrist, hard. He swung over to kick at the vague shadow, but he was grasped at the ankles as well, and a bag was forced over his head, followed by a return to sleep that would have been gentle if part of him wasn't screaming to the rest that he wouldn't ever wake up.

He did wake again, however. The bag and the cloying scent of somniculous remained, but the drug itself was obviously dissipated. He was lying on a hard but inconstant surface, and he soon recognized by the motion that he was in a boat, on water. His hands and feet were efficiently bound. His captors did not speak, but he could hear their breathing and exertions at the oars. He couldn't make out anything through the sack except light, but he felt the sun on his skin and guessed it was approaching midday.

Not much later, there was a bit of jostling and then the shock of the boat coming on shore. He smelled pine.

They cut the bindings on his feet and made him walk. He kept thinking he ought to say something, but his kidnappers behaved so professionally he knew there wasn't much point. There was no talking them out of whatever they were doing with him. All he could do was wait, and wonder. Would he feel it? Would he know anything had happened?

Colin killed a man once. He died confused, begging, unwilling to admit even as the knife cut into him what was happening.

He wished he could have seen his mother again, and—realizing he was weeping—felt ashamed. He'd wanted to be braver.

The hand on his arm came away. He tried not to shake.

Then one of the men made a peculiar sound, a sigh like a very tired man finally lying down.

"What?" the other asked, before sucking a sharp breath.

Colin heard two distinct thumps—then for a moment, nothing. He wondered if he should run.

"Who do you work for?" a feminine voice asked.

He recognized it, and a deep chill wracked through him. The last time he'd heard that voice had been in a house in the Market District, just before its owner slaughtered at least eight men.

"Come," she said. "Tell me."

"I'm not at liberty to say," he replied.

"Keep still," she said. A moment later the sack came off his head.

And there she was, regarding him, Letine Arese. Her small frame, turned-up nose, and short blond hair made her seem almost like a little girl, but he knew her to be thirty-one years of age, and her blue eyes held a cold intensity that was quite un-childlike.

Those eyes narrowed now.

"You look familiar," she said. "I've seen you. I suppose that makes sense."

He glanced behind her, at the two bodies on the ground. Both were male; one was an Argonian, the other a Bosmer. They both seemed quite dead, although he could not see the cause.

"They brought you out here to kill you," she said.

"I gathered that," he replied. "I'm grateful you stopped them."

"Are you? We'll get back to that in a moment." She folded her hands behind her back. She was dressed in Bosmer woods-man style, with high boots and soft leather vest and breeches. It was an odd look for her, in his experience—he'd only ever seen her in relatively fashionable city attire.

"What would you say if I told you they worked for me?" she asked.

"I would be confused," Colin said carefully.

"Yes, I should hope so," she told him. "They noticed you spying on me and brought it to my attention. So of course, I did a little checking of my own. Colin Vineben, from Anvil. Your father is dead, and your mother does laundry. You were recommended for and received training for the Penitus Oculatus, and recently were named an inspector in that organization. It was you who discovered the massacre of Prince Attrebus's personal guard and the apparent murder of the prince, and you who suggested to the Emperor that the prince wasn't actually dead. Which, as it turns out, you were right about. And now you're spying on me, but without, it seems, any official authority to do so. So I wonder if you're employed by someone else."

"Why did you kill them?" he asked.

"Because otherwise, I would have had to kill you," she snapped. "Now I have to account for them, pretend I sent them on a mission to someplace fatal. Otherwise, the two of them would have wondered why you were still walking, and after a while that wonder would have spread its way up to the minister himself."

"I don't understand," Colin said.

"I'm risking my neck for you, you idiot," Arese snapped suddenly. "Can't you see that?"

"I can see it," he replied. "I just don't get why."

She pulled a knife from her belt and stalked toward him. His chest tightened, but she merely cut the ropes that held his hands behind his back. Then she stepped back a bit and untied her pants, loosening the laces and pulling one side down, exposing her hip.

"You know what that is?" she asked, indicating a small black tattoo of a wolf's head.

He did, of course. It was the Emperor's personal brand, worn only by his innermost circle.

He didn't say anything, but she saw he recognized it, and pulled the breeches back up, tying them again.

"He put me in the minister's office ten years ago," she said. "No one knows but him and me. And now you."

"Why are you telling me this?"

"Because I need help, and I think we may have a common purpose."

"What's that?"

"To discover why Minister Hierem wants Prince Attrebus dead."

"Does he?"

"I should know," she said. "I made the arrangements for the ambush on his orders."

"Why?" Colin exploded. "If you're loyal to the Emperor—"

She barked a laugh. "You *knew*," she said. "You were there, weren't you? When I took care of Calvur and his thugs. I *knew* someone was there!" She closed her eyes for a moment, looking very tired.

"I didn't mean for the prince to come to harm," she said. "If I could have gotten word to the Emperor, I would have. It was impossible at the time, at least without revealing myself to Hierem. In the end, a decision had to be made."

"And you decided you were more important than the prince?"

"Yes. If you knew anything about him, you would probably agree."

"And yet Hierem wants him dead."

"Apparently."

"Then why hasn't the Emperor had the minister arrested?"

"When the Emperor first placed me in the ministry, he didn't have any particular worries about Hierem, only the sort of general paranoia a successful monarch must have. For most of the past ten years, the minister has been above suspicion, but a year or so ago he began testing me, first subtly, then overtly. It became clear he wanted his own private intelligence and eliminations organization, one not connected to the Penitus Oculatus or known to the Emperor. The attack on Attrebus was—surprising. I didn't see that coming. It's only because some of the assassins got greedy that the prince survived. The Emperor isn't ready to move against Hierem yet because he doesn't believe we know everything, and because the minister is politically important—very important. The Emperor has survived because he waits until he knows where all the forces are and their strengths before he strikes. Right now, Hierem thinks his actions are invisible. We want to keep it that way a bit longer. That's where you come in, if you're up to it."

"Up to what?"

"Hierem trusts me now, completely I believe. But that limits me. And I can't trust anyone else in the ministry. I can open certain doors, but I need someone who can walk through them. Can you be that man?"

Colin considered for a moment. Arese might be telling the truth and she might be lying; in a way, it didn't matter. If he agreed to help her, it gave him a chance to find the answers he sought, even if she was steering him away from them. If he told her no, it was pretty certain he was staying on this island for eternity.

"I can be that man," he told her.

TWO

When he smelled blood, Mere-Glim turned in the deep waters of the Marrow Sump, trying to find the source. Blood wasn't an unusual smell in these waters; bodies were dumped here every day, many still feebly struggling against death. But this blood was not only fresh, it had a certain rotten scent he'd come to know all too well.

He closed his eyes and flared his reptilian nostrils, and when he identified the current that carried the smell, he struck out along it, his webbed hands and feet propelling him swiftly through the clear waters. It took him only a few moments before he could see the erratically twitching figure trying to reach the surface.

By the time he reached her, the life was dimming from her eyes. He wasn't sure if she ever actually saw him. Blood still roiled in clouds from her nostrils and gaping mouth. He reached around her from behind and kicked purposefully toward the surface, but by the time he reached it, she had gone limp.

He took her into the skraw caves along the shoreline anyway, and laid her out on the little bier his coworkers had made from woven cane and grass for the dead to rest on. In the sunlight she'd looked old, worn, with black bags beneath her eyes and hair like lank kelp, but here in the phosphorescence from the cave walls she appeared younger, more like the ten or fifteen years she probably actually was. On Umbriel, people were born as adults, and those born to be skraws, to tend and harvest the sump, had nothing that resembled a childhood.

He heard others approaching and looked over his shoulder to see his friend Wert and a young skraw named Oluth.

"Joacin," Wert sighed. "I knew she couldn't last much longer."

"I'm sorry," Glim told him. "I couldn't reach her in time."

"It wouldn't have mattered," Wert said. "If you had, she might have lived another day."

"A day is a day," Glim said.

Wert knelt and studied the woman's face for a long moment, his own visage more long and doleful than usual.

"When do we move forward?" he asked without looking up. "Isn't it time to take the next step?"

"We're done with the maps," Oluth blurted. He was young, probably no more than three years old; his skin had only the barest hint of the jaundice that plagued the older skraws.

"Good," Glim replied.

"So—like Wert said—what's next?" the hatchling went on eagerly.

"I'm still planning that," Glim told him.

"You excited everyone, Glim," Wert said. "You gave us all hope. But now—some say that you're stalling."

"We have to be prepared," Glim said. "We have to be careful. Once we start, there's no turning back. Does everyone understand that?"

"They do," Wert said. "They're ready to do what you say, Glim. But you have to say something."

Glim felt his heart sink. "Soon," he said.

"How soon?"

"I'll let you know."

Wert frowned, but nodded. Then he turned to Oluth.

"Go with Glim. He'll show you about the lower sump. You'll be working down there with him."

"It'll be an honor," Oluth said.

Glim waited for Oluth to go take the vapors and felt guilty. The caustic fumes allowed the skraws to breathe underwater, but they also killed them young, as they had just killed Joacin. Of all the skraws, he was the only one who hadn't been born on Umbriel, the only Argonian—the only one who didn't need the vapors to breathe beneath the surface.

When the youngster joined him in the shallows, Glim took him down below the midway of the cone-shaped body of water and showed him the cocooned figures fastened to the wall. Inside each was something that had started as a worm smaller than his least claw, but were now in various stages of becoming inhabitants of Umbriel. He brushed against one near term, a lanky female who—in appearance—would be human. Next to her grew a brick-red creature with horns, and farther along a man with the dusky skin of a Dunmer. All began as worms, however, and beneath appearances they were all Umbrielians. He tried not to be annoyed by Oluth's eagerness as he explained the procedures for tending the unborn and moving them to the birthing pools when their time came, and how to know that time. He could tell the boy was only half paying attention. He kept glancing around, especially down, to the bottom of the sump, where the actinic glare of the connexion with the ingenium lay.

"You're curious about that?" Glim asked.

"That's the ingenium," Oluth said. "That's the heart and soul of Umbriel. If we controlled *that* . . ."

"Even if we could do it," Glim said, "that would be too much."

"But if we're to really revolt, carry the fight to the lords—"

"SSht, husst, slow down," Glim said. "Who ever said anything about taking the fight to anyone? Or fighting at all?"

"Well, I guess we thought it would come to that," Oluth said.

"Who is 'we'?" Glim asked.

"Oh." He looked embarrassed. "I wasn't supposed to tell you."

"Tell me what?"

"The younger skraws. We call ourselves the Glimmers. We've pledged to follow you and help you."

Glim absorbed that, feeling claustrophobic.

"Listen to me," he said. "Our goals are simple: We want a substitute for the vapors, so you don't have to tear your lungs up and die early just to do your job. We're looking for ways to inconvenience the lords, to make them aware of your needs. We don't want it to come to a fight."

"Right," Oluth said. "Inconvenience them. Like how?"

"Well, what do we skraws do? We keep the sump working. That means food, water, nutrients for everyone on Umbriel and the fringe gyre—and of course, we bring the newborns into the world. We just need to emphasize our worth by showing what happens if things don't get done down here—or if things break, clog up, and so forth. Do you understand?"

Oluth nodded vigorously. "I do!" he said. Then his gaze darted past Glim. "What's that?"

Glim followed his regard to a small embryo sac, nearly transparent, and the thing curled in it. It was still small, but it wasn't like a baby—more like an unfinished and undersized adult. It had scales and was a pale pink color with huge eyes and tiny little claws.

"It's an Argonian," he said.

"It looks a little like you."

"Soon enough it will look a lot like me," Mere-Glim said. "I'm an Argonian."

He'd known it was going to happen, but now that it had, he felt a sort of sick spot in his gut.

He needed to see Annaïg.

———

"I really am sorry I tried to kill you," Slyr told Annaïg.

Annaïg blinked and glanced up at the gray-skinned woman fidgeting across the table from her.

"Have you tried again, or is this still about last week?" she asked.

Slyr's red eyes widened. "I haven't tried again, I swear."

"Right. So you've apologized already," Annaïg said. "This means you're now wasting my time."

Slyr didn't reply, but she didn't leave either, just stood there, shuffling her feet a bit. Trying not to let her irritation show, Annaïg bent back to her task of emulsifying horse brains and clove oil, whisking the gray matter vigorously and adding the oil a few drops at a time. When it reached the consistency of mayonnaise, she set it aside.

Slyr was still standing there.

"What?" Annaïg exploded.

"I—you haven't assigned anything for me to do."

"Fine. I assign you to go sit in our quarters."

"I have to work," Slyr said. "Toel thinks little enough of me as it is. If he finds me idle—I worry, Annaïg."

Annaïg closed her eyes and counted to four. When she opened them, she half expected to see Slyr lunging at her with a knife, but Slyr was still just standing there looking pitiful.

"Go husk the durian," she said.

"But—"

"What now?"

"Durian is so *smelly*." She waved the back of her hand at Annaïg's preparations. "What are you doing there?"

She's just spying, Annaïg thought. Trying to steal my ideas. It didn't matter, though, did it?

"I'm extracting terror," she said.

"Come again?"

She lifted the emulsion. "Terror, fear, happiness—any strong emotion leaves something of itself in the brain."

"But if the soul has fled, hasn't all of that gone with it?"

Annaïg smiled, despite the company, and scraped some of the emulsion into a glass cylinder, divided three-quarters of the way down by a thin membrane.

"What's that?" Slyr asked, indicating the divider.

"It's the humorous membrane from a chimera-eel," she replied. "It's what allows them to change color to suit their emotions. I've altered this one to let only terror through."

"You're filtering horse-terror through eel-skin?"

"Very specially prepared eel-skin," she replied. She placed the tube in a small centrifuge and cranked the handle, spinning the vial. After a few moments she detached it and held it up, showing a pale yellow ichor in the bottom.

"That's terror?" Slyr said. She sounded skeptical.

"Do you want to understand this or not?" Annaïg asked.

"I do. Please. I'm sorry."

"Sit down, then—you're making me nervous, hovering there."

Slyr scooched onto a stool and folded her hands in her lap.

"You were right, in a way—terror—or any emotion—isn't merely chemical. But the substance acts as a vessel, a shaper of soul stuff, just as—at a higher level—does the brain and body." She opened a small valve on the bottom of the tube and let the liquid empty into a small glass cone. She then sealed a second, identical cone base-to-base with the first to form a spiculum. She shook the container so that the liquid coated the interior surface evenly, then slid the whole thing into a coil of translucent fibers that in turn was connected to a pulsing cable of the same material that came up through the floor and workbench.

"Now we pass soul energy through it," Annaïg said. "The chemical terror will attract what it needs to become the real thing."

For a moment nothing happened; then the spiculum took on a faint lavender glow, and quite abruptly became opaque. Annaïg waited another moment then removed the spiculum and shook it again. The coating inside the crystal sloughed free and settled into one end, a viscous powder. She unsealed the hlzu gum that held the spiculum together with spirits of coatin. Then she emptied a bit of the newly formed substance into a horn spoon and carefully handed it to Slyr.

"And there you have it," she said.

Slyr blinked at the lavender stuff.

"Am I to taste this?"

"You may if you wish."

"Perhaps not," Slyr said, dipping her finger into it experimentally. A bit clung there, and she rubbed it back and forth. "It feels—" But then her face transformed; her eyes became huge, and the veins on her neck stood out as she suddenly began shrieking. She fell from her stool and twisted into a fetal position, fighting for the air she needed to keep screaming.

"Or you can just touch it," Annaïg said. "It's absorbed just as readily through the skin."

Slyr's only response was to quiver uncontrollably—she was past screaming now.

For Annaïg, the next few seconds stretched thin and brittle; part of her wanted to continue watching the other woman suffer. Anger was beautiful, because its core was the absence of all doubt. When anger wrapped you up in yourself and you knew that you were right and righteous—that the very universe was in agreement with you—at that moment you were a god, and anyone who crossed or disagreed with you was worse than wrong, they were heretics, apostates, twisted in the very womb. Slyr deserved this. And much, much more.

Then why, beneath the wonderful, purifying rage, did she feel sick? Why did she suspect that *she* was the one in the wrong?

Because she wasn't really angry at Slyr. She was angry because all her hopes of escaping Umbriel were destroyed. She was angry at the stupidity of a little girl who thought she could save the world like a hero from the songs, and now was going to spend what little of her life remained in a disgusting place among disgusting people.

And one of those people was Slyr. But somehow she couldn't watch her lose her mind.

So, with a sigh, she unstoppered the bottle she'd fixed for herself, in case she had an accident during the experiment, and waved it under Slyr's nose. The other woman inhaled, gasped, gave one great shake, then sagged. She was still breathing hard but her eyes were clear.

"S-Summmpslurry," Slyr managed, her breath still ragged.

She traveled her gaze over her body, as if fearing she was missing limbs.

"You stopped it, didn't you? You could have let it go on and on."

"For a few hours, yes."

"It would have driven me mad."

Annaïg shrugged, still feeling angry and helpless, and now trying not to cry. What was wrong with her?

"I'm not so convinced you're sane as it is," she said.

Slyr chuckled harshly. "I soiled myself," she said.

"I didn't need to know that," Annaïg replied.

"I guess not." Her eyes dropped down. "Toel doesn't care what happens to me. No one does. No one would have even reprimanded you—"

"I'm not like you, Slyr," Annaïg said.

Slyr shakily came to her feet and gathered her clothing around her.

"Maybe not," she said. "But you're closer than you were."

And then she left. Annaïg almost thought the woman had a faint look of triumph on her face.

When Slyr was gone, Annaïg's tears came.

For a long time after being trapped on Umbriel, she hadn't cried. She watched the city she grew up in destroyed, and although she hadn't seen it, in her heart she knew her father was dead, and Hecua, and every other soul she had ever known before coming to this place, to Umbriel—which was responsible for all of that murder. She had kept it all in, bound up with hope and purpose, freighted by the need to survive to get from one day to the next—and yes, at times by wonder, by the sheer alien assault on the senses that was Umbriel.

But after Slyr poisoned her, those bands began to fray, and when at last she was ready to escape, to leave Umbriel, they had broken, because she wouldn't have to live each day in fear any longer, because she didn't need such unnatural control. And then she and Mere-Glim had flown out across the night to where Prince Attrebus was waiting, with *his* strength, his courage to sustain her.

But Umbriel hadn't let them go, and now . . .

"You cry far too much," a soft voice said behind her.

She closed her eyes, but he knew, so she didn't bother to

wipe them. It would only show further weakness.

She turned with her cheeks still glistening and stood up from her stool.

"Chef Toel," she said.

When she first met Toel, she'd thought him darkly, devilishly handsome, and his unbelievably blue eyes had absorbed her. Now he only seemed dangerous, like a viper.

He looked meaningfully at the purplish substance in the crystal cone.

"What have you there?" he asked

"Terror, Chef."

"Well, give us a taste, then."

She hesitated. "It's quite strong, Chef."

"I'll take care, then."

She doled him out a bit and watched as he carried it to his lips and let it touch his tongue. His eyes widened dreamily and he hissed before taking several shuddering breaths. Little sparks danced on his skin, and she felt the tiny hairs on her face pull toward him.

Then he looked down at her, his gaze still a little strange.

"Exquisite," he murmured. "You have so much talent, little one. Such beautiful ideas. If only you had—well, a little drive. A bit of ambition."

He smiled slightly. "I saw Slyr. She looked as if she'd seen the worst thing in the world."

"She tasted it, Chef."

"You let her?"

"I did."

"Well, well. An improvement. But why is she still walking?

She hasn't a constitution for such things, as I do. I think it should have destroyed her mind."

"I gave her an antidote," Annaïg admitted.

He stared at her a moment, then made a slight tsking sound beneath his breath. His eyes—which had held her with a certain sparkle—dulled and shifted.

"Very well, then," he said. "Bring that around. I've a mind to use it in seasoning the suspiration of hare and sulfur I'm preparing for Lord Irrel's thirty-third course. A little something different for him. And perhaps, if you could, also make me a bit of remorse?"

"I'm not certain a horse can feel remorse, Chef."

"Very well," he said. "Kohnu was badly burned this morning distilling phlogiston. I shall send his brain over."

"But if he's still alive—"

"Healing him would take time and resources, and he wouldn't be able to work for weeks. He'll serve me better this way."

She knew Kohnu. He was funny, always telling little self-effacing jokes and clowning about with the produce.

"Chef—" she began.

He rolled his eyes. "It's not as if you have to kill him yourself," he said. Then he left.

She sat back down, trembling.

"What am I doing?" she whispered. She needed Glim.

"What *are* you doing?" Mere-Glim asked the next night, at their weekly meeting. It took place in an old slurry filter, empty and forgotten a few yards below the pantry. From it Annaïg could hear what was going on in the kitchens—which at night was usually nothing—and Glim was only feet away from the tube that would take him back down into the sump, if anyone approached.

"I'm trying to figure out why we can't leave," she told him. "It's got something to do with the way Umbriel uses souls, I'm pretty sure. At least it's a place to start. But I can't just experiment without producing anything, or Toel would start thinking I'm no longer useful. And if that happens, well—it's over. Just ask poor Kohnu."

"You're doing what you have to do," Glim said. "You can't feel bad because of what Toel does."

"He might have let Kohnu live if it wasn't for me."

"Might-have and mud are fine places to wallow," Glim said.

"That's easy for you to say," Annaïg replied. "You haven't gotten anyone killed." She clenched her fists. "I've gotten a lot of people killed, Glim, not just Kohnu. Everyone in Qijne's kitchen. And probably Attrebus."

"Still no word from him?"

"No," she said miserably. "I talked to him just before we tried to escape. He was in our path, Glim. I fear the worst."

"You don't know, though," Glim said. "He might have lost Coo, or maybe he's somewhere the enchantment doesn't work."

"Maybe."

"But even if something happened to him, it's not your fault."

"If I knew more, had more to tell him—"

"You've done more than he could have ever expected," Glim replied. "More than I've ever done."

"Nonsense. If it weren't for you, I wouldn't understand half of what I do. You found me, Glim. I couldn't have found you. And all of those maps—I still don't know why the skraws helped you with that."

"Well," Glim said, sighing, "I sort of promised them something."

"What do you mean?"

He was silent for a moment. "Do you remember, back when we tried to escape, you said something about having invented a way of breathing underwater?"

"Sure. Why do you ask?"

He wiggled his hands in clear agitation.

"What?"

"The skraws," he said at last. "Those who work in the sump, like me—none of them can naturally breathe underwater. They inhale vapors that allow them to, but the vapors are really bad for them. They live in agony and die young." He looked up. "I was wondering if you could make them something else, something that won't hurt them."

She thought about that, and then found herself answering carefully.

"I could," she said. "It's easy for me to sneak the things I need to make an ounce or two of anything. But you would need more than that—a lot more than that—to make a difference. I would have to set up a generation vat. I don't think I can do that without permission, but if I managed to, it would be noticed and I would be in big trouble."

"Maybe you can get permission," he said.

"If I bring up the skraws, Toel will wonder why I know anything about them and why I care. He considers caring a weakness, and he already thinks I'm about as weak as they come.

And he might find out about you." She paused, and then went on even more cautiously. "Anyway—our goal is to bring Umbriel down, remember? Before it destroys our world?"

"The skraws don't have anything to do with that," he said. "They just work and die."

"Are you—" She laughed suddenly.

"What?"

"After all that making fun of me and my causes. You've got one, haven't you?"

"They—They sort of made me their leader."

"Why?"

"I told them we might be able to make things better if we—umm—organized a little."

"Organized? You're leading a *revolt*?"

"I didn't mean to," he replied miserably. "I mean, they kind of got the idea from me when I stood up to an overseer, and then—well, I might have suggested that they make some maps for me."

"Maps?"

"So I could find you. So we could escape."

"Oh. And now that we're stuck here—"

"They seem to expect me to follow through."

"Well, I guess they do," she said. "Will you?"

His pupils expanded and shrank, and then he nodded. "I think so," he said. "It's not right, how they live."

"You can think of it this way, too," Annaïg told him. "The more of them you've got looking for ways to sabotage things, the more likely you'll find some way to stop Umbriel altogether. That connection with the ingenium you told me about, for instance. We need to know more about that."

"Right," he said, but he sounded a bit uneasy.

"Glim," she said, taking his chin between her fingers.

"Yes?"

"I'm glad you care about these people. I'm glad you found a cause. And if there is any way to save the skraws, I'm all for it. But if it comes down to them or our world—if all of these people and the two of us thrown into the bargain have to die to stop this thing—that's what we have to do. You know that, don't you?"

He nodded, but there was an odd stiffness to it.

"Look," she said. "The kitchens are highly competitive, right? If the skraws raise enough ruckus, the lords may start looking for an alternative to the vapors. I've got one, ready to go. I just need Toel to ask me for it—understand?"

"I understand," Glim replied.

"We'll start there. But meanwhile you have to keep gathering information, okay? I mean, if I solve the problem of getting us off of this rock, maybe we can take your friends with us. The more information I have, the more alternatives that gives us."

"That makes sense," Glim breathed. "I'll see what I can do. But you—what about this woman who tried to kill you? What about Toel? If what you say is true, and if he thinks you're weak—I don't want to find you in the sump one day."

"You have your situation to manage," she said softly. "I have mine."

She hugged him and watched him go, but she felt troubled afterward, wondering if she and Mere-Glim were really on the same side anymore.

THREE

A soft cough drew Colin from the papers massed on his desk. Intendant Marall stood a few feet from his table, hands clasped behind his back.

Colin pushed his chair back and came to his feet.

"Intendant," he acknowledged.

"Inspector," Marall nodded. Then he just stood there.

"Can I help you, sir?" Colin asked after the moment drew uncomfortably long.

"I'm just wondering if you have anything to report."

Colin blinked.

If I had anything to report I would have—he began thinking, but quashed it, lest it show on his face.

"Not much, really, sir," Colin said. "Is there something wrong?"

"You received the latest interceptions."

"I did, Intendant," he replied. "I still can't find any connection between the Thalmor and this—flying city."

"And yet they must be up to something."

"Oh, yes, sir, they're up to plenty," Colin said. "Thalmor agents continue to harass the refugee communities in Sentinel and Balfiera—there has been a series of murders in the latter we can pretty confidently assign to them. The pattern is typical—the victims were all of mixed blood or had associations considered by the Aldmeri Dominion to be unclean. It's much worse in Valenwood—our supplies are no longer reliably getting to the rebels there. Sixty were caught and executed last week, along with four of our own men. There's a leak we don't know about, someplace. They know too much about our movements."

"But in all of that—"

"Nothing. No Thalmor connections to the east at all."

Marall looked sour. He took the other chair in Colin's nook, slid it toward Colin's desk, and sat down.

"Have you seen the reports concerning the flying city?"

"I haven't, sir. Since being taken off the Attrebus case—"

"I'm sorry about that. The more so because you were right about everything. But you made Administrator Vel look foolish, and there you go. At least I managed to get you back on something—eh—important."

"I appreciate that, sir."

"I'm going to tell you a few things, Inspector, because I hope you may have some thoughts on them. But you understand you may not repeat them."

"Of course, sir."

"You're aware, I imagine, of the stories in popular circulation concerning this—Umbriel."

"I am. They are based, as I understand, on letters written

by Prince Attrebus and sent to his biographers—before he vanished again."

"Yes. They've rather captured the popular imagination. A flying city from Oblivion, populated by strange creatures, destroying all it passes over and creating an army of living dead from the corpses."

"I've heard all of that."

"Well, we've a good bit of information from our scouts now," Marall said. "It's all basically true. There are just a few new details. Umbriel—apparently the name of this thing—landed at Lilmoth and proceeded in a straight line toward, it appears, Vvardenfell. It is indeed accompanied by some sort of reanimated corpses, and those who die beneath it also rise again. But here's the thing—the cities of Gideon and Stormhold were both overrun. Do you see what that means?"

"Neither lies between Lilmoth and Vvardenfell," Colin answered after a moment's thought.

"Correct. Apparently this army of the walking dead needn't remain near its creator."

"But do they continue to grow in numbers away from the island? Do they reproduce themselves?"

"That is unclear," Marall replied. "What we do know is that a large force of them has entered Cyrodiil and seems to be making its way toward the Imperial City."

"I see," Colin said.

"Are you certain you've seen no evidence that they might be colluding with the Thalmor? If they strike from the east, and the Dominion from the west, or up the Niben, we could find ourselves in a very precarious state."

"I've seen no evidence that the Thalmor are aware of these goings-on, much less that they are involved with them. Why—if I may ask, sir—why do you feel the Thalmor must be involved?"

"Well, if not them, someone." He tugged at the slight beard under his chin. "You were educated concerning the Oblivion crisis, of course."

"Yes, sir."

"The received wisdom in the highest circles is that Tamriel can never be invaded from Oblivion again."

"And yet we have been."

"Yes and no. Umbriel is apparently not entirely in our world."

"I don't understand."

"It exists in a sort of pocket of Oblivion."

"And yet it can affect our world, obviously."

"Yes. But the consensus opinion of both the Synod and the College of Whispers—who never agree on anything—is that even given its strange nature, Umbriel could not have come into Tamriel even so much as it has without being asked."

"Asked?"

"Summoned. Conjured. Facilitated. The sort of wizardry one naturally associates with the Thalmor."

Colin nodded. "More than ever, then," he said, "I think we're looking in the wrong place. Once it becomes clear we're being attacked, I have no doubt that the Dominion will take some advantage of it, but in my opinion that would be to consolidate their hold on Valenwood while our attention is elsewhere. They have a plan, a plan laid out in decades—I don't see them rushing into some strange alliance with an Oblivion prince or what-have-you."

"Who then?"

"Why not the An-Xileel?"

"The lizards?" Marall's voice dripped with contempt. "They're entirely parochial. Even if they could muster the sort of arcane knowledge this would require, why would they bother? They're content in their swamps."

"They invaded Morrowind."

"For revenge. They stopped their advance decades ago, and haven't showed the slightest interest in doing anything since then."

"Except keeping the Empire from reclaiming their territory," Colin pointed out.

"To my knowledge, we've never tried to invade Black Marsh. Who wants it?"

"I just think they might bear looking at," Colin said. "After all, that's where Umbriel first showed up."

Marall looked unconvinced, but then he nodded. "Very well," he said. "I'll make the appropriate reports available to you, and send any requests for whatever else you may need through my office. You were right about the Attrebus thing, after all. But—keep your head low, yes? I don't need this getting back to Vel."

"Understood, sir."

He watched Marall go, and then returned his gaze to the papers, but he wasn't really seeing them.

The Intendant was probably right that the An-Xileel were not a threat. They were entirely nativistic in their views, interested only in purging the former colonial influences and returning Black Marsh to whatever state they imagined it had been in before it was ruled by foreign powers. And technically, of course, Umbriel had appeared somewhere out at sea, so one might just as well suspect the elusive Sload of having helped the flying city conjure its way into Tamriel. After all, they were supposed to be great sorcerers.

He turned it around a few ways and didn't get anything, so he directed his thoughts to his other "case." There wasn't much there either. Despite her dramatic recruitment of him, he hadn't heard from Arese, and since he didn't have anything to tell her, he didn't see any point in risking contact with her.

He got the intelligence from Black Marsh a few hours later. He started with the most recent stuff; both the College of Whispers and the Synod had collected intelligence remotely, but there were also a number of on-the-ground reports. A few had been relayed by riders, but most were also transmitted through sorcerous means. It was mostly information regarding the size and travel path of Umbriel, and the accounts of Stormhold and Gideon seemed somehow light. Feeling he was missing something, Colin turned to what little they had in the way of information regarding the An-Xileel.

He found something very interesting indeed.

———

It had rained, and Talos Plaza was awash in reflected torch and lamplight. The air still smelled clean as Colin stepped through the puddles. A troupe of Khajiit acrobats was performing nearby, gracefully tumbling, forming unlikely structures with their feline bodies, juggling sparkling torches. A crowd clapped and tossed coins at their feet. He passed through a group of kids enthusiastically swinging at one another with wooden swords, and felt stiffness in this throat. He'd been like them once. He remembered playing such games. But he couldn't remember at all how it felt.

A few steps to the right, and he stood in the near utter darkness of an alleyway. Here, a man could die—or kill—and those in the plaza with its light and merriment would never be the wiser.

She noticed him too late. If he'd meant to end her, he could have, and she knew it. For the first time since he'd met her, Arese's controlled expression cracked, and he saw something that looked very much like fear. He could almost hear her heart pounding.

"Easy," he said. "I needed to see you. I was afraid to send any sort of message."

She took a step back, swallowed, and the mask went back on.

"How did you know I would come this way?" she asked.

"You usually do. You're on your way to meet your sister at the pub, and you always cut through here." He indicated the narrow lane with a slight twist of his head.

"You've been spying on me?"

"Not lately. Before. I wondered why you come through here rather than staying on the street."

She vented a self-deprecating chuckle. "So I can hear if anyone is following me," she replied. "No one ever is, and so I've gotten careless. What do you need?"

"I was looking at reports dealing with Black Marsh," he told her. "They've been censored—by Minister Hierem's office."

"That's not terribly surprising," she said.

"How is that?"

"Hierem made a secret trip to Black Marsh last year, ostensibly to negotiate with the An-Xileel leaders. He would have had anything suggesting his presence there removed."

"That explains the older reports," Colin said. "But I'm talking about intelligence gathered recently, concerning the attacks from the flying city."

"That's interesting," Arese replied. "That's really very interesting. You think there's some connection between this and the attempt on Attrebus?"

"I don't think there's any doubt about it," Colin said. "Attrebus was on his way to attack Umbriel. We know that from several sources, including the broadsides posted on every street corner. Clearly Hierem wanted to prevent that, to delay any Imperial confrontation with this thing for as long as possible. Now we know a force from the city is already in eastern Cyrodiil."

"Umbriel has also turned," Arese said. "It is now moving over the Valus Mountains toward the Imperial City."

"Well, then," Colin said, "what we have to ask ourselves is why Hierem wants Umbriel to attack the Imperial City. What's his relationship with it? Do you have any ideas?"

"None. Do you?"

"Well, I think Hierem summoned Umbriel," he said. "Helped it come here, whatever. That suggests he has some sort of bargain with whoever is master of the flying city."

"It does, doesn't it?" Arese said. She frowned. "It will be trouble to get the uncensored documents. He keeps things like that—if he keeps them at all—in his private rooms."

"Did anyone go with him to Black Marsh?" he asked.

"Yes, let me think. He took—" Then her eyes widened. "Well, that's no good," she said.

"What?"

"He took Delia Huerc. But she's dead."

"Dead? Murdered?"

"An illness of some sort, according to the report, and there wasn't any reason to doubt it. Now—well, what's to be done about it?"

"Anyone else?"

"He hired a merchant ship and traveled in disguise. I'm sure the name of the ship has been removed from any records."

"He had to pay for it."

"He didn't want the Emperor to know, so he probably paid out of pocket. He's not without his own wealth." She looked around. "This is going on too long," she said. "Is there anything else?"

"Delia Huerc. Where did she live?"

"I don't know, but I can get that. Look for a message from me."

"Okay."

She started to go, but then turned. "Good work," she said.

"Thanks."

"Next time, come to my house. Do you know where it is?"

"Yes."

"Of course you do. Come to the window above the alley and tap it four times. If I'm there, I'll come. And watch your back. Things are getting very paranoid in the ministry. There are questions where there shouldn't be."

"I'll be careful," he said.

She nodded and started walking.

"You be careful, too," he said.

She paused for an instant, but didn't look back, and then continued on her way.

FOUR

Annaïg stared out at the shimmering green sump and delicate, insectile buildings that climbed and depended from the stone walls of the conical valley at Umbriel's heart. Above, shining through the glittering strands of what resembled a giant spiderweb or some vast sea invertebrate, shone the sun of Tamriel. The sun she had been born under. It made her feel tight, claustrophobic, to know the light of that sun could illume the flying city, touch her, warm her—but that she could not go up through that sky, be in the wider world that orb washed with its radiance.

"You've not been here in a while," Toel said.

Annaïg forced herself to look at him. She had first seen Toel when he and his staff had slaughtered everyone in her former kitchen—everyone but Slyr and her. Even then, surrounded by brutally murdered corpses, he'd been calm, serene really. She had been terrified of him then, and was even more so now. She felt that at any moment he would stand, take her by the shoulders, and push her over the balcony to her death. Afterward, he would never think of her again.

But showing her fear would only get her killed more quickly. Toel had no use for the weak. She had to present him with something else.

"You've not invited me," Annaïg replied.

He shrugged and breathed in mist from the long, curved glass tube he held.

"I'm aware of why you haven't been here," he said, frost forming on his nostrils. "Are you?"

"You're disappointed that I asked you to spare Slyr, after she poisoned me."

"It goes beyond that. I thought you were like me, driven to excel, to rise. But you hold yourself back, and there isn't anything I can do about that."

"Then why am I here?" she asked.

"Because still you intrigue me. You invent marvelous things. I hope to reach you, at last."

The hairs behind Annaïg's ears pricked up at the ominous sound of that.

"I do wish to please you, Chef," she said.

"Do you?"

"Yes. But in my own way."

"By definition, you can only please me by catering to my desires."

Annaïg shook her head, tightening her belly to act bold. "That is only the beginning," she said. "A child's idea of pleasure."

"What is a child?" Toel asked.

"It doesn't matter," she replied. "My point is that the best chef cooks what the patron never knew he wanted."

"And what is it that I don't know I want?"

"That is for me to show you," Annaïg said, trying to sound playful. "And it cannot be rushed."

"And yet, I feel impatient," Toel said, "and perhaps a bit condescended to."

She forced a smile. "But still I intrigue you."

"I cannot deny it," he said, inhaling again.

He looked off into the distance for a long moment, and then returned his attention to her.

"There will be a banquet," he said, "some days hence. It will be for the court of Umbriel himself. Four kitchens have been invited to present a tasting for Lord Rhel, Umbriel's steward—mine, and those of Phmer, Luuniel, and Ashdre. Whichever kitchen pleases the steward most will cook for Umbriel. I need not tell you that it must be my kitchen that wins."

"It goes without saying, Chef."

"Phmer is our chief competition, to my mind. She is known for her creativity. Before Phmer, there were only eight essential savors: salty, bitter, piquant, sweet, sour, ephemerate, quick, and dead. But Phmer found a ninth sensation of taste, which has no name, and all attempts to duplicate it or ascertain how it is created have failed. And so, Annaïg, although you may tantalize me with these desires you know I have which I myself do not, this is what I tell you now: You will find this ninth savor for me. If you do not, any other plans you have to gratify me are moot. Do you understand?"

"I do, Chef," Annaïg said. "I won't fail."

"Indeed," he replied. She couldn't tell if it was an affirmation or a question. "Now you may go."

"A few questions, Chef," she said.

"What are they?"

"Do you have a sample of this ninth taste, so that I might know what I'm trying to duplicate?"

"I don't have any, no."

"Have you ever tasted it yourself, Chef?"

For a moment his face might have been cast in stone.

"No," he finally said.

"Can you at least tell me if it is a spiritual or gross substance?"

"We may assume spiritual, as only the highest lords have tasted it."

"Thank you, Chef."

———

Her knees were shaking when she left, and she felt profoundly unreal, as if she were watching this all happen to someone else. She returned to the kitchens, attempting to stay calm, to focus—trying to understand where she had to start.

She was sure she could duplicate anything she could taste, but that wasn't in the offering. That left her with what seemed an impossible task, but it was pointless to entertain that notion, wasn't it? She had to assume that it was possible. Phmer had done it, after all. Had it been an accident, or a design?

She went to her private bench, far from the hustle and bustle of the stations, and began idly thumbing through the various powders, liquids, distillations, and ferments in her cabinet. She fiddled with the flow of soul force through the refraxor, but after an hour of that pushed back and placed her face in her palms.

Her brain didn't seem to work at all. Sighing, she went back to her room, but her thoughts flowed no better there, so in the end she gave up and opened a bottle of wine.

She was on her second glass when Slyr entered.

"I'm sorry," the other woman said. "You're never here this early in the day. I—"

"No, join me," Annaïg said. "I'm just thinking."

"Well, I've no wish to disturb you."

"Sometimes talking helps me think." She pulled over a second cup and poured more wine. "Have a drink, talk."

Slyr looked uncertain but did as she was told.

"What do you know of Phmer's ninth savor?" Annaïg asked.

"I've heard of it," Slyr said cautiously.

"Before I came to Umbriel, I knew of only four or five essential flavors. When I was taught to cook, I was told that the success of a good dish was in the inclusion and balancing of these sensations. When I came here, you, Slyr, taught me that there were three more, all of a spiritual nature."

"Quick, dead, and ephemerate," Slyr supplied.

"So I'm thinking," Annaïg said. "I taste the five gross senses on different parts of my tongue, and I read long ago that the tongue is grown to interpret such flavors. But I cannot, like the lords, taste the difference between quick and dead. I might discern that a wiggling shrimp is alive and a still one dead, but the taste is the same, because my tongue isn't designed for that distinction. And as for ephemerate, that's another thing entirely, isn't it? Those are the 'flavors' we make with souls. The tongue doesn't taste them, although that's generally how they are introduced, since they're presented as food. But really, the skin or eyes can taste them equally as well—and ephemerate isn't a single kind of flavor, but hundreds, thousands, of very different things made possible by the cuisine spirituelle. Like the terror you tasted the other day, or the joy I could create tomorrow. How does that compare with the electric vitality of raw, unrefined soul energy, or the needling pleasure of filple?"

Slyr took a drink. "So you're thinking that the ninth savor can't be ephemerate, then? That it must be a new material flavor?"

"Or something completely different, as different from the ephemerate as the ephemerate is from salty and piquant."

"How can such a thing be discovered, then? If one knew only piquant, sour, and sweet, how would you guess that salty existed and learn how to make it?"

Something shaped itself in her mind then, a worm that might become an idea.

"Especially if one had no tongue," Annaïg pursued, her thoughts racing. "That is our dilemma."

"Our?"

"You are still my assistant, Slyr."

"I know that," she said. "I only thought—"

"I'm giving you another chance," Annaïg said. "One more, do you understand?"

Slyr nodded vigorously, and then her eyes narrowed.

"You've thought of something, haven't you?"

Annaïg smiled. "It's not what you think."

"What, then?"

"I think I might be able to hit twice with the same stone," she said.

"What do you mean?"

"Toel believes that I am not ambitious enough, that I'm not willing to do what I have to do to survive and get ahead."

"Yes," Slyr said. "I've heard him say so."

"I'll get the ninth savor," Annaïg promised. "And I'll show Toel just how far I'm willing to go."

"How?"

"I'm going to steal it from Phmer."

Slyr's eyes widened and her mouth parted.

"That's impossible," she said.

"Look," Annaïg said, drinking a bit more wine. "We can work for two weeks to invent this thing—and probably fail—or we can go where we know it already exists, and spend that time learning how best to use it to please Umbriel." She sat back. "I think it's what Toel intends me to do. I think this is a test he has devised."

"That does sound like him," Slyr admitted. "But to invade another kitchen, to pass all their safeguards and survive, much less escape being caught—I can't imagine how it could be done."

"I can," Annaïg told her. "I know how to learn secret ways, and I know recipes for concealment that—with a bit of work—ought to keep me undiscovered."

"I'm not sure you understand," Slyr said. "Even if you escape—if Phmer finds any evidence that you stole from her, she can demand Toel give you to her, and he must do so. That is the law. Perhaps that is even what Toel has in mind for you."

"Then I had better not be caught," Annaïg said. "Or leave trace of my visit."

Slyr's face hardened into an expression of determination.

"Tell me what I can do to help," she said. "I will not fail you."

"You had better not," Annaïg said. "This really is your last chance. You must understand that."

"I understand," Slyr replied.

"Good. I'll let you know when I need something."

———

Glim unfolded the note from Annaïg the skraw Jernle had handed him. It was written in the jumble language of their childhood—which only the two of them understood—although Glim hadn't seen any evidence that anyone on Umbriel could read in any language. Still—avoiding leeches was better than picking them off.

What are you up to, Nn? he thought. For a moment he considered refusing the request until Annaïg agreed to make something to replace the vapors. He followed her logic, understood why she couldn't do it, but still, something about her refusal bothered him. Maybe it was because she didn't take him seriously, that she thought her cause was bigger than his. And it was, wasn't it? How many of his people—his relatives—had died because of Umbriel?

But the skraws weren't to blame for that. They didn't even know it had happened.

But someone was responsible.

He turned to Wert, who was watching him patiently.

"I need detailed information concerning the kitchen of Phmer," he said. "Bribe the pantry workers, if you must."

"More maps?" Wert inquired.

"No. More than that." He paused. "And let's see what happens if some of the middens stop draining. That should get someone's attention."

Wert's face broke into a huge grin. "At last!" he said. "Which ones?"

"You decide," Glim said. "I need to have a second look at something."

———

Everything led to the sump, which meant lots of things led away from it as well. Early on Glim had found his way to the trees of the Fringe Gyre.

The flying island of Umbriel was a rough cone, with the apex pointed down. The sump was a basin in that cone, and most of the population of the city lived in warrens in the stone. The lords lived on the upper edge in their delicate habitations of metal and crystal. But another world sprouted from the verge of the rim, enormous trees whose roots sank deep into the rock where vesicles from the sump fed and watered them, and whose boughs and branches flowed far out from the island like a sort of lacy collar, bending in a rightwise whorl. It was a world of strange birds and weird gardens growing from intentionally rotted places in the wood, of fruits and nuts and warbling monkeylike things.

Next to the sump, he liked this place most, and sometimes better. Part of it was the feeling of freedom the place afforded, but part of it was a familiarity that spoke to him almost below the level of consciousness, a sense of intrinsic belonging he'd lost months ago.

The view, however, was disturbing. If he looked to the

horizons, he saw plains and forest, softened and made beautiful by distance. If he looked down, however, that was another story. Any open ground revealed the thousands of corpses walking, animated by Umbriel's larvae.

The ground was very open now. Umbriel had changed direction, taking them east over vast mountains, and below them was heath and snow, and few trees to hide the undying. They seemed numberless, and—perhaps worst of all—organized, marching in a rough semblance of ranks.

"I haven't seen you lately," a pleasant feminine voice quietly said.

He glanced up but already knew who it was.

"Hello, Fhena," he said.

With her charcoal complexion and red eyes, Fhena might have been a Dunmer woman of about twenty years. But she was no more Dunmer than Wert was human, and since Umbrielians were born adult, he'd reckoned from their earlier conversations she was probably no more than five or six years old. She wore her usual blouse and knee-shorts; today the former was green and the latter yellow.

"Did you bring me more orchid shrimp?" she asked hopefully.

"No," he said, "but I thought you might like these."

He handed her a pouch, which she took with an expression of purest delight. But when she saw what was inside, her look wandered toward puzzlement.

"Kraken barnacles," he explained.

She pulled one out of the bag. It was about the size and shape of a large shark tooth, smooth and dark green, with a wet, tube-like appendage sticking out of the wide end.

She bit the tooth-shaped shell.

"Hard," she said.

"Here," he said. "Let me show you."

He took the barnacle, gave it a squeeze so the shell cracked, then pulled out the soft mass inside by the projecting stalk. He handed it to Fhena, who bit into it, chewed a moment, and then laughed.

"Good, yes?" Glim said. "Those are native to the seas around Lilmoth, where I grew up. The taskers must have collected some and brought them up, because they've suddenly started growing in the sump."

"Delicious," she agreed. "You always find some way to surprise me."

"I'm glad to be of service," Mere-Glim said.

"But I'm not often able to repay the favor," she replied.

"You might today," he said. "Tell me about the trees."

"The trees?"

"Yes." He tapped on the nearest branch.

"I'm not sure what to say about them," she replied.

"Well," he said, trying to think how to go about this, "I've noticed that they produce nuts and fruit and even grains, of a sort. But what else?"

"What else?" She clapped her hands. "Salt and sugar, acid and wine, vinegar and sulfur, iron and glass. The trees have a talent for making things—they just have to be told how."

"Who tells them?"

She looked thoughtful. "Well, I'm not sure," she said. "They've been making most things for so long, I think they may have forgotten. Or at least they don't talk about it. They just tell us when something needs doing, or collecting, or when something isn't right and them in the kitchens must help."

"Wait a minute," Glim said. "The trees talk to you?"

"Of course. Can't you hear them?"

"Almost," Glim said. "Almost. But what does it mean?"

Her eyes had widened, and he realized his spines were puffed out and he was giving off his fighting odor. He tried to calm himself.

"What's this about, Glim?" she asked.

"It's about me," he said. "It's about my people, and why they died."

"I don't understand," she said. "But I can see how upset you are. Can you explain?"

Glim thought about that for a long moment. Annaïg would tell him not to trust the girl; she didn't trust anyone on Umbriel. But Fhena had only ever helped him.

"I would like to explain," he finally said. "Because it might mean something to you. It might make you think of something. So don't be afraid to interrupt me."

"I won't," she replied.

"I've told you before; I'm from a place named Black Marsh. My people call themselves the Saxhleel, and others call us Argonians."

"I remember. And you said all of your people are the same."

"The same? Yes, compared to your people. We all have scales, and breathe beneath the water, that sort of thing. Umbriel chooses your form when you are born. Mine is chosen by—ah—heritage."

"What do you mean?"

"It's not important right now. We can talk about that later. What's important is this; there is another race in Black Marsh—the Hist. They are sentient trees, and we are—connected to them. They are many and they are one, all attached at the root, and we, too, are joined to that root. Some say we were created by the Hist, to see for them the world where they cannot walk. They can call us or send us away. When we are named, we take of the sap of the Hist, and we are changed—sometimes a little, sometimes very much."

"What do you mean, 'changed'?"

"A few twelves of years ago, our country was invaded from Oblivion. The Hist knew it was going to happen, and called our people back to Black Marsh. Many of us were altered, made ready for the war that we had to fight. Made stronger, faster—able to endure terrible things."

"I'm starting to understand," Fhena said. "You're saying the Hist are much like the trees of our gyre."

"Yes. But not the same. They don't speak to me as the Hist did. But you say they speak to you."

"Not in words," she replied. "They dream, they experience, they communicate needs. I can't imagine them making a plan, as you describe."

"But their sap can alter things, like that of the Hist."

"Oh, yes. But as I said, usually they have to be told." She put her hand on his shoulder. "I still don't understand why this is so upsetting to you."

"The Hist are supposed to be unified," Glim said, "but at times certain trees have gone rogue, broken away from the others. It happened long, long ago in my city, and I think it happened again, not long before your world entered mine. A rogue tree helped Umbriel somehow, do you understand? It helped kill many, many of my people so they could serve Umbriel as dead things. And now I think it may have helped summon Umbriel here in the first place. Can you remember—"

But Fhena's eyes had become unfocused with memory. He stopped and waited.

"We were in the void," she said. "Nothing around. And then the trees began to sing a strange song, one I had never heard before. They sang and sang. It was beautiful. No one could remember such a thing happening before. And then we were here. They still sing it, but quietly now. Listen."

She took his hand and pressed it to the bark. It was strange, the roughness of the tree and the supple warmth of her hand, and for a moment that was all he experienced. But then she began to hum, and something seemed to turn in his head, and the soft burring that was all he had ever heard from the Fringe Gyre before suddenly sharpened and he heard it in tune with Fhena's humming, a faint, rising and falling tone, along with a thousand harmonics, as if each seed and leaf had its own note to add. And he knew that melody, had known it since before his birth. The Hist sang it.

But the Fringe version was a little different—simpler. Still, it drew him, pulling him out of language and thought, and for a long, long time he knelt there with Fhena's hand on his, feeling newborn, empty, at one.

FIVE

Most traps are simple, Colin thought. It's why they work.

Delia Huerc's apartment had seemed simple. It had been reoccupied since her death, so he'd had to wait until the current owner—a Khajiit rug-seller named Lwef-Dim—was gone. It was an old place, full of shadows, once-weres, and might-have-beens, and so opening his spectral eyes was easy enough. And there she was, a slip of a ghost, still waiting. Ghosts usually moved on, except in locations with the power to hold them and feed them, but this place had given him hope—and it hadn't disappointed.

But then he saw that it wasn't Delia. It wasn't even a ghost. It was *something* left to deal with the likes of him. It contorted in his overvision, a chimera that refused to settle on a shape, then bloomed fully into Mundus, the world, and brought harm to him. He failed to dodge its blow, but whatever hit him still wasn't actually matter; it was worse, traveling though his arm, through every layer of muscle, every vessel of blood, the bone and spongy marrow, leaving detailed and unbelievable agony behind. At first he thought the arm was actually off, but then he saw it was still there, a mass of spasming muscle.

He tumbled away without thinking and drew the blade from his belt as reflexively, his training working well below the level of thought. The thing came for him and he cut at it with the translucent weapon. The apparition shivered and made a sound he hardly heard, so high-pitched was it, but the windows of the apartment shattered.

So it didn't like the blade, which was good. He'd brought it in case he had to fend off a ghost, and luckily whatever this was, it was at least offended by the consecrations bound into its crystalline metal.

But he wasn't sure if he'd actually hurt it, so he backed away, trying to focus on it, to forget the feeling of death eating at his arm and understand what he was facing.

It came again, and this time he noticed a sort of center and stabbed at that. He felt resistance, and it made the sound again, but this time shudders of pain that weren't his own racked through him, so he thrust again, and then again. A yellowish mist whipped at his head, he felt something like a razor pass through his brain, and colors exploded, seemed to spill out of him. He couldn't feel his limbs, and realized he was in a jumble on the floor.

The presence loomed over him.

Feeling oddly detached, Colin closed his eyes against the thing and reached into the middle of himself, where his little star was, the tiny piece of him that had come from beyond the world and even Oblivion, from Aetherius, the realm of pure light and magic.

As pain and then cold gripped him, he made the star a sun.

The force and light of it blew his eyelids and mouth open, and radiance shredded through the specter like a high wind through smoke. This time it didn't manage to make a sound, but was instantly and utterly gone.

Colin lay there then, watching the slight rise and fall of his chest, unable to remember what he was supposed to be doing. He didn't recognize where he was either. And he couldn't move.

He ought to have panicked, but he was too tired.

Across the room, a woman he did not know was watching him, silent, unmoving.

He remembered being a boy in the city of Anvil, tarring boats and staring out to sea, dreaming of distant lands. He remembered his mother, her back permanently bent from her work scrubbing clothes.

He remembered killing a man. He hadn't known his name. It was on a bridge, and the man was looking out across water at a light. The man had seen his knife and tried to fend off the sharp blade with his hands. He tried to beg, but Colin had stabbed him until all of his life spilled out.

He remembered that was his final test before becoming an inspector.

As his memory returned, so did the feeling in his legs and arms. It was as if a million needles had been thrust into them.

By the time he could push himself up, he knew where he was again. He faced the woman, who still hadn't said anything. She was a Redguard, with tight, curly hair and a strong, handsome face. She was probably about fifty.

"Are you Delia Huerc?" he asked.

Her eyes moved at the sound of her name, but otherwise she didn't react.

Some ghosts remembered everything, some nothing. Some didn't even know they were dead.

"You went to Black Marsh, with Prime Minister Hierem. Do you remember that?"

Her head turned a bit. She looked down, and her hand came up a little.

He followed the gesture and saw she was pointing at one of the baseboards. He went over to it and found it loose. In a hollow in the wall he discovered a soft leather bag, and in that a book.

"May I look at this?" he asked.

Her hand dropped back to her side but she didn't answer, so he opened it. It was written mostly in Tamrielic, with some asides in Yoku, which he had passing knowledge of. It was a journal, and flipping toward the end, he found several pages of entries about Black Marsh. He'd only read a page when he heard steps in the hall and realized he'd been on the floor most of the day.

He went out the empty window, taking the book with him. Delia watched him go without objection.

———

There wasn't much sun left, but he wanted to be in it, to try to forget the thing in the apartment. He went through the Market District and bought apples, pork pies, and lemon water from street vendors, then found a good place on the roof of a building overlooking the alley behind Arese's house. There he ate and read the journal, stalked by pigeons trying to get at his scraps.

Huerc described the preparations for the trip in detail, and it became clear to him that she thought the Emperor, at least, was aware of the trip. Hierem had explained that the secrecy and misdirection were to avoid any of the Emperor's enemies learning what he was about. She hadn't been privy to the meeting with the An-Xileel, but worked out that some agreement had been reached. She'd been led to believe that Hierem was there to propose an alliance against the Thalmor. But he was vague about what the negotiations actually entailed. Most interesting, the agreement involved Hierem performing some sort of ritual at the City Tree.

She had written:

The tree is enormous. The only one I have ever seen taller was in Valenwood, but the Hist was more massive, more spread out. And I could feel a palpable presence in it. I had never quite credited the Argonian claims that the trees are intelligent, but when I stood in its presence, I could no longer doubt it. Further, I thought I felt a certain malevolence in it, but that might well have been my imagination, for the whole situation was anything but friendly. The An-Xileel have been uniformly rude and arrogant, the city itself is a festering, putrid place. From the moment I entered Lilmoth, I have wanted nothing more than to leave it.

The minister, on the other hand, seems quite excited, almost jubilant.

The An-Xileel sang to the tree, an awful cacophonous chant that went on so long that I might have drifted off a bit. At some point, Hierem added his voice to theirs, but in a sort of counterpoint. He lit a brazier, and I'm sure he did some sort of sorcery. In his younger years he was in the leadership of the Mages'

Guild, before that organization utterly collapsed, and so I know him capable of these things, but I was still somehow surprised.

It was my impression that he was calling something, for he repeated the word "Umbriel" many times. It seemed like a name, although the language he spoke was not one I knew, and so I may have been mistaken, for nothing came, although everyone seemed pleased anyway.

Tomorrow we sail for home, and I could not be happier.

He read on, but the only other passage of interest to him was one in which she began to question whether the Emperor had authorized or was aware of their trip, and she had determined to ask Hierem about it.

He read the final few sentences with a little chill:

At lunch today Hierem repeated his assertions, but I still have my doubts. I have a meeting with the Emperor tomorrow. I will ask him myself.

I hope I shall feel better. My stomach is unsettled, and there is pain in my joints. Perhaps the soup did not suit me.

Colin thumbed back through earlier parts of the book, but it was dark now. He settled against a chimney, watching Arese's unlit window. Neither moon was in the sky, but there were no clouds, and the stars were glorious. He rested there, letting the fall of night ease into him; first the swifts, then the fluttering of bats, the lonely imprecation of a barn owl. Tree frogs chirped and insects whirred. A dog barked somewhere in the Market District and was answered nearby, which set off a chorus of canine comment from all quarters of the city. A couple argued not far away about what the proper price of the cockles for dinner might have been, and the strains from a lute drifted along in the breeze.

Arese would be with her sister now. He had a few more hours to wait, a little more time to decide what to do, whether to show Arese the journal or not. Was she really an agent of the Emperor?

He'd been assigned to find Prince Attrebus. The prince had gone, against his father's wishes and in secret, to find and fight the menace of the flying city. He hadn't gotten far; Colin had found his entire bodyguard slaughtered—and it seemed, at first, the prince, too. Attrebus, it turned out, was a careful creation of his father and his ministers. All of the battles and duels he had won were set up that way, and the bards and authors who sang and wrote of him were heavily subsidized by the court. The prince himself hadn't known this; few outside his guard had. Whenever the prince decided to go off on some sort of adventure, his right-hand man Gulan always reported it to the office of the Prime Minister, and it had been handled.

But not this time—or at least not the way it usually was. This time the prince had been ambushed. That was what had led Colin to investigate Arese; he knew Gulan had gone to her, as usual. He discovered that she had set up the attack on the prince herself, and later followed her to a house where—as he listened—she killed the crime boss who had facilitated it, along with all of his guard and household. He still didn't know if she had summoned something or *transformed* into the nightmare that had turned the house into an abattoir.

And yet, Arese had admitted this to him. She had offered an explanation for it.

Most traps are simple.

He sighed, ran his hand through his hair, felt the breeze on his face.

He heard a faint noise that seemed somehow out of place and opened his eyes.

Fifteen yards away he saw the shadowed figure of a man, dressed in the black quilted jerkin so many of the Dark Brotherhood affected these days. The fellow was in profile, kneeling on the roof of the building across the alley. As Colin watched, he slipped like a spider down a rope too dark and thin to make out from his vantage point. He settled, still like a spider, on the casement of Arese's window. After a moment Colin saw the window reflect starlight as it swung open, and then, a few heartbeats later, shut again.

The breeze picked up. It felt cool, and Colin realized he was sweating.

Someone wanted Arese dead.

He hesitated long enough to feel ashamed, trying to sort out what the smart thing to do was. If she died, he could step out of this whole thing.

But then he would never know what was going on, and maybe he would have to watch the Empire collapse knowing he might have done something.

But it was more than that. There had been something about her, brittleness, vulnerability . . .

He recognized her, he understood in that moment. She was what he might become after a few years of this. He had seen, however briefly, the hollow place in her, the weariness. He still wasn't sure if he believed her or if they were on the same side.

But he didn't want her to die.

He looked back up at the sky. Almost time for her to come home, of course. The assassin would know that, too, wouldn't he?

He didn't have any rope or cord. He could make the jump to the window, maybe, but the odds were against it, and it wouldn't be quiet. But he could jump to the next building, get to her front door before she did, and avoid the whole confrontation.

But then he saw light in the window—not in the room itself, but diffuse light, coming from another room.

Muttering a curse, he stepped back a few paces, assessed the distance, and leapt.

His toes hit the window ledge and he curled forward, elbows over his eyes. Glass panes shattered but the wooden frame did not, and so he bounced back, spine toward the street thirty feet below. He kicked a foot through one of the broken panes and managed to hook it on the wood, which swung him back and smacked his shoulders into the brick. Gasping, he jerked up, tightening his stomach muscles, and drew himself up to the window.

By the time he got it open, of course, someone was coming for him.

He dove past and to the side of the dark blur and rolled toward the lantern-lit room farther in, drawing his knife. He absently noticed that his hands were slick with blood.

A knife thudded into the floor next to him as he scrambled up, and the assassin was close behind; he had a dark blade in his left hand and was drawing a bright one with his right from beneath his jerkin. Colin's breath rushed in, and for an instant everything slowed and golden light seemed to infuse the room. His arms moved but he seemed outside of it. The next thing he knew, he hit the wall hard, pain trying to make him scream as he fell, but his throat wouldn't open to let it out.

His attacker was leaning against a bookcase across the room. He made a sort of snarling sound and took one, two steps toward him. With the third step his knee kept bending and he slammed face-first into the floor. Colin could see the bloody point of his knife standing out between the downed man's shoulder blades.

Groaning, he pushed himself to his feet, feeling them wobble beneath him. Under his breath he said a little prayer to Dibella, but he couldn't tell if she heard. He wasn't sure how long he could stand. He made it to the fallen man, though, and took the black knife from his hand. He stuck it in between the first two vertebrae below the skull and wiggled it. Then he had a look at himself.

His arms were cut up from the window, nothing so deep as to be dangerous. The assassin's other knife had driven through the pectoral muscle where it stretched up to meet his shoulder. The feeling of the impact came back to him, and he realized the blade must have hit a bone and skipped up instead of slipping through to his heart. In any event, if the dagger hadn't been poisoned, he was probably going to survive.

Then, from the corner of his eye, he saw a second man, coming from the direction of the window, and he tried to turn, far too slowly.

But there was a clap like thunder, and the man went staggering back, and in the next instant something appeared, something horrible. Colin had a glimpse of slits of green balefire, scales, and claws like sickles. The man almost managed to scream before his lungs and viscera were spattered across the room. Then the thing turned on Colin, snarling.

"Stop!" a voice shouted, and the daedra stopped, panting.

Arese stood behind him, her eyes wider than he had ever seen them. It made her look very young. The sleeve of her white shirt was soaked in blood, and a red patch on her temple and eye would probably soon prove itself a bruise.

"Hunt and guard," she told the daedra, and it turned and reluctantly slouched back toward the window.

"How did you—" Arese managed. She was breathing so hard and shallowly it worried him.

"Come here," he said. "Are you cut anyplace else?"

"I never saw him," she said, staring down at the body. "Never heard him. I didn't have time to do anything."

"Let me look," he said. "You got your arm up," he remarked, examining the defensive wound on her wrist. It wasn't deep.

"I heard a crash, like glass breaking. I guess I threw up my hand when I turned, but he was there already."

"The crash was me," Colin said, searching for punctures anywhere vital.

"I don't understand."

"I was waiting on the roof across the alley. I saw him come in."

"He came to kill me." Her breath was still too quick, and her skin was hot, much hotter than it should be.

"That seems obvious," he said.

"They would have killed me if not for you."

"Well, that second guy would have had me," he said.

"Divines, you're bleeding everywhere."

"Nothing serious," he said. "But speaking of bleeding, your arm—"

She looked at it, then back at him. He realized he had one hand on her shoulder and another on her stomach. He felt her belly quiver, and something happened to her eyes.

Stupid, he thought. This is stupid.

Her skin felt almost molten. She gasped when their lips came together, as if trying to get the air from his lungs. He smelled something like burning cloves and felt a shock of energy race through him like nothing he had ever known before, filling the emptiness left in him from two hard fights with impossible strength. She buried her face in his neck and he in hers, and they went down on the rug in a tangle, both wrestling furiously at ties and buttons.

Slick with blood, the salt from their sweat burned his wounds, but not enough to matter.

————

Later, much later it seemed, he lay back while she cleaned his wounds, first with warm water and then with a white ointment that left a pleasant warmth behind it and smelled a little like mustard. It did more than feel good; he could see the flesh draw together almost as if stitched. They had moved to her bedroom, where she had laid out a thick cover over her sheets and let him rest stretched out. She sat on the edge of the bed, the skin of her throat and breast like pearl in the moonlight—except for where the streaks of dried blood still clung.

"Feel better?" she asked.

"Much," he said. "Although I have to say, I didn't feel it that much a little while ago either."

She looked down. He thought she seemed embarrassed.

"Reaction," he offered. "When you realize you've almost died, sometimes—you know."

She shook her head. "When I summon daedra, I have to touch them with my mind. I have to be strong enough to keep them from turning on me. Daedra are—violent, passionate. Sometimes I feel something of what they do." She looked away. "I think—" She shook her head and dabbed at the cut on his chest. "It's also been a long time, for me. I haven't felt I could trust anyone enough to—do that. I haven't felt secure enough."

"And you trust me?"

She smiled. "No. But—" She smiled. "Reaction. And there *is* something about you." She cocked her head. "You've no reason to trust me either, I know. I've given you every reason not to. But I'm just trying to get through this. Alive. And sometimes it doesn't seem worth the cost."

"Cost?"

"This isn't a life, Colin. I'm thirty-one years old. I've been a spy in Hierem's ministry since I was twenty-one. I've been with one other person in that time, and it was a disaster. I work, and I fear, and sometimes I do awful things. I have drinks with my sister for an hour or two most evenings and come home. I can't talk to her about what I do. She stays out, gambles, goes for rides in the country, has affairs. I'm careful. I protect myself. And now I'm going to die anyway."

"They failed," he pointed out.

"But someone sent them, probably one of my rivals or Hierem himself. They'll send more. I've made a mistake somewhere—probably to do with those two on the island. They know." She lifted his hand and kissed it. "You're very young," she said. "You can get out of this. You should. I won't stop you."

"Are you giving up?" he asked.

"No. No, I can't do that. But I don't have to pull you down with me."

He sighed. "I was in this already," he said. "I have to—I have to do something right. Do you understand?"

"You did something right tonight," she said. "You saved my life. Can't that be enough?"

"Not if you die tomorrow."

"We all die. You gave me at least a day more than I would have had. And not a bad one."

"It's not enough," he said.

"Why?"

"It's just not."

"Don't get angry," she said.

"I'm not," he replied.

"You sound it."

"Okay," he said, closing his eyes. "I'm not, though." But he was, wasn't he?

She didn't say anything, but then he felt a tender kiss, just at the edge of his lips.

"It doesn't have to be rough," she said. "I can be gentle."

He thought of the two men she had killed on the island, of the many who had perished in that house he had followed her to. He thought about the assassin he had just slaughtered, and realized he felt nothing.

He kissed her, and outside the night birds sang as if everything were normal, quiet, and in its place.

SIX

"Halt here," Captain Falcus shouted. "Brennus, Mazgar—take three more and check out the village."

"On it, Captain," Mazgar said, trying to keep the fatigue out of her voice. Then realizing she'd spoken out of turn, she looked to Brennus.

"I'm not trained for this," Brennus said. "We both know that. You choose."

She nodded. "Merthun, Tosh, Na-Nasha, come on."

The others were as weary as she, and in fact she was beginning to worry about Brennus. He was a scholar, not a warrior or battlemage, although his skills had saved her a few times in the past weeks. But he didn't have the constitution or the training for this sort of forced march, and it was starting to show.

They had managed to fight their way through the southern end of the encirclement on the ridge, but none of the horses had survived and they had lost almost half their number. Since then they had been able to keep ahead of the undead creatures, but only by pushing themselves to their limits. What provisions they had were now gone, and they couldn't stop to hunt or fish, because the band that attacked them wasn't alone; it was part of a massive wave moving across the mountains into Cheydinhal County.

They half trotted, half stumbled down the hill to the village, if village was even the word for ten houses arranged around a central area of bare dirt and a well. She looked longingly at the latter, but had a job to do before she could drink from it.

There were about seven people in the square when they entered it, but within moments more began appearing from the houses. They didn't look threatening; none of them even seemed to be armed.

"We're Imperial troops," Mazgar shouted. "Who's in charge here?"

An older Redguard woman with frizzled white hair stepped toward her.

"I suppose that would be me," she said. "I'm Sariah, charter-holder of Mountain Watch, such as it is."

"Sariah," Mazgar said, "just keep your people still for a moment. We mean you no harm."

They went quickly house to house, despite the sudden burst of protests and complaints from Sariah and a few others in the square, only confirming what Mazgar already reckoned—that this was a bunch of farmers and hunters. Then she whistled—one short, one long, two short.

A few moments later Captain Falcus and the rest came down.

"Captain, this here is Sariah," Mazgar said, introducing her, "the charter-holder."

"What's this about, Captain?" Sariah demanded. "Since when

can Imperial troops search houses without permission?"

"By order of his majesty, or in time of war, lady," Falcus said. "You and all of your people are about half a day from being dead, every one of you."

"What are you talking about?" Sariah asked.

"Mountain Watch, eh?" Falcus said, and spat. "You aren't watching too well." He raised his voice. "Listen up! You people have fifteen minutes to pack. Take nothing you can't eat, drink, or fight with, and I mean it. Any horses you have, bring those up now, and bring my men provisions."

"What gives you the right to order us out of our homes?" Sariah snapped.

"I don't aim for any of you to die," Falcus said. "I intend to get you all behind the gates of Cheydinhal ahead of what's coming. But if you delay me with this senseless prattle—if anyone does—it means some or all of you are going to die. Even now it may be too late. Now—do what I told you. Now!"

The charter-holder's eyes widened, but she didn't dissent anymore. Nobody ever argued with Falcus when he used that tone of voice. He might as well have been the Emperor himself.

They took turns at the well, drinking and filling their skins, and those not at the well helped gather up the grand total of six horses the village had to offer. They hooked four of them to two wagons, to carry the youngest and the infirm. Falcus and Kuur, the battlemage, took the other two.

A bit of grumbling started to resurface, and it took more than fifteen minutes, but within the hour they were shepherding forty people ranging in age from two months to sixty-something down a weather-worn track that couldn't quite be called a road.

Mazgar and Brennus took positions along one of the wagons. Brennus looked pale.

"There's room in the wagon," Mazgar suggested.

"I'm fine," he murmured. "Thank Akatosh I don't have to carry around all that muscle and bone, like you do."

"No, all of your weight is in your head," she replied. "Seriously. A little rest will help you."

"He can have my place," a child's voice said. "I want to walk."

Mazgar glanced in the wagon and saw that the speaker was a little human in brown twill breeches and a yellow felt shirt.

"See?" she said. "The boy is willing to give up his spot for you."

"Yeah," the kid said, "but I ain't a boy."

Mazgar studied the short brown bangs, snub nose, and slight frame.

"The girl, then," she corrected.

"It's all right," Brennus said.

"Come on," the girl said, hopping out. "I'm seven now. I can walk as good as anyone and better than most."

Brennus shook his head, but in the next step he stumbled.

"Well, considering that," he sighed.

"Right," Mazgar said. "We need you fresh when the wormies catch up to us, and that's no lie."

She expected a quip back from him, but he just nodded and started trying to clamber in. She gave him a little shove to help him along.

"There," she said. Then she looked down at the girl. "Think you can keep up with me?"

"I can keep up with anybody," she said.

"We'll see about that."

"You're an orc," the girl said.

"Is she, now?" Brennus said, perking up a little. "Here I've been thinking that somewhere out there a bear and a pig are living in wedded bliss."

"What do you mean?" the girl asked.

"Don't pay attention to him," Mazgar said. "He's only trying to get me to mash his face in."

"Why?"

"Some people are funny that way," she replied.

"Well, I'd like to see it!"

"Maybe when he's feeling a little better. What's your name?"

"Lorcette, but everybody calls me Goblin."

"Why?"

"I don't know, they just always have. Mom always said I had ears like a goblin."

"Huh," Mazgar said. "Now that I look, you sort of do. Which one of these is your mom?"

"Oh, she's gone," Goblin said. "Died when I was six."

"Mine died when I was seven," Mazgar said. "At the sack of Orsinium. They say she killed thirty before death took her."

"My mom didn't die in a battle. She just got sick." The girl cocked her head. "Who was your mom fighting?"

"Redguards and Bretons," Mazgar replied.

"You became an Imperial soldier because of her?"

"I became a soldier because of her. I became an Imperial soldier because if it hadn't been for the Seventh and Fifteenth legions, a lot more of us would have died. They put themselves in harm's way for us, got the survivors to safety in Skyrim."

"Kind of like what you're doing now."

Mazgar remembered the terror, the chaos, the walk that went on for weeks through bitter cold—and never having enough to eat.

"Let's hope not," she said.

"What's a wormy?" Goblin asked after a few moments of silence.

"What?"

"You said something about wormies catching up with us."

"Yeah. That's what I call 'em. They used to be people—then they died and some kind of witchery brought them back, and now they're all full of maggots and such—so I call 'em wormies."

She thought the girl would look scared, but instead she looked thoughtful.

"My mom is buried back there," she said. "Do you think they'll bring her back?"

"Nah, they like fresher bodies than that. Anyway, it wouldn't really be your mom, just your mom's body with a daedra in it."

"Why would anyone do that?"

"To conquer Tamriel, it looks like," Mazgar replied. "But I wish whoever it is who had the itch to do that would have chosen less smelly troops."

"I could say the same about some of his majesty's elections," Brennus said.

Mazgar was preparing a retort, but then she saw his eyes were closed. "Mauloch," she muttered. "Even when he's asleep."

They marched along like that, with the girl prattling and keeping good pace. When night fell, however, she and Brennus switched places. The mage seemed much better for the rest, and Goblin dropped off pretty swiftly.

"You let that girl talk your ear off all day," Brennus said, "and you never once looked like you were going to clout her in the head. That's not like you."

"Isn't it?"

"Remember that kid that hung around our camp on the way up—that little mountain town? The one you threatened to tie to a tree by his bowels?"

"Well, he was annoying."

"About the same as this one, really," he said. "Something's changed in you."

"In me?" she snorted.

"I think maybe you're starting to think about spitting out a few little bear-pigs yourself, that's what I think."

"You're more out of your mind than usual," she said. "Children? Me?"

"Just an observation," he rejoined. "You're not getting any younger, and we've lost a lot of comrades. Makes you think."

"Makes you think," she said. "And way too much."

"Still—"

"Rest it!" she snapped.

She must have said it louder than she meant to, for a number of heads turned her way.

She couldn't tell if the look on Brennus's face was smugness or contrition.

Humans.

———

A bit after noon the next day, Mazgar saw the high steeple of the chapel of Arkay peeking up through the trees below them. On foot they would have been there quickly, but the wagons were having a hard time going downhill. Mazgar felt the familiar itch of danger at her back growing more and more pronounced, and glanced often over her shoulder, though Coals and Merthun were on the rearguard and both were more than competent.

But it wasn't Coals and Merthun who sent up the alarm—it came from the north, their left flank, from Na-Nasha and Glavius.

The two men arrived a few moments behind their signal.

"They'll cut us off from Cheydinhal if we don't hurry," Na-Nasha said, wriggling his reptilian fingers oddly, as he often did when agitated.

"That's it for the wagons," Falcus said. He turned to the refugees. "We're going to make it, but we're going to have to run. Leave everything, you hear? Cheydinhal is just down this hill, not even half a mile."

Mazgar dumped her backpack and reached for Goblin, but the girl shook her head. "I told you, I can run. Carry Riff Belancour, there—he's got a funny foot."

Mazgar nodded and took up the boy, who was probably about six and weighed half as much as her pack. The horses were cut loose and the most elderly put up on them in tandem. Mothers clutched their infants.

Falcus set the pace, a slow trot, and the boy on Mazgar's shoulders giggled, obviously thinking it was all a game of some kind. True to her boast, Goblin kept up, running alongside her.

Falcus picked up the tempo a little as they burst into a field; the walls of Cheydinhal were visible through the next line of trees.

But the wormies were coming fast, toward their left flank, ranged in a rough phalanx, and Mazgar could easily make the calculation that they weren't going to make it. A few of the townsfolk screamed or began to cry, but most broke into full-on, terrified flight.

Falcus began shouting orders, but Mazgar couldn't make them out. A moment later, though, Na-Nasha, Coals, Casion, and Sugar-Lick broke off and formed a semicircle with Kuur behind them.

"Captain!" she shouted. "Permission to join—"

"Denied," Falcus shouted back. "Keep with your charge. Make it count. Go!"

She exchanged a glance with Brennus.

"I'm with you," he said. "Whatever you want to do."

Mazgar glanced down at Goblin, felt the weight on her back.

"I don't make the orders," she snarled.

So they ran.

She looked back once before they reached the trees, because she felt the heat on her back and heard the dull thud of an explosion. She couldn't see anything but black, greasy smoke and billowing flame.

They came through the trees into the clearing around the walls. The gate was off to the right. It was open, and a picket of about a fifty soldiers was formed up there.

They had maybe thirty paces to go when Goblin shrieked. Mazgar looked back and saw six wormies coming up fast.

She set Riff down and drew Sister.

"Get them through the line," she howled at Brennus. Then she got her footing and charged.

Sister caught the first—a half-charred Dunmer man—right at the juncture of clavicle and neck, and the heavy blade clove halfway through his ribs and stuck there. Bellowing, she punched the next in the face as he lifted his heavy curving blade, and had the satisfaction of feeling the cartilage and bone crush under her knuckles. She used Sister to turn the corpse into the next two, temporarily deflecting them while she reached for another, this one unarmed, and she roared the battle cry her mother had in her last battle. Red sleeted before her eyes, and rage took everything.

The next thing she knew, Goblin was shouting at her. She looked dully down and saw the pile of bodies, Sister still stuck in one. Twenty yards away, about sixty wormies were charging toward her.

She put her boot on the dead thing and heaved out the sword, then turned and pounded toward the gate, where the others were waiting.

———

Falcus ordered them all to eat and rest, and no one argued. The wormies didn't have siege engines, and Cheydinhal had its own soldiers, after all, and a mixed company of Imperial troops as well. Within an hour a camp had been set up near the castle that dominated the north end of town, and Mazgar had the first hot food and cool ale she'd had in a long time.

She didn't remember falling asleep, and the next thing she knew was light coming softly through an open tent-flap.

She left her armor in the tent and went outside to stretch, wandering down to the river that flowed through the city. The sun wasn't showing over the walls yet, but things were waking up. Wagons of bags and crates made their way across the bridges, pulled by thick, sturdy horses. Across the river, a Dunmer woman was casting a net, which came up wriggling. Mazgar could smell sausage frying somewhere.

But most of the people she saw were up on the walls.

She watched the river flow for a while.

She knew Brennus by the sound of his gait.

"Nice place," he said. "Have you ever been here before?"

"No," she said. "The houses look funny." She nodded across the river. The timbers of most of the structures in town were exposed. In the lower floors they were covered with stone, but the upper ones had plaster between the beams and struts, which were often arranged in whimsical patterns. The roofs were concave peaks, and the shingles looked like scales.

"That's called half-timbering," Brennus said. "It's Morrowind architecture, really—or was."

She tossed a twig in the river and watched it float off.

"Have you heard anything?"

"No," he replied, "but I need to have a look with my instruments."

"Going up on the wall, then?"

"Higher," he said, pointing to the structure of stone and stained glass that towered over everything else.

"I'll go with you," she said.

"I don't think I need a guard at the moment," he said.

"You never know," she replied.

———

Inside, the chapel of Arkay was all hush and colored light.

They found a priest who, after a bit of explanation, showed them the way up to the highest spire.

From there even the people on the walls looked small. She gazed first out over the forest, hills, and distant Valus Mountains. Only reluctantly did she focus nearer.

The wormies had taken up positions a few hundred yards from the gates.

"They're out of range of ballista and catapults," she said. "They're not stupid."

"No, they aren't," Brennus replied. "Necromancers have been known to make such creatures as these, but they are generally mindless. And slow. We're dealing with something new here. Did you hear what happened last night?"

"What do you mean?"

"A man died of natural causes and rose up as one of these. The watch got him, and afterward they put out the alarm. There were three more cases."

"Just like Jarrow, and the others we lost on the hill."

"Right. Whatever spirits animate them clearly can travel more than a few paces."

"Every time we kill one, we risk a corpse waking up in town."

Brennus nodded.

"What do you reckon, then? They'll try to starve us out?"

"No," the mage replied. "I think they're just waiting for reinforcements." As he said it, he pointed.

She saw it then, pale as a cloud with distance, unmistakable. Umbriel itself was coming for them.

SEVEN

Annaïg picked at the flesh of the green nutlike thing and popped it into her mouth, chewing slowly. She felt a little heat like black pepper, followed by a rush in her nose like fiery mustard and green onions. The texture, though, was like a boiled cashew.

"That's great," she told Glim. "What is it?"

"Something new," he said. "Maybe from Morrowind."

"Maybe," Annaïg said dubiously.

"Wert says that sometimes the sump will go for years without producing a particular thing, then start again, while something else vanishes for a time."

"How does it do it?" she wondered. "Does Umbriel store seeds and eggs someplace?"

"I don't think so," Glim told her. "I think it's the trees."

Glim had a sharp, excited scent about him, and he seemed to be barely holding something in.

"The trees?" she asked.

"The trees in the Fringe Gyre," he said. "You saw them when we tried to escape."

"Well, yes," she said. "But it was dark, and I was distracted by—well, escaping."

"I believe that they are cousins of the Hist."

"That's interesting. I can't imagine what that means."

"Well—think of water oaks and white oaks in Black Marsh. They're both oaks because they have acorns; their leaves are arranged in a spiral. But other things about them are different. Like cousins."

"Okay," Annaïg said. "I follow that, although I never thought of it that way. So are you saying that the trees in the Fringe Gyre are intelligent, like the Hist?"

"Yes and no. They communicate, as the Hist do, but in different tones. I didn't really learn to hear them until Fhena showed me, and then—"

"Fhena?"

"Yes, one of the gardeners in the trees. She helped me find you. Surely I mentioned her."

"No, you surely did not," Annaïg said.

"Well, she's just someone I talk to," Mere-Glim said. She thought he sounded defensive.

"A woman?"

"She is female, yes."

"Uh-huh."

He made a low growl in his throat, which she understood as embarrassment. "It's not like that," he said. "She's not—I mean, she's an Umbrielian. She looks like a Dunmer."

"Fine. I'm just wondering, if you're so friendly with her, why you haven't mentioned her before."

He blinked at her, and she realized she sounded stupid.

Jealous. And what did she have to be jealous over?

But the fact that after all of these years as best friends, he hadn't mentioned her . . .

She pushed it off.

"The trees," she said.

"Yes," he replied. "Some of my people believe that the Hist came to Tamriel from Oblivion. Umbriel is from Oblivion, too, so it doesn't seem too far-fetched to me that they could be cousins."

"Yes, but it would be a huge coincidence."

"I don't think it's a coincidence. I think the city tree somehow called Umbriel, or the Fringe Gyre trees may have called to the Hist—but I think there was some sort of collusion."

"Are the trees here malevolent?"

"No, they are—vaguer than the Hist. Not as intelligent maybe, or maybe just in a different way. Simpler. But like the Hist, they can form their sap into different things, the way you do with your equipment. And they can shape life, change its form."

She thought about that for a moment.

"That—makes sense. One of my tasks is to take raw ingredients from the sump and transform them into nutrients for the trees, but part of that process involves getting the roots themselves to release substances. I haven't worked in the large fermentation vats, but I have noticed there are always roots involved."

"I think it's the trees who remember all the forms of life on Umbriel," Glim said. "I think they produce the proforms—the little worms Umbrielians start as. Then the ingenium gives them a soul, and they grow according to some sort of plan the trees remember."

"Well, that's really interesting," Annaïg said. "If we could poison the trees, destroy them, that would in essence destroy Umbriel."

Glim's eyes went wide. "But you can't—" he began, then stopped. "It would take a long time," he said. "And it might not be possible."

"If they are all connected at the root, like the Hist—sure, they all draw nourishment from the sump."

An expression flickered across his features that she had never actually seen before, but it reminded her of anger.

"Look," she said, "you're saying these trees are responsible for the murder of almost everyone we know."

"I'm not," he said. "I'm saying they were used. Someone used them."

"Glim, you can't—I know how you feel about some of these people, but—"

"I don't think you do," he said. "You hate everyone you know here."

"Glim, the one person I showed friendship to tried to kill me."

"I know," he said. "But the skraws are different. And Fhena."

She sighed. "Look, let's take one thing at a time. What about Phmer's kitchen? Can I get in?"

"You can't get in far," he said. "Any more than I could get into your kitchen."

"But here we are."

"No, no. I can get to your pantry, and so could someone from another kitchen, in the proper disguise. But to go any farther would raise all sorts of alarms and protections. Some are in the walls, living things that see and smell the uninvited. Others, as I understand it, are sorcerous in nature. All I know is, they say at least twenty people from other kitchens have tried to invade past Phmer's pantry; all were caught or killed. Almost as many have tried to get into Toel's kitchen since you came to work there."

"I haven't heard anything about that."

"That's because they all went into the sump," he said.

"Huh. But you think I can get into the pantry."

"At night, if you're very careful."

"Suppose I was invisible, had no scent, made no sound?" she asked.

"You might make it another fifteen paces, as some of the others did."

"Well, then," she said. "Thanks, Glim, that's very helpful."

"You're going to get yourself killed," he said. "You remember the last time you tried to make someone invisible? For a week all my organs were on display for everyone to see."

"I've learned a lot since then," she assured him.

"I hope so. When are you going?"

"Tonight."

————

Annaïg was wakened by a gentle pressure on her arm. She opened her eyes and found Dulg standing there, his little frog-like form perched on the stool by her bed.

"What is it?" she asked.

"Chef Toel requires your presence," he said.

She stirred, rubbing her eyes. "What's going on?"

"That's not for you to ask," Dulg replied.

She looked around. "Where is Slyr?" she asked.

"Summoned earlier," Dulg supplied.

"Did she wear my gold-and-black gown?"

Dulg looked a bit puzzled. "You said I could offer it to her."

"Right. I did, didn't I? Well, just fetch me the black one."

Dulg nodded and bounded off.

An hour later, properly dressed and coiffed, she met Toel on his balcony. He wasn't alone this time. His underchefs Intovar and Yeum stood on either side of him. Intovar was a spindly fellow with dirty yellow hair and an air of the rodent about him. Yeum was a thick woman with an appealing, heart-shaped face and dusky skin. Neither had ever spoken to her except to give her orders.

Slyr was also there, of course.

On the other side of the balcony—as if relegated there by an invisible line—stood another party. The obvious leader was an impressively tall, narrow woman with close-cropped hair and large emerald eyes. She was accompanied by two men, one brick red with horns and the other a merish-looking person who looked perpetually surprised.

"Chef Toel," Annaïg said, bowing her head slightly.

He smiled oddly and gestured at the green-eyed woman. "I should like to present you to Chef Phmer, and also her assistants Jolha and Egren."

"An honor, Chefs," Annaïg replied.

Phmer smiled, but it reminded Annaïg of the toothy grin of the piranhas that lived in the dunkwaters.

"I'm told you are to thank—or blame—for many of the fads passing through some kitchens," she said. Her voice was silk, coiled thick and made into a noose.

"I suppose I might be," Annaïg replied.

"And yet your inventiveness would appear to have its limits."

"Everything has limits," Annaïg said cautiously.

"And yet fetching up against these limits has tempted you to do something rather costly," Phmer went on.

Annaïg looked at Toel, whose expression was blank.

"I don't understand," she said.

Phmer's expression changed, going from one of apparent good humor to barely checked rage.

"Do you deny you broke into my kitchen last night in an attempt to steal the secret of the ninth savor?"

"Chef," Annaïg said, "I do. I certainly do."

"And yet we have testimony that you did. And other evidence."

"Testimony?"

But she couldn't miss the suppressed look of triumph on Slyr's face.

"If you did this thing," Toel said, "you know I must give you over to her. It is the law."

"It's permissible to invade another kitchen wholesale and slaughter everyone there, but not to sneak into one to steal?"

"I obtained permission for my raid on Qijne's kitchen," he replied. "Nor is that here nor there. You are not the head of a kitchen. Did you do this? Did you try to steal from Phmer?"

"I've already said I didn't," Annaïg pointed out.

"Well, we shall see about that," Phmer said. She gestured at a box on the floor, and her red-skinned underchef bent to it. He unlatched one side of the thing, and something crawled out.

She thought at first it was a spider, but its legs weren't rigid; nor were they as supple as those of a squid, but something in between. And—she realized as it unfolded them—it had wings, rather like those of a mosquito, and in fact now it somewhat resembled one, albeit one that could fit into the palm of her hand.

The wings blurred into motion, and the little creature lifted into the air; three stalks or antennae began probing about as it approached her. She remained still, wondering if it had some sort of sting, and if she had made a mistake. She tried to slow her heart with simple willpower, but it thudded on irrespective.

The tentacles tickled across her face and down her dress, lingering on her left hand, but then the creature darted over to Slyr and began to make an annoying high-pitched sound. Phmer frowned, but Toel's lips turned up.

Slyr just looked puzzled, then aghast.

Toel lifted his hand toward Phmer, then turned it gently toward Slyr. Two of his guards took Slyr by the shoulders, and the woman looked wildly at Annaïg.

Phmer reached into one of Slyr's pockets, and then the other. From the second she withdrew a small vial. She uncorked it, sniffed it, and then tasted a bit on her finger.

"This is it," she said. "The scent of my kitchen is on her dress, the ninth savor in her pocket. Do you need more?"

"I do not," Toel said. "The evidence is clear enough."

"How did you do it?" Phmer asked Slyr. "There was sign that you had been in the kitchen, but my best safeguards are those around the taste itself, and you left no trace there. I must know how you did this."

"I didn't!" Slyr exploded. "It was Annaïg! Somehow she

made it look as if—why would I warn you she was going to steal from you if it was really me coming? Why would I— This is her doing!" She plucked wildly at her clothing, as if discovering it was made of fire. "This is her dress! She's tricked us all somehow."

"Let me understand this," Toel said softly. "You warned Phmer against someone on my staff? Behind my back?"

Slyr shrank back, like a cornered animal, a little whimper escaping her.

"She remains mine," Phmer said.

"Oh, you may have her," Toel replied. "I have no doubt you will extract revenge enough for both of us."

"First there will be questions," she said. "Many, many questions." She nodded at Annaïg. "I would question her as well."

"There is no evidence against her other than the testimony of a thief," Toel replied. "You may not have her."

Phmer lifted her chin haughtily, but she didn't argue. Instead she signed for her creature to take Slyr.

"Annaïg, please," Slyr whimpered.

She felt her heart soften, remembering her first few weeks in the bowels of Umbriel, nights with Slyr, gazing at the stars.

"It's not in my hands, Slyr," she said quietly. "Your own actions brought you to this."

And so they dragged Slyr off. She didn't beg or plead again, at least not in Annaïg's earshot.

When they were gone, Toel indicated one of the chairs.

"Sit," he said.

She did as he commanded.

"How did you do it?" he asked.

"Chef—" she began.

"You are safe," he replied. "Unless you left some sort of evidence that might turn up later, you are safe. I can easily see how you manipulated Slyr into going to Phmer, and how you used the chemical stains of that kitchen to implicate her, how you might scrub them from your own person. But I ask you again, how did you do it—how did you pass the inner safeguards and steal the savor itself?"

Annaïg felt her fear melting, then transforming, igniting into triumph.

"I didn't, Chef," she said.

"What do you mean?"

"I only entered the outer corridors of her kitchen, to taint the dress. The ninth taste I invented—or reinvented, I suppose—on my own."

For perhaps the first time since she had met him, Toel's mouth moved as if in speech but without producing any sound.

"How?" he asked.

"All I had to do was think about it a bit. Once I understood the principle, making the taste was simple enough. And just now, Phmer confirmed that I was right. Until then I couldn't be sure."

"What is it, then? Do you have more?"

"I can make more," she assured him. "For obvious reasons, I don't have any with me."

"But what is it?"

"The ninth savor is the opposite of all other tastes. It is the utter absence of flavor."

Toel's pupils constricted, then widened again, reminding her of Glim.

"Like the space between words," he murmured.

"I thought of music," she said. "There are many pitches, chords, harmonies, and dissonances—but silence—that, too, is a part of music."

His smiled broadened a little and he tapped the table with his forefinger.

"I had given up on you, you know," he said. "I thought all of that talk about showing me what I didn't know I wanted to see was desperate nonsense, and yet you've done it. And Slyr—she never saw it coming. But why did it take you so long?"

"I do things in my own time, for my own reasons," she said.

His gaze intensified and he placed his hand on hers.

"You've pleased me more than you can imagine," he said. "Come with me now, and let me please you."

She squeezed his hand, leaned forward—and with a slight hesitation, brought her lips to his. They were amazingly smooth, like slippery glass, and an unexpected tingle fizzed down to her belly, leaving her feeling both excited and somewhat sick. He responded, lightly at first, but as he grew hungrier she pulled away.

"In my own time," she said softly. "For my own reasons."

For a breath or two she didn't think he would relent, but then he laughed. "I will have to kill you one day," he said. "But for now, I love you. Go now; invent delightful things for Lord Rhel. I will see you tomorrow."

In the corridor, her knees wobbled.

"Xhuth!" she swore.

She hated Toel, *hated* him, now more than ever. And yet her body didn't care about that at all. It was disgusting.

Later, in her rooms, she drew out her locket. Maybe tonight Attrebus would answer, finally.

But did she want him to? What would she tell him? How could she explain what she had done to Slyr? Or talk about what had happened with Toel?

She couldn't. And so she closed the locket and sought sleep, turning so she could not see Slyr's empty bed.

EIGHT

Colin woke sometime after midnight. At first he thought he was alone, but then he noticed Arese standing at the window. She reminded him of one of the white poplars that grew along streams in the hills outside of Anvil.

She heard him approaching and glanced over her shoulder, but her features were shadowed by the moonlight behind her.

"I shouldn't still be here," she said.

"Right," he replied. "Why are you?"

She shrugged. "I guess I thought we weren't through."

She must have seen the expression on his face, because she laughed. "No, I think we're done with *that* for the night," she said. "I mean—you came here for something, right? To tell me something?"

"Yes," he said, surprised at how unimportant it seemed at the moment. But he explained it anyway—about what Hierem did in Black Marsh.

"That only seems to confirm what we already thought," she said.

"It's something," Colin replied. "The journal is proof, isn't it?"

"It is proof," she said. "Just not very good proof."

"How good does it have to be? The Emperor was suspicious enough to plant you in Hierem's ministry. Shouldn't this be enough to convince him?"

"I don't know," she said. "What do you know about Hierem?"

"Not much," Colin admitted.

"He's been around forever. He had a position in the old Empire—he was an ambassador to Morrowind. He was a minister to Thules the Gibbering, the witch-warrior who ruled what little remained of the Empire before Titus Mede took it from him."

"I remember. Not a well-liked ruler."

"Maybe not beloved, but he was Nibenese, and despite his various perversions, many on the council favored him over a Colovian usurper. Hierem is from an old Nibenese family, with a lot of connections. He smoothed over the conquest, helped convince the council to accept Mede as a liberator rather than a conqueror. He's also extremely influential with the Synod. He's the second most powerful man in the Empire, despite his servile public appearance, and if Mede were to move against him without an unimpeachable reason, it could lead to civil war."

"I find that hard to believe."

"Only because you don't know Hierem. I feel certain that Mede would win any such conflict, but it would be costly."

"What then?"

She turned back to the window. "Don't worry about it," she said. "I'll work something out."

"Your life is in danger," he said. "Go to the Emperor, tell him what you know. Get out."

"It's not enough," she said. "And any cover I might have left—"

"Surely you have some means of communicating with him. Secret means."

"There is a secret word," she said. "If it reaches the Emperor's ear, he will know to go to a certain place. But if I do that, he may do exactly as you say."

"Would that be so bad?"

"Yes, because we fail to stop Hierem. After ten years—I have to have something."

"Then let me go," Colin said. "I'll speak for you. I'll explain it all."

He didn't hold his breath, but he felt like it.

She saw right through it.

"You don't believe me," she said. "You think I'm lying about working for him."

"I want to believe you," he said.

She looked back out the window and chewed her lower lip.

"Jasper," she said. "The word is Jasper."

———

The second time Colin met the Emperor it was in a narrow, unfurnished room. He'd been brought there bound and blindfolded, and he didn't see a door. The stone was the same color as the interior of the White-Gold Tower, but beyond that he had no clues at all as to where he was.

This wasn't court, and the Emperor wasn't dressed for it. He wore a plain Colovian soldier's tunic of dark gray wool and leather breeks. His crown was a plain gold circlet. A broadsword in a battered scabbard hung at his side. Two soldiers stood yards away, but Colin suspected that if he tried anything, he would be dead at Mede's hand before either of them could move.

"I know you," the Emperor said. "You're the young man who told me my Attrebus wasn't killed when his men were massacred."

"Yes, sire," Colin replied.

"You're an inspector in the Penitus Oculatus."

"Yes, sire."

"And yet you've come to me over all of your superiors, using a password and sign that only I and one other know."

"Knew, sire. I know it now, as does the man who brought it to you. It's as few as I could manage to involve, but more than I would have liked."

Titus Mede conceded that with a nod. Then he signed for the guards to leave, and Colin was alone with the most powerful man in the world.

"Who sent you?" the Emperor asked.

"Letine Arese, majesty," Colin said.

"Why didn't she come herself?"

"Two members of the Dark Brotherhood tried to kill her a few nights ago. She's afraid that if she came to you herself, she would be followed. She's in hiding."

"Who sent the assassins?"

"I wasn't able to discover that, sire. Both men are dead, and I cannot find any trace of their shades—it's rumored the brotherhood has ways of ensuring their members don't leave behind talkative ghosts. Not surprisingly, they had no material evidence to connect them to anyone either."

"But surely Arese has suspicions about who might try to murder her."

"She suspects your minister, Hierem, majesty."

The Emperor nodded. "Of course. How are you mixed up in this, inspector?"

"Arese asked for my help," he replied. "In finding proof to implicate Hierem in the massacre—in the attempted murder of your son."

"That's funny," the Emperor said. "Hierem has supplied me with some evidence that Arese was behind that herself."

"She arranged the attack," Colin said, "but the order came from higher."

"From Hierem?"

"She believes so."

"Believes so?" Mede paced, hands clasped behind his back. "Ten years she's been there," he muttered. "In all of that time, no proof. Nothing I can use against him."

"Sire, I don't understand. If you're suspicious of the minister . . ."

"It's not so simple," the Emperor said. "I can't risk an internal conflict—especially when we face this—bonewalker army, if it can be called that."

"Sire, Arese and I believe that's no accident," Colin said. "We believe Hierem is somehow involved in this Umbriel business."

He outlined what they had learned about Hierem's trip to Black Marsh. When Colin was done, Mede stood still and silent for a long time, his forehead wrinkled.

"You have the journal?"

"Yes, sire."

He handed the Emperor the book and waited while he read it.

"Why didn't you go to your superiors with this?" he asked when he was finished.

"I wasn't sure I could trust them, majesty," Colin said. "I really don't know who to trust anymore."

"I can see your point. But now I wonder who *I* should trust. This might all be true, and it might all be some fabrication of Arese's." He stroked his chin. "Find me proof," the Emperor said. "Real proof. Something the council can't argue with."

He leaned against the wall.

"You know, we had a letter from Umbriel, delivered by a . . . *rotting thing* . . . to one of my generals."

"Really, sire? A letter?"

"Yes—very politely written, supposedly from the very hand of the master of that place, who also calls himself Umbriel. They have besieged every path to the Imperial City in the East, and soon enough they will probably hold the West as well. Yet we are told we are free to leave the city unharmed—with all of our arms and possessions. Umbriel wants this city, not its inhabitants. The offer remains good until Umbriel arrives. Doesn't that seem peculiar?"

"Didn't your majesty offer the chance of surrender to any city he besieged?"

"Yes. But according to our reports, Umbriel requires the souls of the living to remain aloft—and no defense has been found by either the College or the Synod to prevent its method of slaughter. Why would they allow the fuel that keeps their engines burning to simply walk away?"

"Obviously, majesty, they want something more than fuel. Something here in the city."

"Or perhaps Umbriel has no interest in the city, but rather is aiding the ally who summoned it here. If I take my army and leave, what will Hierem do? Take possession of the throne and then send Umbriel to destroy my army and me?"

"From what we know, it seems a possibility," Colin said.

"But not yet enough of one to risk a civil war if I'm wrong. So find out. And involve no one else, other than Arese."

Mede reached into his pocket and produced a small metallic key.

"Use this carefully," he said. "It is a key to Hierem's ministry and rooms. If he finds it on you, he will know it came from me, and things will go bad very quickly. If he is connected to Umbriel, he may know something of its secrets, who commands it, how to stop it. Find these things out for me, and do it quickly. I am not squeamish about methods—you understand? Our time grows short. If you find nothing, he will have to be questioned, no matter the consequences—before the enemy arrives."

"I understand, majesty."

NINE

In her third hour of sleeplessness, Annaïg gave up the fight and sat up in bed. Despite her earlier misgivings, she tried the locket, but Attrebus still didn't answer, and she didn't really expect him to. She was beginning to think he was dead.

"I'm not sorry for what I did to Slyr," she muttered, under her breath. "I had to do it."

But for what? And what now? She could play Toel along for a bit, but soon he would get impatient, and she would have to refuse him outright or comply with his desires.

Would it be that bad?

"Yes," she told herself. But if it worked, if it moved her nearer to discovering how to rip Umbriel from the sky, then fine. But it wouldn't work. If she became his mistress she might rise a bit in position, but then he would become bored with her, as he had with Slyr, and she would be worse off than before—or at least no better.

What she had to do was escape him, and that meant moving up on her own merit—without him.

And her best chance at that was coming up all too soon, and it might not come again. If she could cook the perfect meal, draw the attention of those Toel called "lords"—then she would really be in a position to do something.

She had started something and she couldn't stop now. If she cooked the best meal Lord Rhel had ever eaten—if she could impress him beyond measure—then maybe he would make her a chef, give her her own kitchen.

And so she began to plan, and that calmed her down, and finally she slept, and dreamed of cooking.

———

She met Glim again, this time by the light of the two moons, high up on one of the massive boughs of the trees. She strained to see something of the land below, but mist and clouds obscured almost everything. Glim was curiously silent.

"Are you listening to the trees?" she asked.

"I'm thinking," he replied softly. He sounded strange—upset.

"I didn't want to do it," she said. "I had to."

"It's not about Slyr," Mere-Glim said. "It's about this new request of yours."

"It should be easy," she replied. "Even if the skraws never get past the pantries, they talk to the workers there—I know they do. A little information is all I ask."

"No, you're asking for a lot of information. And the skraws have already given you a lot of information—for which they haven't been repaid."

"Is that what it's come to be between us?" she asked. "Glim, I have to know I can count on you. I have to know you're my friend."

"I am your friend," he said. "Of course I am. And I've been doing what you ask, haven't I? All I am saying is—maybe it's time you helped me."

"I'm still in no position to manufacture enough water-breathing serum to make a difference," she said. "I would if I could."

"I understand that," he replied. "What I need right now are weapons."

"What?"

"The tubes that bring processed waste from the midden to the sump are living things. There is a series of sphincters that pass the waste along or hold it back, as needed. I need something that will paralyze the sphincters and an antidote for that. I need concoctions to taint foods, to make them unpleasant or inedible without rendering them poisonous. I need weapons of sabotage for the skraws to wage their rebellion with. I won't need large amounts of them—just enough. You know how to make these things."

"I do," she said. "Let me think a moment."

She closed her eyes and felt the pull toward the world below, so close, so impossibly far away. So far, none of her experimentation had given her any hope that she and Glim could leave without fading into nothingness. But there was still some chance she could destroy her prison. Glim was giving her an opportunity to learn how to sabotage Umbriel, and a network to do it with. How could she refuse?

"Okay," she said finally. "But we have to do this carefully. We have to be smart. The first thing is, Toel's kitchen has to keep running, at least for now. At the same time, we can't be seen as immune to these attacks, or we'll draw attention. I think it's also best that—at first—no one knows the skraws are doing this."

"I don't understand," Glim said. "We're trying to pressure the lords into doing something about the vapors. If they don't know it's us—"

"I really don't think you know what you're dealing with," Annaïg told him. "As soon as they suspect the skraws, the kitchens—or worse, I'm sure, the lords—will come after you. I've seen what that means."

"They can't kill us all."

"No, but they can kill you. They can find out who the other leaders are and kill them."

"Maybe."

"Try it my way," she urged. "When everything is completely bollixed up, when they see how vulnerable they are, you step in and set things right, asking only that the vapors be replaced by something more humane."

"What's your way?" Glim asked.

"Well—at first we make the kitchens think they're attacking one another."

"How is that?"

"The banquet, the one I needed the ninth savor for. Umbriel himself will be in attendance. Four kitchens are competing to win the honor of cooking that meal. Would it be so surprising if they started sabotaging one another?"

"Now I'm starting to see," Glim said. "And of course, your kitchen would in the end benefit the most from this—competition."

"Yes."

Glim scratched his arms. "I don't hate this idea," he said. "But why do you want Toel to succeed?"

"Because if he succeeds, I succeed. He might get advanced and take me with him."

"Why do you care about that?"

"Because the closer I am to the heart of things, the more damage I can do. And the more I can help the skraws."

He nodded. "That makes sense," he said. "I'll talk to the others."

"And I'll start work on the things you need. Now come on, let's go back down before we're noticed."

"I'm going to stay up here awhile," he said. "Listen to the trees."

"I'll see you later, then."

She felt stirrings of guilt, because she didn't like to deceive Glim, but he had lost all sense of things. She loved him, and she needed him—and if she had to, for both of their sakes, and the sake of the world—she would use him.

———

Toel's expression began as disgust but quickly became so murderous that Annaïg felt a rush of fear. Then she noticed it wasn't the vaporessence of fermented duck egg she had given him to try that he was reacting to—he was smelling something else more generally in the air.

"It's the water filters," she explained. "Sump slurry has them clogged."

"I know what it is," Toel said, his voice cold. "Do not presume, you. I know every scent of this kitchen. If a single lampen invades the cilia tubules, my nose aches from the stench. We are sabotaged—again. I will not bear it. I will not bear it!"

"But who would do such a thing?" Annaïg asked.

"Phmer possibly," he snarled. "That's the problem, isn't it? It could be her, or it could be Luuniel or Ashdre."

"Why? Is this kind of thing usual during a competition?"

"Not at all," he fumed. "It is far outside of the bounds. Very far. Too far." He slammed the flat of his hand on the table. "This sort of contest happens all the time. We are all of us rivals. But never before has this sort of wholesale sabotage occurred. Now they strike at us, we strike at them—it escalates."

"Wait," Annaïg said. "We've been doing this as well?"

"Well, of course," he replied. "Once a war is begun, only a fool will not fight. But after our last response to Phmer's affronts, I should have thought the matter settled. But now she—or one of the others—they come back at us."

"Why don't the lords step in?"

"Because there is no law concerning this. Outright invasion is governed by strict rules, but this picking and *picking* at things . . . Anyway, even though we're usually able to discover who has been tampering with us, it's not enough proof for a lord, you understand. They do not understand instinct and intuition the way we do."

"Who started it?" she asked as guilelessly as possible.

"Most think it was Ashdre. He had the least chance of winning." He chuckled a mean sort of laugh. "He has none now. Between Phmer and us, Ashdre's kitchen is crippled. Luuniel isn't much better off."

"That's good, then," Annaïg said. "It seems we're faring better than the others."

"It seems, it seems. But all of the others hate me, you know, because I rose up from below. They disdain me, they pine for my failure. And lesser chefs, they are watching this. Possibly they are even behind some of the vandalism, hoping to see me fall and take my place. And sooner, not later, they will think to come against me together."

"Have you no protection? Couldn't you post guards?"

"Post them where? In the sump? In the midden? Below the filters? Even if I had a hundred guards, there would be no way to cover every vulnerable place. No, the only thing we can do is set a harsher example. And that I will do. I will show them what real retribution is."

With that, he left her, and she worked in silence.

She felt like humming, but suppressed the urge for fear that her good cheer might be noticed. Her plan was working better than she had ever imagined. This was the first time Toel had said anything about it, but the rumors had been thick this last week, and Toel had come to ask her to develop a recipe for breathing underwater. All of the major kitchens were at one another's throats, and they were all so vicious and mean it didn't occur to any of them to question closely how it had all started. Glim and the skraws didn't have to do much to keep things going—just a little nudge here and there. In fact, for the first time since she had been in Umbriel, she heard people talking about the skraws in glowing terms—how quickly they fixed what was broken, how good and uncomplaining they were. That was very good news, because it meant that Glim might achieve his goal without ever having to risk a confrontation between the skraws and the lords—when Toel's kitchen was triumphant, she could reasonably suggest a replacement for the vapors as their reward. She'd already been given the perfect excuse to invent a safer drug.

That wouldn't matter in the long run, of course, but it would make Glim happy.

The other thing that had Annaïg suppressing her humming was how well her menu was coming along. Thanks to the skraws, she knew the tastes, fashions, and fetishes of not only Lord Rhel, but also most of those attending his tasting. She knew which ones Rhel liked and which ones he despised, and part of her planning was that the meal itself subtly insult and discomfit the latter. She knew he had a great sense of whimsy, and above all that he was partial to the new, strange, surprising—but also that he prided himself on a sort of coarseness of taste, of mortal indulgence. In this, he seemed to ape Umbriel himself, the eponymous master of this place, who was known to dine on the lowest sorts of matter at times. Rhel had been heard to say that such tastes reflected not the lack of refinement, but the fulfillment of it.

She worked, and her mood only improved as the day went on.

———

Glim rode the tree and bellowed in delight.

His claws gripped about the tendril-thin branch tips, and the wind, the spin of Umbriel, and the long rippling undulation of the trees did the rest. Fhena's musical laugh sang nearby, where she clung to her own branch.

"I told you!" she shouted.

"You did!" he admitted. "It's better than flying, I can tell you that."

"You've flown? How?"

"Never mind," he said. "It doesn't matter."

It was merely exciting, at first, but after a few moments he began to feel the trees, their own joy in their existence, in the process of merely being, and he felt himself gently tugged into a state of pure thought, where no words existed to constrain his feelings, where no logic tried to make sense and order of the world, and there was only color, smell, touch, feeling, motion. When Fhena finally cajoled him back to thicker branches, he went only reluctantly, and he felt more refreshed—and more himself—than he had in a long time.

"Thank you," he said. "That was—wonderful."

"Isn't it?" she said. "Sometimes I dream of just letting go, of never coming back."

"Right," Glim said. "But you have to come back."

"Why?" she asked.

"Well, because—you would die."

"And return to Umbriel and be born again. People do it all the time."

"Die?"

"Ride the branches and let go. They say sometimes the mood just hits you and you can't help it."

"How do you know what someone who lets go was thinking?"

"Well, my friend Jinel got the feeling, but Qwern caught him. But he just went out the next day and let go anyway."

Glim remembered the ghost of the feeling, of near-perfect peace.

"You didn't think to warn me about that before I did it?" he wondered.

"Warn you? Why?"

"Because—" He stopped, then started again. "Listen, don't do it again, okay? I don't want you to die."

"Well, I wouldn't die, silly, just go back into Umbriel."

"Right—and be born as someone else, someone who doesn't remember me, who isn't my friend."

"I wouldn't have to remember you," Fhena said. "I would know you, Mere-Glim, whatever form I wore." She brightened. "Maybe I would even be born in a form like yours. Wouldn't that be fun?"

Something like a quick hot tide seem to fill him up, and his mouth worked in embarrassment.

"What's wrong?" she asked.

"Please," he said, "just promise me—no more branch riding."

"That's an awful lot to promise," she said. "But if you're asking, I guess I will."

"Good. Thank you."

But she had reminded him of something he'd been trying not to think about.

"What now?" Fhena asked.

"Now?" he sighed. "Well, speaking of being reborn, I have to go back to the sump and check on the recent implantations."

"Stay a little longer," she pleaded.

"I have to go," he said. "Besides, you've got your own work to do. I don't want to get you in trouble."

"Well, very well. Tomorrow?"

"Tomorrow."

He left, but the thought of Fhena as an Argonian—or at least in the form of one—stayed with him. In fact, he was so distracted that he realized he'd reached the implantations and had just been staring at them for several moments before he really saw them.

They looked so much like small Saxhleel. Their eyes were very large.

He'd known since he first saw them, but put it off. He couldn't face it then.

No matter what happened with the kitchens and the lords, the skraws wouldn't be free of the vapors. They would die, one by one, and be replaced by things that looked like him, that didn't need the vapors to breathe beneath the waves. When they were all dead, the agony of the skraws would be over.

But that meant Wert and Oluth and everyone he actually knew was going to die horribly. He'd hoped to save them, to give them a better life, but instead his mere existence as a template had doomed them irrevocably to misery.

And they were so close. Toel's kitchen would win, and the skraws would be rewarded with a healthier life. Then let the worms become Argonians, and the skraws live out their remaining years decently.

So he did what he had to do. He carefully killed them all, took them back up the Fringe Gyre, and threw them over the edge, where their tiny figures became smoke and then nothing.

———

It was the morning before the day of the banquet when Toel came to her, his eyes icy with fury. He wore a shirt and pair of breeches that appeared to be made of sharkskin, or something similar. He placed garments like them on her table.

"Put those on. You're going with us."

"Chef?"

"I have good information that the sump feed from our midden is going to be sabotaged again," he said. "Soon."

"But that's okay," she said. "That won't affect the meal, at this point."

"It's not that," Toel shouted. "I've simply had enough of this. Someone is going to die for this presumption, and I'm going to be there to see it. And so are you."

———

Mere-Glim drifted nearly still amid twenty-foot-long strands of slackweed, watching the party approaching the maw where the midden was supposed to empty into the sump. They weren't skraws, and swam even more clumsily. They were armed with long, wicked-looking spears, and there were six of them.

He waited until they had passed into darkness, then followed behind them into the dark fissure, trying to decide what he could do.

He hoped the armed figures would make some noise his comrades would hear, but they moved pretty quietly and altogether without talking.

They stopped to examine the tertiary sphincter, already closed, and then swam to the side, toward the maintenance tunnels. These were narrow, flattened tubes that worked around the big valve into the last of the seven chambers that waste from the middens passed through. It was dark with sludge, but not nearly as thick as it should have been. They produced some sort of underwater lanterns, and the beams stabbed through the murk, revealing a wide-eyed Wert holding a nutrient injector.

"You there," a man's voice said. "What are you doing?"

Wert's mouth worked soundlessly for a moment.

"Just checking the muscle, sir," he said. "These have been seizing up lately."

"Yes, they have," the man said. His companions were positioning themselves in a hemisphere around Wert. "I wonder why you have a nutrient injector. Those are used by farmers, on the Fringe Gyre. To my knowledge they have no purpose in the sump."

"Well, it fell, I guess—from up there," Wert attempted lamely. "I was wondering what it was."

"Don't lie to me!" the man exploded. "Unbelievable! Phmer has turned the skraws against me! No wonder!"

"Phmer?" Wert said, puzzled.

"Not just the skraws," another said. "The nutrient injector—they must have help from the Fringe Gyre."

"Well," the man said. "We'll see about all of that. If the skraws and the farmers are involved, the lords will have to take notice." He poked his spear toward Wert. "You'll tell us everything, skraw."

"It's just me," Wert said. "No one else is involved. Just me."

"I doubt that. But we'll be sure before it's over. I'll find everything in that little mind of yours."

Glim was convinced the man was telling the truth. That

meant trouble not only for the skraws, but for Fhena.

The first man probably never knew he was there before Glim's claws sheared through his neck. The second had only time for a short shriek. The third—the man doing most of the talking—he was quick. He managed to get his spear up fast enough to cut a gash along Glim's belly before Glim grabbed the shaft and slammed his thorny crest into the man's face, the man then gurgling and drifting toward the bottom.

Glim spun in time to avoid another spear, this one wielded by a red-skinned woman with horns. They were all so clumsy, so slow. He dodged the tip and disemboweled her. A merish-looking woman was thrashing about with the injector in her back, and Cilinil appeared from somewhere and wrapped her long legs and arms around another, while Wert drove one of the spears through that one's neck.

Glim felt a humming in his veins he'd never known, a terrible, black joy that made it hard to think.

The fellow he had butted was coming back. Glim swam down, caught him by the hair, and pulled him up to eye level.

"Incredible," the man said weakly. "Do you know who I am? Have you no idea what you've done?"

"None," Glim snarled.

"I am Chef Toel. Do you understand? Now let me go."

"I don't think I can do that," Glim said.

"No?" Toel's eyes suddenly glowed a strange silver color and the water started to hiss with bubbles.

"Xhuth!" Glim gasped as agony coursed up his arms. The muscles clenched uncontrollably and his fingers lost their grip. Toel came toward him, snarling, and his remaining companion was coming from the side, quickly. Wert and Cilinil were much too far away to help.

It was almost over before Annaïg realized what was happening, that it was Glim attacking them. She struck toward him as he confronted Toel.

She saw the water around Toel stir, and Glim was suddenly thrashing, choking with pain. Toel steadied himself in the water, and the familiar look of self-satisfaction on his face was suddenly more than she could bear, much more. As she approached, his lips curled up and he started to say something, but something he saw stopped him.

What he saw was her.

She felt the blade snick out from her arm, and she acted on instinct, slashing clumsily with the invisible knife. Toel managed to get his arm in the way, and the blade sliced cleanly through the joint of his elbow. She felt a terrific shock, and her lungs stopped working. All she could see was his face.

"I was wrong about you," Toel gasped. Then his features seemed to blur into light and dark arabesques that made no sort of sense.

She came to herself again in Glim's arms. They were still underwater. The two skraws were looking on in shock at Toel's body, which besides missing a forearm, was now mostly decapitated.

"Glim," she murmured.

"I didn't know who you were," he said. "I might have killed you. What the kaoc' are you doing down here?"

"He made me come," she said. "He was furious—wanted

to set an example, or something."

She looked back at the destroyed body. "Oh Stendarr, Glim, what did I do? I've never—"

"Neither have I," he said.

She felt flimsy, like wet paper. She could see the dead bodies, the dark blood swirling in the water, more black than red, like chocolate.

But none of it seemed real. She had just been talking to Toel. She had kissed him!

"What do we do?" Wert sputtered. "You killed a chef! That's almost as bad as killing a lord!"

No, no, Annaïg thought. No one is dead. It's a mistake. You weren't supposed to be here . . .

"The first thing," Glim said, "is we clean up."

That sank in a little. Yes, they had to do that, didn't they? What a mess.

"But he's going to be missed," Wert went on. "They'll send more divers to look for him."

"Right," Glim said. "That's why we're going to fix it so they don't find him. Or any of them."

"How can we do that? Even if we cut them up and put them in a midden, a sniffer could find them."

"Don't worry," Glim said confidently. "I know what to do. They won't be found."

"Then they'll start interrogating us."

"The four of us are the only ones who know what happened," Glim said.

"What do you mean by that?" Cilinil asked, swimming away a bit.

"No one's going to hurt you," Glim said. "That's not

what I'm getting at."

Something suddenly fit together inside Annaïg's head.

"Listen to me," she said. "Just listen. No one knows the skraws are involved, right? Each kitchen will think the other killed Toel. We don't need to get rid of the bodies—they need to be found. But they need to be found hidden in Phmer's midden. Everything here—and I mean everything—must be cleaned up. I can make a scrub that will scour this place as if we were never here. Then you can make it look like Toel was killed trying to invade Phmer's kitchen, you understand?"

Glim's membranes filmed his eyes and then drew open again.

"Did you—" he began, then stopped.

But he didn't have to finish. She knew what he was thinking.

"No, Glim," she said. "I didn't plan this. It never occurred to me to—you know. But if we play this right, it can work. For all of us."

"They'll suspect you," Glim said. "The only survivor."

"Everyone who knows I came down here is right here," she replied. "When Toel can't be found, I'll be as surprised as anyone as to where he went in the first place."

Glim seemed to sort that for a moment before nodding.

"If you think it will work."

"It's a gamble," she admitted. "We could be found out. We could die horribly. But that was probably going to happen anyway, right?"

"I suppose so," Glim agreed.

"Well, then," Annaïg said. "Let's go do what's needed, and try to live until tomorrow."

And so they began doing that.

PART II

ONE

⎯⎯⎯⎯⎯⎯⎯

It happened around midday, beginning as a murmur ghosting up from the pantry and swelling. Toel's underchefs—Intovar and Yeum—got into a shrill argument in the hall.

When Lord Irrel came down, everything hushed.

Annaïg had never seen a lord before. She had supposed they looked like everyone else, possibly in finer clothes.

She was right about the clothes. Irrel's robe seemed to be made of black smoke within which winked thousands of tiny sparks. The form-fitting garment beneath might have been made of liquid iron.

Irrel himself was somewhat translucent. When he turned his head, flashes of skull showed through his fine, long features. His large eyes glowed with a soft purple light that shone through his lids when he closed them. He stood a head taller than anyone else in the room.

"Toel is dead," he said. His voice was soft, but it carried easily to every corner of the kitchen. "Who is his second?"

Intovar and Yeum glanced at each other, and then Intovar

stepped forward.

"I am, Lord Irrel."

Irrel nodded. "The contest tomorrow. Can you win it? Tell me now, and do not dissemble."

Intovar cleared his voice softly. He looked terrified, and Annaïg could see his fingers shaking.

"Lord, without Chef Toel, our chances are much diminished."

"Much diminished?" Irrel said, raising an eyebrow. He gestured—as if flicking something from his finger—and Intovar shrieked and dropped to his knees before falling on his face. He didn't move.

"I'll ask the question again," Irrel said. "Can we win it?"

"N-No," Yeum stuttered. "We cannot, lord. Not without Chef Toel."

Irrel nodded, and Yeum flinched.

"There," he said. "A simple answer to a simple question. Thank you." He sighed. "It is an unpleasant inconvenience to withdraw, but better that than to look foolish." He turned and took a step toward the door. Annaïg closed her eyes and pushed back her fear.

"We can win, Lord Irrel," she said.

A little gasp went up around her, but she kept her gaze focused on the lord.

"And you are?" he asked.

"Annaïg, lord," she replied.

"Ah. Toel's whimsical inventor."

"Yes, lord."

"I have been pleased with many of your creations," he said. "But that does not make you a chef."

"We can win, lord. The menu is planned, the preparations are made. We will not make you look foolish—we will make you proud."

Irrel glanced at Intovar's body, then back at Annaïg. "It would irritate me greatly to learn this is false bravado," he said.

"It is not, lord," she replied forcefully.

"Very well, then," he said. "We'll just see."

No one uttered a word until he was out of sight and presumably out of earshot. Then it began.

"Are you insane?" Yeum shouted. "You've just killed us all!"

A chorus of agreement went up from the staff.

"What did you think was going to happen anyway?" Annaïg asked. "Irrel must have a kitchen, and he must have a good one. Did you think you were going to be made chef, Yeum, for telling him we aren't—you aren't—competent? He would have brought in a new chef, with a new staff, and most of you would end up in the sump."

That struck home—she could see it, so she pressed. "We can do this. We don't need Toel. If you agree to follow me, cook what I say the way I say to, we can win. I know it."

"I don't understand," Aelo—one of the dicers—said. "You're probably right about what would have happened to us—all of us except you. Any chef would be pleased to have you. Now, if you fail—"

"I'm tired of being passed around," she said. "If we win, Irrel will make me chef, I'll keep all of you, and everything will be fine."

"But I'm the senior cook," Yeum protested.

"No, she's right," one of the others said. "You can't be chef now, Yeum. It has to be her."

"No, she's crazy," Yeum retorted. "Irrel wouldn't . . ." Her
eyes wandered over to Intovar's body, then she shook her head.
"Sumpslurry," she sighed.

Yeum looked back at Annaïg. "Fine," she said. "What are
we cooking?"

———

"But this is absurd," Loehsh asserted as Annaïg looked over
his shoulder at his preparations. "Rhel is a lord—he will not
eat the raw flesh of an animal, no matter how prettied up with
froths and suspirations."

"He will," she replied, "and he'll like it. Just—stop. Give
me the knife."

"Why?" he asked.

"Because you're cutting it wrong," she snapped, reposition-
ing the fat-veined slab of meat on the table and cutting paper-thin
slices from it.

"It won't matter how thin it is," Loehsh muttered.

"Loehsh," Yeum's voice piped up from behind. "You see
how she wants it done?"

"Yes," he said sullenly.

"Then do it that way," Yeum replied. "Would you have
questioned Toel this way?"

"Of course not. But he—"

"Is dead. Unless you wish to join him before even the rest
of us do, I suggest you stop asking questions and do things as
Annaïg says to."

"Very well," Loehsh said sourly. He returned to his task,

this time cutting the meat properly.

"Come on," Yeum said to Annaïg. "We need to talk."

They went into the little room where Toel used to work on his menus.

"You need me," Yeum said.

"How is that?"

"You know how to cook—I look at the menu and I'm amazed, I admit. Maybe we do have a small chance of coming through this. The problem is, you don't know how to be a chef."

"What do you mean?"

"You try to do everything yourself. It's impossible. You have to delegate, and you have to do it with authority. You haven't the most basic idea how to go about it."

"What are you suggesting, then?" Annaïg asked.

"That we work together," Yeum replied. "I know how to give orders and spread the work around. I know how to get things done. You know how to make them *right*."

"Work together," she considered. "I worked together with Slyr and she tried to kill me. Why should I trust you?"

"Because I'm not stupid like Slyr. It's impossible for me to steal credit for this—Irrel was right here. He knows whose dishes these are. I'm only asking that if we succeed, I get to stay here as your underchef."

Right, Annaïg thought. So you can find another time to slip a knife into my back.

"That's reasonable," was what she said, however.

"Okay," Yeum replied. "In that case I have some recommendations concerning the preparations."

"I should like to hear them," Annaïg said.

Yeum paused, and a sly little look passed across her face.

"What?" Annaïg asked.

"Did you kill him?" Yeum whispered.

"What?" Annaïg felt a little chill in her vertebrae.

"The chef. Did you kill him? It was made to look as if Phmer did it, but I can't imagine her being that sloppy. If, on the other hand, you set it up to look like that—"

"I'm not going to dignify that with a denial," Annaïg said.

"Don't misunderstand me," Yeum went on. "If that were the case, you would have nothing but my admiration. Do you know how many people Toel murdered to get here? It's how things are done."

"Well, it's not how I do things," Annaïg snapped back. She was outraged. Yes, she had killed him, sort of, but it had been an accident. She wasn't what Yeum thought she was.

Yeum shrugged. "Anyway," she said.

"Do you have those recommendations or not?"

"I do."

———

She slept a scant three hours that night; even with Yeum's organizations of the kitchen, there were hundreds of details that only she could handle.

Rhel, fortunately, was not like Irrel, who preferred up to a hundred distinct dishes at a meal. From what she had learned, Rhel considered himself more essential than that, and thus she only prepared three, each to be served in a separate course. She scrutinized each plate as it went to the servers.

First came the quintessences of sulfur and sugar, congealed into a glutinous web that held suspended drops of human blood and denatured snapadder venom, which glittered pleasingly—like tiny rubies and emeralds. The web stretched over the cavity of a halved and hollowed durian fruit, whose sweet, garlicky scent she had enhanced with metagastronomics and infused with the lust of a monkeylike creature from the Fringe Gyre, killed just as it was about to mate.

Next came the thin, translucent slices of raw bear loin, collected like the durian from the world below. She had turned the fat of the bear into a room-temperature vapor that clung to the tiny bits of meat, which were pillowed on a nest of glassy yellow noodles that, when bitten, would erase the taste of everything else within a few seconds, but leave deep longing to remember what had been lost.

An hour passed after the second course went up, and Annaïg began to feel nervous. The third course—a complex preparation based on the smoke of clove, cardamom, cumin, mustard, pepper, hornet, black widow, and rage—would begin to mellow and lose its edge if it wasn't served soon.

The servers finally came a half hour later, a few minutes too late for the smoke to be at its best, but there wasn't anything she could do about it.

When the final dish went up, Annaïg wiped her brow.

"I'm going to lie down," she told Yeum.

"We did well," Yeum said. "I wonder about your choice to include so much carnal matter, but what you did with it—Toel could not have done better." She hesitated. "Do you still believe we will win?"

"I don't know," Annaïg replied. "But I'm too tired to worry about it anymore. If I'm going to die, I want a little rest first."

She wasn't sure how long she dozed, but when she woke, at first she thought it was Lord Irrel standing there, for he had the same translucence. But then she noticed the slow, constant shifting of color beneath his skin, the squarer face and voluptuous lips.

"Lord?" Annaïg said, coming shakily to her feet.

"Rhel," he murmured in a detached manner, as if he wasn't so much speaking to her as recalling the conversation out loud. "How did you know?" he asked.

"Know what, lord?"

"The first dish made Lord Ix vomit, which I much enjoyed, and it made Ghol laugh, which is extremely pleasant. Each dish was for me perfect, but affected my companions in ways that I very much appreciated. How could you have known all of these things? Are you able to pick into my mind? I sense no such talent in you."

"Does this mean we won?" Annaïg asked.

"Yes," Rhel conceded. "And yet in doing so you have raised questions, you see."

"I can't explain it, lord," she lied. "It is my art, that is all. When it comes to food, I know what people want. I believe one of the gods must have blessed me."

His gaze settled for a moment, and then he blinked.

"You are from below—from the world we travel through."

"Yes, lord."

He smiled. "I think I shall enjoy your world, when we are done."

"Done with what, my lord?"

He waved his hand.

"Oh, never mind that. You are my creature now, and I value such as you. I look forward to the day that you have full access to the goods of your world, rather than just the smatterings the taskers bring up. In any event, Irrel will have to find another chef."

"And my staff?"

"Keep those you wish—dismiss the rest. Three days from now you will cook another meal, this one for Umbriel himself. I will be interested to see if you can please him as much—and as specifically—as you did me."

"Thank you, lord," she said. "I endeavor to do my best."

"Of course," he replied, and then left.

She passed a terrified-looking Yeum as she left the kitchens for her quarters.

"We won," she said. "You'll stay. We begin preparing tomorrow."

Then she found her bed, and slept more soundly then she had in a long, long time.

TWO

Mere-Glim was finishing off a sheartooth steak when Wert burst into the chamber they shared with four other skraws, a damp stony room grown up in phosphorescent moss. He had an agitated look on his face, even for Wert. Oluth came in right behind him.

"They're coming for you," Oluth gasped. "You have to go."

"What? Who is coming for me?"

"Guards from one of the lords—Ix, I think. They've been questioning people. They broke poor Jith. I know he didn't mean to—"

"You have to hide someplace until they're gone," Wert said.

"That will only put you in more danger," Glim replied. "If they're after me, they probably know you're my second. I'm not going to leave you here to face them."

"I'll run, too, just in a different direction," Wert said. "Glim, we need you. The skraws need you, especially if they've caught on to us. You know how to think about these things—we don't."

"It's just I don't see how they found out," Glim said. "It was supposed to look like the kitchens were doing it to each other. It was working, I'm sure of it."

He saw Oluth start at that, but before he could say anything, Wert began trying to push him into the water.

"Go," he said. "Go someplace deep."

———

He saw them as soon as he was in the water. They were smart; they probably had sent someone to run him down in the caves, but figured he would come out here—and he had, right into their hands—if not their net, which he saw descending from above.

He only had one way out, and the four figures ahead were blocking it, so he went straight at them with all the speed he had, which was clearly more than they were expecting. He avoided their spears and bowled right through them, diving for the Drop.

He thought he was free when something hit him in the side, hard. He spun down to his right, but after a few yards something yanked him back and sent waves of agony through his ribs.

He looked back into a cloud of blood. His blood, pouring from where a harpoon was stuck in him. One of the men was lashing the other end of the line around a spike of coral.

With a harsh cry, Glim hurled himself back at them, but they were more ready for him this time, three of them setting their spears and the harpooner reloading his weapon, which looked a lot like a crossbow.

He jagged at the last moment, but one of the spearmen managed to shift his point so it hit him in the forehead. He screamed as the tip found his skull and deflected, slicing all the

way to his ear. The pain was terrific, but it only seemed to make
him stronger as he jerked his way down the shaft and buried
his claws in the man's throat. One of the others gripped him
from behind, and then they all had him. He rolled and pitched
furiously, smashing them into coral. Two let go, but the other
managed to hold on by grabbing the harpoon, and this time his
senses were shattered by the pain, and for a moment he wasn't
sure what was happening.

The next thing that came to him clearly was Oluth, trying
to say something. Blood was coming from his mouth. A quick
look showed his attackers all dead or too badly wounded to do
anything.

"What?" he asked Oluth.

"I'm sorry," the boy said. "We did it, the glimmers. We
thought it was what you wanted."

"What?" Glim demanded. "What did you do?"

"They were supposed to know, so they would do something
about the vapors. We were proud, proud to be a part of—" He
coughed, and a great gout of red poured from his mouth.

"We broke a tree-root feed," he said. "We left our sign there,
the sign of the vapors."

"Sign of the vapors?"

"Right," Oluth said weakly. "You wouldn't have seen it. It's
on the door to the chamber. Four wriggling lines, in a spray."
He closed his eyes. Glim saw the wound now. The knife was
still in it.

"Let's get you fixed up," he said.

"No," Oluth said. "More coming. I'll wait here for them."

"I can't let you, not alone."

"Please," Oluth said. "Please, for me? If you forgive me, please go."

Glim cut the line to the harpoon and was trying to pull it free when several figures emerged from the cave entrance. Oluth launched himself forward.

"Go!" he screamed. Glim saw he had the harpoon gun.

More guards came out, seven now.

So he did as Oluth asked and swam deep.

———

When Glim had put some distance between himself and his pursuers, he found a crevice in the side of the sump, wedged the other end of the harpoon into it, and finally managed to yank the barbed head free. He almost passed out, and for several long breaths he couldn't swim, but then he started stroking again, trailing more blood than ever.

He couldn't get Oluth's last words out of his head. Where had he gone wrong? Hadn't he explained well enough? And what were they doing breaking a tree-root feed? That hadn't even been one of the targets he had approved.

But it did give him an idea. He took a twisting course, past where a cluster of middens emptied into the sump, hoping the turbulence would disperse his blood trail, then swam toward the capillaries that drew water up to the Fringe Gyre. It took him a few minutes, but he found the one with the lines crudely etched into the stone above—the sign of the vapors. They had smashed the filter, so the capillary was pulling up debris that in time would choke the feed. Hoping it wasn't blocked already, he went up it.

It was nearly too tight for him; he had to writhe up the thing
for the first hundred feet or so, but finally it met a larger tube
and he let himself drift for a moment before continuing on.

He'd never been in these passages before for the simple
reason that none of the filters were ever broken. Older skraws
who had made repairs said they formed a webwork that brought
water to the roots of the Fringe Gyre. He hadn't wanted to take
his usual path up, because it would have been far too easy to
track him. Now, as he passed dozens of branching tubes, many
far too small to admit him, he wondered if he hadn't merely
managed to trap himself. If they found him here, his speed and
maneuverability wouldn't count for much.

Not that he had that much of either left anyway. He didn't
know how much blood he had lost; his wounds stanched themselves pretty quickly, but he was still bleeding.

Hoping he wouldn't pass out before he found a way up,
he swam on, through passages that became increasingly more
dizzying and labyrinthine.

THREE

Attrebus fell, but before he could start a scream he crunched into something cold and wet. Gasping, he came to his hands and knees, swiping at the clotting stuff on his face, wondering what horrible Oblivion realm Malacath had banished them to. But then he understood that he'd landed in snow, and the air coming into his lungs was clean and filled with evergreen scent. When he looked up, the sky was blue and traced with high, thin clouds.

"He did it," he said.

"So it would appear," Sul replied. "This is not Oblivion, at least."

"It's cold."

"If this is Solstheim, that makes sense."

Like him, Sul was still naked; his dark skin stood in sharp contrast to the snow and spruce trees surrounding them. Near him lay a bundle, and the older man stepped over to it, discovering their clothing, weapons, and armor.

Everything was still torn, filthy, and blood-caked, but Attrebus felt warmer and more secure back in his gear.

"Which way now?" he asked. They were on a low ridge. Jagged peaks stood off in one direction. "I thought he would drop us right in front of—wherever we're going."

"That's not always possible, even for a daedra prince," Sul replied. "He probably put us as near as was convenient." He looked around, and then jerked his chin toward the peaks. "I've no interest in climbing mountains just for sport. Downhill is likely more hospitable, and we're more apt to find someone to ask directions of."

"I won't argue with that," Attrebus said.

The land rolled up and down, but took them generally lower, until they came to a little valley with a small but enthusiastic river laughing over polished stones. They began following that downstream. It was about midday, and the sun was warmer, the ice turning to mush under their feet.

As the sky paled to slate and the outlines of the moon Secundus began to brighten, the snow began to crackle under their feet, and the inadequacy of their clothing became clear. They searched the valley wall for a rock shelter, but failing to find one, they stopped, gathered wood, and built a fire to huddle around.

"I thought we would find people sooner," Attrebus said, watching the flames dance and trying to avoid the resinous smoke.

"Why?" Sul asked.

"Well, because so many Dark Elves came here after the red year—" He broke off, realizing he was in uncomfortable territory, but Sul clapped his hands together and rubbed them over the fire.

"I had many unpleasant surprises after returning from exile in Oblivion," he said. "I knew that Vivec City was destroyed. Vuhon told me he had seen as much, when he was torturing me. But it wasn't until I went there that I understood how badly my homeland had been ravaged, or how they had suffered from the Argonian invasion. Still, I had an idea. But that Skyrim had offered Solstheim as a haven for my people, after ages of enmity between our races—for that I was unprepared."

" 'Untithed to any thane or hold,' " Attrebus quoted, " 'and self-governed, with free worship, with no compensation to Skyrim or the Empire except as writ in the armistice of old wheresoever those might still apply, and henceforth let no man or mer say that the Sons and Daughters of Kyne are without mercy or honor.' "

Sul raised an eyebrow.

"I learned it from my tutors," Attrebus explained. "I memorized it. I've always been moved by it."

Sul poked at the fire, his brow furrowing, then tossed his head to indicate their surroundings. "It's not the most fruitful land," he said. "And in my day almost unpopulated, and then by scraggly tribesmen with no clear allegiance toward Skyrim or the Empire. Morrowind had always laid theoretical claim to the place. If Skyrim hadn't given it freely, odds are the refugees would have settled here anyway, forcing the Nords to either fight or lose face. This way they came out looking like saviors."

"Stendarr," Attrebus swore. "Can't you ever imagine that people actually act from kindness? From mercy?"

"People might, or at least might imagine that's what moves them," Sul said. "Nations don't."

"I don't believe that," Attrebus said. "Nations are ruled by people. When did the Nords ever back down from a fight with Dunmer? Your people were weakened, Sul—battered, without home or resources."

"They were desperate," Sul replied. "Desperate and dangerous. You've too many romantic notions in your head."

"Maybe," Attrebus said. "And maybe nine times out of ten, you're right—nations act from cold self-interest. But sometimes, at their very best, they act for a greater good, just as some men and women do."

Sul waved that off. "I'm not going to argue any further," he said. "Believe what you want. But to return to your question, my guess is that most Dunmer settled in the South and along the coasts, and I think we're in the interior."

"You've been here before?"

"No, but as I said, it was always a disputed territory, and therefore its essentials were a part of my education in the ministry."

Despite Sul's pronouncement, Attrebus wanted to press the debate, but at that moment he heard a soft noise from his haversack, both artificial and birdlike.

"Annaïg," he whispered. "She's alive. I tried to contact her earlier but—"

"Go on," Sul said. "But don't stray far from the fire."

Attrebus nodded and stepped a bit away from the flames, into the muffling spruces, for a bit of privacy. Then he hesitated at the cold, wondering why he *needed* discretion, why Sul assumed he did . . .

He pulled out Coo, the mechanical bird, an exquisitely crafted object, detailed down to the feather. He opened the small latch on its belly.

And there she was, Annaïg, with her curly black hair and mouth curving up in a wide, happy grin.

"Attrebus," she said. "I—I thought you were dead. It's been so long."

"Has it?" he asked. "I'm afraid I've lost all sense of time."

"What happened?" she asked. "Where are you?"

"Things didn't go exactly as planned," he said. "Sul and I reached Umbriel, but Vuhon was too much for us. We barely escaped into Oblivion with our lives, and there—we were quite busy. I tried to contact you a few times but I never managed it." He felt sick as he said it, and realized he was holding his gut scar. He forced a smile. "But now we have returned to Tamriel."

"Vuhon? Who is Vuhon?"

"You haven't heard of him? He's the lord of Umbriel. He created it."

Her brow furrowed.

"When they speak of the lord of Umbriel, they call him Umbriel," she said. "I've never heard of anyone named Vuhon."

"That's odd," Attrebus said, but he remembered Vuhon suggesting that he didn't go by that name anymore, that he was only answering to it out of convenience for Sul. Then he caught the tense of her verb. "You speak as if you're still there," he said. "I thought you had managed to escape."

"My plans didn't fare so well either," she replied. "It seems Umbriel has some hold over us. We flew out a few hundred yards and our bodies began to—ah—evaporate."

"Evaporate? Like the larvae you told me about? I remember you said the inhabitants of Umbriel all believed they couldn't leave."

"And it seems they can't. And now Glim and I can't."

"I'm sorry," he said. "All this time I thought you were safe. I tried to contact you once from Oblivion, when we had a moment's respite, but there wasn't an answer. There must be some way."

"There is, I'm sure," she said, but her eyes shifted away and her tone was unconvincing.

"What's wrong?"

"I just haven't made much progress, that's all," she said.

"We learned a few things from Vuhon that might help you," he told her.

"Really?" she asked. "Such as?"

"Umbriel used to be a city in Oblivion, in the realm of Clavicus Vile. Vuhon—the lord of Umbriel—was trying to escape that realm with his companion, Umbra, but Vile essentially hardened the walls of his domain so no one could leave it. Vuhon found a way to sort of turn space around the city, though, and then break that free, like twisting a sausage casing and then tearing it."

Annaïg blinked. "So Umbriel is in a bubble—a bubble of the wall Clavicus Vile made it impossible to pass through?"

"I think that's right," he said. "Sul has tried to explain it better, but we've been rather busy—"

"But that helps," she said excitedly. "Attrebus, that helps a lot. If I were there I would kiss—"

But she broke off and blushed.

"You know what I mean," she said after a moment.

"I think I could suffer through a kiss from you," he said.

Her brows drew in. "Oh, could you?" she asked.

"Sure—if it wasn't too long, or wet."

"I'll keep that in mind, your highness," she said. But then her face changed, as if she'd just remembered something awful.

"What's wrong?" he asked. "Is someone there?"

"No," she replied. "No, privacy isn't the problem it used to be."

"How is that?"

"I've—moved up. I'm the chef of a kitchen now."

"That's good?"

"I think so. It puts me in a position to learn more about Umbriel. I think I may have found some weaknesses."

"That's wonderful, then. Are you safer?"

"I don't know," she said. Her good mood seemed to have all but left her. Now she sounded tired. "In a way, certainly. But every step up just means a new kind of danger. In two days I will make a meal for Umbriel himself."

"Vuhon?"

"I guess so. I don't know."

"He's a Dunmer, Annaïg. From Morrowind." A thought occurred, but he felt reluctant to voice it. She must have seen it on his face.

"You're wondering if I can poison him."

"No," he said. "It's too dangerous."

"I—" She closed her eyes. "I'm confused, Attrebus. To survive, to get to this position—I've had to do things. Things I'm not happy about or proud of."

"I'm sure everything you've done was necessary," he said. "Look, I know you're not an assassin. I shouldn't have—"

"If I thought I could succeed, I would do it," she said. "The fact that he was once an elf, a person of flesh and blood like you and me—that's interesting. But I don't think he is that anymore."

"No," he said, "you're probably right. He said that everything on Umbriel was a part of him, and he part of it. And he was so strong . . ."

Her expression had changed again, become thoughtful.

"If that's true . . ." she began.

"Yes?"

"I'm sorry," she said. "I need to think about this. Tell me everything you remember him saying, everything you know about Umbriel."

He recounted the meeting with Vuhon and everything he could remember Sul saying about him, Clavicus Vile, and Umbra, continuing long into the night.

"I should go now," she sighed. "I have more privacy, but I have a kitchen to run. I'm—it's good to talk to you."

"To you, too," he said. He hesitated, then went on. "There's so much that's happened, so much I want to tell you about when we really have time—"

"I never got that description of Rimmen," she said.

"I know. But gods willing, I'll get the chance to give it to you. When you're free, and alone, always try me. I'll answer when I can."

"I know you will," she said.

Her image persisted a moment, and then vanished as she put away the locket.

It was only then that he realized he was freezing.

———

"Watch it," Sul warned.

Attrebus looked down and realized he was about to put his foot into a jagged crevice a yard deep.

"Thanks," he said.

"Just—watch yourself."

"I didn't really sleep last night," Attrebus explained.

"Cold and hard dirt can do that."

"That wasn't it. Believe it or not, I've slept perfectly peacefully under those conditions before. I just couldn't stop thinking."

"I can believe that," Sul grunted.

Attrebus felt irritation flare but pressed it down.

"Look, until a few weeks ago I thought I was a warrior, a leader—a hero. I slept like a baby because I didn't have any worries. Every fight I was ever in, I won, every battle went my way. And I was too stupid to figure out the whole thing was a sham."

"You're not that stupid," Sul said, to his surprise. "That's an easy sort of thing to believe, when you're young. I thought I was invincible at one point, too, and I didn't have any of the excuses you do for thinking so."

"Well, that's—thanks."

For a moment he continued in silence, wondering over the rare almost-compliment.

"Sul," he finally began, "you made me face the facts, and then you gave me a way of making it through with my sanity. You told me to try to become the man people think I am. And I am trying."

"Good for you."

"But I need you to tell me something. I need you to tell me if you think we have any chance at this, or if you're just so angry and guilty . . ."

Sul drew to an abrupt stop.

"Do you think I'm out of my mind?" he asked quietly.

"What?"

"I asked," Sul said, his voice rising to a shout, "if you think I'm out of my mind?"

Attrebus felt a stir of fear in his gut. If Sul chose to kill him, there was no way he would be able to stop him.

"I don't know," he finally said. "If everything Vuhon said was true, I honestly don't know."

"Does it matter?" Sul asked.

"Yes, it does. Umbriel is headed toward the Imperial City. Toward my father, my mother, everyone I know. And yet here we are, halfway across the world, looking for a sword that *might* help us destroy Umbriel. But I've met Vuhon and seen his power. Even with all of your art, we barely escaped with our lives, and I hadn't the slightest chance against him. I don't see how this sword is going to change things."

"It might not," Sul admitted. "But what else would you do?"

"You could take us back through Oblivion, get us to the Imperial City before Umbriel reaches it. We know things that can help the Empire against Vuhon."

"We do? What would you tell him?"

"Everything we know."

"And how would that help him? Have you worked out how to destroy Umbriel?"

"No," Attrebus said.

"Neither have I," Sul replied. "Until we know that, I can't see what use going there will do. Even assuming I could do it at this point, which is anything but given. You've seen now what can happen if I don't have my trail to follow through the realms."

"We know Vuhon wants the White-Gold Tower for something. My father's mages might be able to figure out why."

"They might," Sul conceded.

Attrebus paused, uncertain if he wanted to continue, but he knew he had to.

"We could go to Clavicus Vile," he said.

"Now there's an idea," Sul replied. "And you're wondering if I'm out of *my* mind."

"But it makes sense. Vuhon is fleeing Vile, trying to be free of him. If we tell Vile where he is—"

"Vile can't come into Tamriel, at least not in an aspect potent enough to do anything about Umbriel. And if he could, he would probably make a far bigger mess than Vuhon will. If Clavicus Vile could take his power back from Umbriel, he already would have. What he needs in order to do that is what we're looking for."

"You're sure of that?"

"No. But Vuhon went way out of his way to try to retrieve the sword. Azura gave me visions of it, and even Malacath seemed to think we're on to something. Anyway, our last little forays into Oblivion have left me weakened. If I dare try going there again anytime soon, it will have to be for a very good reason, and not just because you want to be with your daddy."

"Look—"

"The Imperial City is that way," Sul said, pointing. "You're free to go there anytime you like."

Attrebus pursed his lips and drew himself a little straighter.

"Did you kill your lover? Did you destroy Vivec City?"

Sul's bloody eyes narrowed. "I did what I did," he said. "I bear some of the blame. But Vuhon made this as well, and when I am done with him—" He stopped abruptly.

"What?" Attrebus asked. "Yes, what then?"

"Come with me if you wish," Sul said. "I won't speak of this anymore."

And with that he started walking again, his lean legs stretching in long strides.

Attrebus watched him for a moment, sighed, and followed.

FOUR

———————

"That was even stranger than the last meal," Yeum said, sipping her wine. The two of them sat at one of the cutting tables. The last dish had gone up for Umbriel's banquet, and the rest of the kitchen swirled around their still point, cleaning up. "I liked it, especially the one with that plant, what is it called . . .?"

"Marshmerrow," Annaïg replied. "It grows in Morrowind, one of the countries we passed over."

"It was delicious. Before, I would have questioned the choice—but I've heard that since Rhel's tasting, the other lords have begun demanding coarser, less spiritual food. You've started a trend."

"More a fad, I would think," Annaïg said.

Inwardly, she wasn't so certain about the meal. She'd heard that Umbriel often ate plain matter, but beyond that neither the skraws nor anyone else knew anything about his specific tastes. She'd had two things to go on—Attrebus's assertion that he'd at least once been a fully corporeal Dunmer, and Rhel's preferences, which seemed in that light perhaps an aping of his master's appetites. In any case, it was done now.

Hours passed and no one came down, so she bid Yeum good-night and went to her bed.

Sleep eluded her, however, despite her fatigue, so instead she rose and went to her old workbench in the kitchens, where the tree-wine vats were, and idly sifted through the powders and potions while she thought.

She was a chef now, master of a kitchen, and not a negligible one. But for how long? She doubted there was anywhere to go from here but down. She might have tried to poison Umbriel, but she knew in her gut that any such attempt would fail, and she'd lose any chance she had of accomplishing anything. But if Attrebus was right, if Umbriel, the ingenium that kept it aloft, and the Histlike trees Mere-Glim had discovered were all connected by a flow of soul-force, then she ought to be able to poison the whole system. Lord Umbriel was likely untouchable; she knew where the ingenium was, but Glim hadn't found any way to reach it other than through the apparently deadly connexion at the bottom of the sump.

But the trees—them, she could reach.

And so she began making a poison.

Some believed that poison was the antithesis of food, but Annaïg knew better. Most food was poison to one extent or another, especially plants, many of which had to be pounded or soaked or boiled or all three to divest them of enough toxins to make them even edible. Too many beans eaten raw could be fatal—the same was true of almonds, cherry pits, apple seeds. Nutmeg, when taken in large amounts, could give strange visions, and in higher doses, death. Alcohol, while pleasant, was indisputably a poison. The body dealt with these things, but over time, eventually, the body failed. Everything one ate brought one closer to one's last meal, and not just in a metaphorical sense.

So while she hadn't made much in the way of poison, it came as naturally to her as cooking or concocting tonics to allow flight or breathing water. And in learning how to use the stolen souls that pulsed through the cables of Umbriel, she now had the knowledge to create a venin of a more than merely physical nature. She could blacken the whole system if she did things right. And she could make gallons of it—tons, maybe—before anyone questioned what she was doing, now that the kitchen was hers.

She worked almost until dawn, when she had something she was almost happy with. The only problem was testing it, and she couldn't think of any good way to do that. In the end she knew she would have to take a risk.

She hid it in her cabinet. Tomorrow she would work on it a bit more, and then set up a larger production in the tree-wine vats—and then, well, she would see.

She had sent Slyr to certain destruction. She had killed Toel. Neither were good people, but if in the end their deaths didn't serve some higher purpose, she didn't think she could bear it. If she was now a murderer, it had to have been for something.

And maybe, as Umbriel died, she and Glim might find a way off of it. Maybe. But if not . . . such was life. Everyone died.

When she reached her room, she found two men and a woman waiting for her. They wore simple robes of gray and white. They didn't seem armed, but when they asked her to go with them, she didn't argue. They took her directly to Toel's balcony. Two of them gripped her beneath her arms, and she gasped as they all lifted silently into the night air, rising up through the glittering, shifting web of glasslike strands she had only seen from below, and farther, to a fragile-looking spire, the tallest in the city. Umbriel was a massive inkiness below, and above, the stars were glorious. Masser was a gargantuan opal dome on the horizon.

They took her through an opening in the spire and put her down. Then they left.

It was more a gazebo than a room, with a floor of polished mica and a dome of nearly black jade supported by silvery filaments pulsing with souls. A single figure welcomed her, a Dunmer with a long white braid, dressed in a robe similar to the ones her escorts had worn.

"I haven't had a meal like that in a long time," the man said.

"I hope it pleased you, lord," Annaïg replied. The words were hardly out before she wanted to suck them back in; the man had spoken in clear, perfect Tamrielic, not the strange Merish dialect of Umbriel. She had answered in the same language.

He chuckled softly, probably at her expression.

"I thought so," he said. "The references to the cuisine of my homeland were rather too obvious."

"Are you Lord Umbriel?"

"I am Umbriel," he said. "I am me, I am my city and my people. You aren't part of me, though. And yet I didn't invite you here or have you captured. They've been hiding you from me, down there in the kitchens. Using you in their little intrigues, I expect. Where are you from?"

"Black Marsh," she replied. "From Lilmoth."

"Everyone in Lilmoth is supposed to be dead, certain particular Argonians aside. How is it you are here, and alive?"

"It was an accident," she replied. "I made an elixir that gave my body flight."

"And you chose to come here?"

"No, I didn't," she replied. "I was trying to flee, actually. Anyway, I was south of Lilmoth, not in the city."

"I suppose you lost family there? Friends?"

"My father," she said, trying to keep calm, to keep away from where her feelings lived. She wondered if her invisible knife could kill Umbriel. Six steps, a swift swing . . .

"And you're angry with me about that?"

"At first, yes," she said. "But I have learned a certain pragmatism. I have done well here in Umbriel. I have risen to a fairly high place in a short time."

"Indeed you have," Umbriel replied. "You made no attempt to poison me last night, which can be interpreted in several ways. One would be that you've no wish to harm me. Another would be that you were too smart to try."

"Or perhaps a little of both," she replied.

"That's an interesting answer," Umbriel said. "I like it."

"My father and I weren't close," Annaïg told him, "and I had no real love for Lilmoth. I always dreamed of leaving, going somewhere exotic and exciting."

"And here you are," he said, a neutral little smile at the edge of his lips.

"Yes, Lord Umbriel."

He tapped his forehead, and the line of his mouth flattened out. "What bothers me is *this*," he said, his voice rising a bit.

It was shocking, like seeing a shark fin break the surface of a perfectly placid bay.

"Part of me, long ago, was Dunmer. How in all of the worlds and not-world could you have known that?"

"I did not know it, lord," she said.

"And yet several of your dishes were obviously inspired by the high cuisine of Morrowind. Why would you make such things if you had no inkling of my history?"

His tone was very dangerous now, and she felt herself trembling involuntarily.

"Lord, since I've been on Umbriel, the familiar components the taskers have brought me were first from Black Marsh and then from Morrowind. I was inspired by the ingredients, my lord. Marshmerrow begs to be made into hluurn or echar, urgandil into vverm. I learned something of Lord Rhel's tastes by asking questions of those who know him. I could find no one to question about you, so I guessed that Rhel, as your valet, would have discrimination similar to yours. There is no more to it than that."

"There isn't?" He seemed to be calming a bit.

"No, my lord."

"Well," he said, pacing suddenly like a caged tiger. "Well, in that case, there is this other thing."

"What is that, lord?"

"There is an Argonian in the sump. Did you know that? Did he come with you?"

She was paralyzed for a moment, but she knew that if she dissembled and he knew she was lying, it was all over. A lot of the people who had actually seen them arrive together were dead, but she could not be certain they all were.

"Yes," she said. "He is my friend."

"Did you have him kill Toel for you?"

"My lord—"

"It doesn't matter," he said, waving her off. "The chefs are always murdering one another. But it seems your Argonian friend is up to a bit more than that. He's organized some sort of rebellion among the skraws. That's going to stop."

"Are you asking me to talk to him, lord?"

"No. I'm asking you to kill him."

Her throat closed, and for a second she couldn't breathe. "L-Lord?" she stuttered.

"He's hard to catch, this one, and the skraws are loyal to him. And even if I were to really bend my mind to it and catch him, killing him would only make him a martyr. I don't need that at the moment, any more than I can afford to slaughter all of the skraws and start again."

She tried to still her shaking, which had grown worse. "What do you want me to do, then?"

"He's the only Argonian in the sump. It should be simple enough to introduce something into the water that will kill him without affecting anything else. I want it to look as if he died of natural causes. Do that for me."

She tightened her mind, pushed herself further out—away from her weak corpus—and met Umbriel's gaze squarely.

"I will, lord," she promised.

And so she returned to her kitchen, and she made a poison.

FIVE

After another two days of mostly silent trudging, Attrebus smelled salt air, and the land dropped jaggedly until they emerged onto a strand of black sand where gray waves lapped halfheartedly at the shore. Up the beach, perhaps a mile away, he could make out what appeared to be crenellated towers rising from a promontory.

"Do you think that's it?" he asked.

"Well," Sul said, "it's someplace." He turned and set off toward the castle.

For a time they saw only sea birds and occasionally odd three-tusked creatures sunning on some of the rocks. They had slick but hairy hides, paddlelike forelimbs with three toes, and no hind limbs at all, but instead a tail shaped like that of a shrimp. On land they were clumsy, but once in the water they seemed at ease, even elegant. Attrebus's stomach was quite empty, and he found himself wondering if the things were edible.

They reached the castle a few hours before sunset, or at least the rock it stood on and the small village between it and the sea.

There wasn't a dock as such, but a number of boats pulled up on the beach—some with substantial keels—suggested deep water offshore. A group of mostly women was crowded down near the boats, picking through fish lying in a couple of large troughs. Most had the flaxen hair and pink cheeks of Nords, although he saw a young Dunmer woman among them.

The village was no more than about twenty buildings, one of which had a placard with the promising words char bucket printed on it. He and Sul made their way there.

It was a tight little place with walls of undressed stone, a shake roof, and no windows, but inside it was warm and smelled pretty good. The oldest elven man Attrebus had ever seen watched them enter with obvious curiosity.

"You want to eat?" he asked.

"That would be good," Sul told him.

"Do you have money?"

For answer Sul tossed a couple of coins onto the counter. The man nodded and left through a side door, returning a moment later with two steaming bowls of something and some bread. It turned out to be some sort of chowder, and despite some unfamiliar flavors, Attrebus thought it was the best thing he had eaten in a long time, possibly because he hadn't eaten *anything* in a long time.

A few moments later two flagons of spiced mead joined the stew, and Attrebus felt officially happy.

He looked up and saw the old man still regarding them.

"It's okay?" he asked.

"Delicious," Attrebus replied. "My compliments."

"You come up from Oleer Mar?" he asked.

"Down from the mountains," Sul said. "Not much to see."

"What is this place?" Attrebus asked.

"The village?" the man asked. "Sathil, after the castle, I guess. We don't call it much of anything."

"Sathil? They were allied with house Indoril, yes?" Sul said.

"Not Hleryn Sathil, not for a long time," the fellow said. "Declared himself independent when he came here back in 'sixteen."

"Why?" Attrebus asked.

"Why not? If the Great Houses couldn't stop the wrack of Morrowind, what good are they?"

"I see your point," Attrebus replied, although it actually made very little sense to him. "Did you come up here with Sathil?"

"No, I settled here a few years ago when my ship wrecked on the coast. I like it up here. It's mostly quiet, not like the city. A few raiders now and then, but Sathil is still capable of handling that."

"Still capable? Is something wrong with him?"

"Never mind," the man said. "I talk too much."

"Do you think he would mind if we pay him a visit?" Attrebus asked.

"Sathil?" He looked surprised, then contemplative. "Well, you never know, do you? He might. Do either of you have any sorcery?"

"A little," Sul said.

"He used to entertain a lot of sorcerers. Not as much lately. Anyway, his gates will be closed by now, but you could go up there in the morning. In the meantime, how about a couple of nice beds?"

"And a hot bath?" Attrebus asked hopefully.

"Now, that's just crazy talk," the fellow gruffed.

———

The beds weren't so nice, but they were better than cold dirt. Breakfast wasn't much either—a thin porridge and a bit of dark bread. But it was enough, and the cocks were still crowing when they started up the approach to the castle.

The path was wide enough for wagons and not too steep for them, but by the time they reached the top of it, Sathil village was tiny below them. The walls of the castle were living rock for the first fifteen feet or so, polished smooth as glass, and then for another ten feet they were carefully fitted stone. It would be a hard place to take; except for the road, there wasn't any place for siege engines, and the two towers that overlooked the gate seemed pretty capable of defending the approach.

The gate, a thick wooden affair heavily banded with steel, was closed, but a fellow on the wall hailed them as they approached. Like most of the villagers, he seemed to be a Nord.

"Haven't seen you before," the fellow commented.

"We're travelers," Attrebus said. "Naturalists, actually. We hope to catalogue the flora and fauna hereabouts."

He saw Sul's eyebrow lift, but otherwise his companion didn't react.

"Do what?" the Nord asked.

"You know—those things on the beach, for instance, with the three tusks . . ."

"Horkers? You've come to look at horkers? Must be a boring place you're from, lad."

"I'm from the Imperial City," Attrebus said. "I've been commissioned as part of a project to write a new guide to the Empire and surrounding countries."

"Well, this isn't the Empire, you know," the man said.

"Right," Attrebus agreed. "Hence the 'surrounding countries' part. I was rather hoping to gain Lord Sathil's patronage for a time, while we're doing our cataloguing."

"Cattle hogging? What does that mean?"

"No, I mean—writing down types of things and describing them."

"You're going to write about horkers?"

"Yes, and whatever other things might be of interest in the area. Wildlife, geography, culture and customs, places and objects of power, those sorts of things."

"Places of power, eh? Are you a sorcerer?"

"I am not. That is my companion's specialty."

"Hang on there, then," the man said. "I'll convey your request to his lordship."

He vanished from the wall.

"Naturalist?" Sul asked.

"I've always been interested in those sorts of things," Attrebus said.

"Not enough to actually read about them, so far as I've seen," Sul said.

"Well, here's my opportunity," Attrebus replied.

An hour passed and most of another before the gate creaked and finally opened. The man from the wall was there, and a thin, ascetic-looking Dunmer woman with a long queue, clad in a flowing black robe embroidered with the stylized form of a draugr. Her gaze flicked over them a bit distastefully.

"Welcome to Sathil Manor," she said. "Isilr was a bit confused about your purpose here. I wonder if I could prevail upon you to reiterate it."

"Of course," Attrebus said. "It's nothing complicated, really. The Emperor in Cyrodiil has commissioned a new guide to the Empire and independent realms of Tamriel. I've been sent here to collect general information on the area for the guide."

"You're not just spying on our horkers, then, but on us as well?"

"Spying? I wouldn't put it that way, my lady."

She smiled thinly. "Don't worry," she said. "I have been instructed to offer you lodging and whatever help you require—within reason, of course."

"Of course, lady. That is most hospitable."

She nodded wanly. "I am Nirai Sathil, daughter of Hleryn Sathil. With whom do I make the acquaintance?"

"My name is Uriel Tripitus," Attrebus lied, "and this is my companion Ozul."

"Ozul," she said. "From what house?"

"I belong to no house," Sul told her.

"I understand you," she said. "We have also foresworn allegiance to the houses. Please, follow me and be welcome in our home."

She led them across a bare stone yard surrounded by what appeared to be barracks and into a central keep that rose quite high before sprouting six slender towers. The place was smaller than it looked from the shore, but still quite large—and to Attrebus's eye, undermanned. He didn't see nearly enough guards or servants.

They entered a large central hall with an enormous table. The walls were hung with the busts of animals—bears, wolves, wild bulls, lions—and also with various sorts of arms and armor, some of which seemed quite exotic.

"I must leave you here," Nirai said, "but servants will attend you shortly. Only tell them your needs, and they will see to them."

And with a whisking of robes, she was gone, and they were alone in the hall.

Attrebus paced, examining the swords, spears, maces, and falchions that adorned the walls.

"What does this 'Umbra' look like?" he asked.

"A black longsword with red runes on the blade," Sul replied. "At least when it was seen last."

"What do you mean?"

"Legend says it has worn other shapes—but it is always a bladed weapon."

Attrebus started in a hurry, but as the minutes stretched to more than an hour, he had ample time to assure himself that no weapon approaching that description was to be found—not in the great room, anyway.

He was just starting to consider wandering through the rest of the castle when he heard a soft whisper, then a giggle.

He turned, and caught a flash of gray vanishing from the doorway. There was a sudden furious whispering he couldn't make out, and then, after a moment, a rounded woman with fading red hair came in. She studied them for a moment, then gave a little curtsy.

"My apologies, sirs," she said. "I hadn't been informed of your presence. May I be of service?"

"I'm not sure," Attrebus said. "The lady Nirai brought us here, and said we would be provided with rooms and so forth."

"Nirai," she sighed, then cocked an eyebrow. "And so forth?"

"Well, I'm here to do a bit of exploring," he said, then rambled off his invented job description.

The woman looked a bit disapproving, but she nodded.

"I'll get rooms ready for you. Meantime I'll take you to the kitchen—I don't know what Nirai is thinking, but there will be no meal in the hall tonight."

"We were hoping to meet Lord Sathil," Attrebus said.

"Were you?" she replied. "Well, perhaps you will." She didn't sound convinced.

———

She showed them to the kitchen, a smoky, low-ceilinged room with an enormous hearth and two massive oaken tables. To Attrebus's vast surprise, about thirty people were seated there. None of them were elves; most seemed to be Nord, although there were two Khajiit. They were dressed in plain working clothes. All stood when they entered.

A gnarled old woman at the head of the table raised her head.

"Who is this, then, Yingfry?" she asked.

"Lords Uriel and Ozul," their escort reported. "From the Empire. Nirai brought them up. They're here to see the country."

"Well," the old woman said, "you gentlemen look hungry. Join us, won't you?"

"We would be honored," Attrebus said.

He heard a familiar giggle, and his attention was drawn to a honey-haired young woman with mischievous green eyes.

"Irinja!" the woman said sternly.

"I'm sorry, Eld Ma," she said. "It's just he speaks so fine, as if he's in court."

"All the more reason to mind your manners," Eld Ma said. "Lords, please, sit."

A couple of men made room on the bench, and Attrebus and Sul were soon seated in front of thick trenchers of black bread, boiled venison (or at least it tasted like venison) with wine and honey sauce, fish with butter and vinegar, and roast duck. Their hosts were silent as the two began eating.

"I hope it is to your liking," Eld Ma said.

"It's delicious," Attrebus replied.

"Very good," Sul added. "Different."

Eld Ma leaned back. "We know the food of Morrowind, lord," she said. "If I had known you were coming, we would have cooked in that manner."

"You misunderstand me," Sul replied. "I was paying a compliment. I don't care to be reminded of Morrowind."

"Ah," a bald-headed fellow piped up. "Lord Sathil is the same; he prefers our cuisine, our ways. But the lady, she prefers the tastes of her people—especially hluurn, and other things made from Marshmerrow."

"Val," Eld Ma said, quietly, "didn't the gentleman just say he didn't like to be reminded?"

"Oh, right," Val said. "Sorry."

"No harm," Attrebus cut in. "We're just glad of the hospitality." He lifted his mug of warm ale. "To each of you," he said.

They all toasted, and when he didn't continue, began talking among themselves, a low chatter rising—talk of tasks to be done that afternoon, complaints about the work of the morning, simple things, confirming his suspicion that these were castle servants, not masters. He ate and listened, hoping to hear something useful, but when the end of the meal came he didn't know much more than when it began.

Yingfry took them up three flights of stairs to two adjacent rooms, both quite large, both with fireplaces already blazing. When she was gone, they met together in Attrebus's room.

"What do you think is going on here?" Attrebus asked Sul.

The Dunmer scratched his chin. "I don't know much about the Sathils, other than remembering the name."

"Don't you think it's odd that we haven't met him yet? That we were left to eat with servants?"

"Not really," Sul said. "I don't know the man. Neither do you. Perhaps he is reclusive. Or very busy."

"Very busy with what?"

"Again, I don't know him, and we hardly know anything about this place."

"Well, if we never see him, how do we find the sword?"

Sul blinked. "Was that your plan? Just to ask him about it?"

"I suppose so."

"Then why this whole demented story about you being a naturalist?" Sul demanded.

"I don't know. 'Hello, I'm crown prince Attrebus, I've just

come from Oblivion, where I was eviscerated by something and then healed by a god so I can try to find the sword that will help me defeat the flying city of Umbriel and its army of undead' just seemed like an implausible way to go."

"Right," Sul grunted. "You had a good instinct. But asking outright where the sword is would seem to run counter to it, wouldn't you think?"

"I could just ask him if he has any unusual artifacts I can write about. We don't have a lot of time, Sul."

"He let us in," Sul said. "He seems to have an interest in sorcerers. Let's continue to follow your first instinct and see what happens. At least for another day."

Attrebus studied Sul for a moment, trying to see if he was making fun of him. Even now it was hard to tell.

"Okay, then," he said.

"Get some sleep," Sul replied.

Attrebus turned in, but every time he closed his eyes, he felt his belly open and the wet, impossible gush of his innards into the basket of his arms. Sleep felt too near death, and after half an hour of lying there, watching the faint crack and glow of the flames, he rose, dressed in breeches and shirt, and quietly padded into the hall. He dithered for a moment, feeling vulnerable in the near-black. He'd thought he might explore a bit, but without a torch or lantern, he wouldn't be able to see much. He took a few steps along the wall and stopped, not entirely sure why.

Then he felt breath touch his face.

SIX

"Anything I can help you with, inspector?"

Colin looked up from the tome he was studying to find a bent and withered fellow in a burnt umber robe furnished with what was possibly a hundred pockets. His nose took up most of his face, but his keen blue eyes were what drew your attention.

"Professor Aronil," he said, standing.

"No need for that, old fellow," the mage said. "Are you finding what you're looking for?"

"I don't really know what I'm looking for," he said.

"Well, that can either be good or bad, can't it?" Aronil said. "But I don't remember you as a browser, Colin. You always wanted to get to the point, to the answer. I don't expect you've changed that much."

"No, I don't expect I have."

Aronil peered down at the pages. "Pneumatology? That's rather your strong suit."

"Well, I thought so," Colin replied.

"Is this about the flying city or what-have-you? Because the

College of Whispers has the most up-to-date information on those things. I've just seen their most recent report—fascinating, really. The things aren't bonewalkers—they're more like flesh atronachs, although they don't respond the same to arcane stimuli."

"No, it's not about that," Colin said. "I'm assigned internally."

"I understand," the mage said. "I shan't pry more."

He began to walk away.

"Actually, I would welcome your help," Colin said. "It could take me weeks at this rate."

"Well, what's the problem, then?"

"The problem is that something nearly killed me the other day, and I don't know what it was."

"Well, the 'nearly' part is encouraging anyway," Aronil said.

"I don't like my chances if I meet another one," Colin said. "I don't know if that's even likely, but I always prefer to be prepared."

"Tell me about it," Aronil said, pulling over a seat.

"I was searching an apartment," Colin began. "At first I thought it was a ghost—"

"Presenting, or had you prepared yourself?"

"I went there looking for spiritual remnants," he admitted.

"So it was probably invisible to the untrained eye."

"Oh, I'm sure of that," Colin replied. "The apartment has a resident. I checked into him a little and he's apparently never claimed his place was haunted or whatever."

"And he isn't a mage?"

"No."

"Fine. Go on."

Colin related the rest of the encounter, and the old Altmer just sat there for a moment, nodding absently.

"And afterward—the spirit you were looking for?"

"She was there. Not much left of her, though."

Aronil stood and took a couple of paces. "You're in danger-ous territory here, Colin. I wonder if you know exactly what you're doing."

"Just my job," he replied.

"I can check that, you know," Aronil said. "I am privy, if I wish to be, to any investigation our organization is running. And one of my charges is to make certain that the library of the Penitus Oculatus isn't being abused in any fashion."

"I'm aware of that, sir," Colin said, as ice formed in his belly. "I don't believe I'm abusing anything."

"Last I checked, you were assigned to find any possible Thalmor connection with our current problem. This seems far afield from that, to me. How did you meet this thing? What did you hope to learn?"

He sighed. He couldn't pretend Aronil didn't have the clearance.

"You're right," he said. "I think the Thalmor angle is a dead end. I'm looking into something else."

"We're alone here," Aronil said. "Tell me."

"I believed there was a connection to Black Marsh," he said. "The spirit I was looking for was of a woman who witnessed what may have been the calling of Umbriel into our world."

Aronil folded his arms.

"I've heard the speculation that it must have been summoned here, or at least invited. It arrived in Black Marsh, so I suppose that makes sense, on the surface of it. Do you have proof?"

"Only a strong suggestion," Colin said.

"Strengthened, perhaps, by the fact that the witness to this event was murdered, presumably for what she saw?"

"Yes."

"Have you gone to Marall with this?"

"No, I haven't," he replied.

"Why?"

"I'm not sure, to be honest," Colin said. "Part of it is that I'm not sure who I can trust anymore."

"And yet you trust me?" Aronil said. "How touching." His kindly tone had been replaced by a dark rasp.

"Well, I hadn't thought about whether I trust you," Colin replied. "I didn't expect to have to."

Aronil snorted. "Well, it's a good thing you can, you idiot." He strode across the room and up a ladder, and without even looking, it seemed, selected a book and pulled it down. It was bound in some sort of dark red leather and blackened iron bands, but it was quite small, not much bigger than his palm.

"The thing you're talking about is a very specific variety of daedra. They were often summoned by the Nibenese battlemages who ruled during the times of the Alessian order, but after the War of Righteousness, the relationship they cultivated with this species deteriorated. The knowledge to summon them was lost, or almost so—confined to this volume, do you understand?"

"I'm not sure I do," Colin answered. "It was powerful, yes—and I don't want to face another one unprepared—but far worse things are conjured now, from what I've heard."

"Of course. It's not the creatures themselves you need to worry about. And that's why I asked if you know what you are doing."

"Sir?"

"There are certain spells here in the library that few know about. If a book is touched, I can tell who touched it. Before this moment, this book hadn't been touched in twenty years, and then by only one man, one of the few not of our order with the authority to do so. Would you care to guess who that was?"

"I'm pretty certain I know," Colin replied. "But it would help me a lot if you told me."

"Minister Hierem," Aronil said, his voice nearly a whisper. "He has a curiosity for knowledge of that era. And so why, Colin, are you investigating the second most powerful man in the Empire?"

"Because I have to," Colin said. "I have no choice."

"Always aiming for the answer? The point?"

"I guess so."

The mage looked at the book for a moment before handing it to Colin. "It can't leave here," he said. "Is there anything else?"

"Maps," Colin replied. "But I know where to find those."

"You should take what you know to Marall. He's a good man. You can trust him. On a more pragmatic level, you might well lose your position for this sort of rogue activity."

"I'm aware of that, professor," Colin replied. "Thank you for your help."

"I always liked you, Colin," Aronil replied. "I'd hate to have to attend your funeral."

"If this goes wrong, I doubt there will be a funeral," Colin said, "a burial, maybe—funeral, no."

———

Far down the corridor, light appeared, orange and shivering.

Shadows moved in it, and then it was gone.

"What was that?" Arese asked, her whisper so faint as to be almost inaudible, though her breath tickled his ear.

"That's one of the main tunnels," Colin said. "I'm sure they're securing them against the siege. They won't bother with this passage because it doesn't go anywhere—or doesn't seem to."

They had to walk crouched over for another hundred feet before he found the recess in the wall and the mechanism it hid, and then they passed into a chamber large enough to stand in. He closed the hidden panel and then produced a stone that, although it glowed only faintly, illumined everything about it at exactly that same dim luminescence, so it did not outshine what it revealed: a largish room decorated in ghoulish splendor; furniture adorned in grinning, gold-leafed skulls and articulated vertebrae, velvet upholstery figured with obscene rituals of sex and death.

"What is this place?" she asked.

"It was a sort of warren for Julius Primus," he said, "about twenty years ago."

"I don't remember the name."

"I shouldn't think so. He rather fancied himself the new King of Worms, a necromancer supreme, a prince of death. In the end he was moderately clever at hiding and being a nuisance. The Penitus Oculatus rooted him out and sent him to his own long sleep."

"It seems a little silly," she said, picking up a carving of a skull with a serpent wound about it. "Pretentious."

"He was theatrical, to say the least. It didn't save him."

"And this is underneath the ministry?"

"Relatively so."

"It's not on any of our maps," she said.

"Well—we have better maps," Colin replied. "We've been at it longer."

"Hmmm. Unless Hierem has charts I don't know of," she said. "After all, he might well have been involved with this Julius character."

"I rather doubt it," Colin said. "Anyway, this place is not connected to anything in or beneath the ministry."

"Then why are we here?"

"Because this is where you're staying," he said, "until I have this sorted out."

"Nonsense," she replied. "We're partners in this. I recruited you, remember?"

"I could hardly forget that," he told her. "But for what I'm about to do, you would only impede me. You have your gifts, but the shadows aren't friendly to you, I can see that much. Here you should be safe. I brought food and wine down yesterday. I also left some little tricks to show if anyone has been here since then, and they haven't."

She sighed. "Well, that all makes sense, but—"

"If I'm not back in four hours, you can worry about your next move," Colin said. "But I'm safest working alone."

She nodded. "I trust you're right," she said.

"I'm often wrong," he replied. "But not about this."

"About being better able to get in unseen, perhaps—but what then?"

"I'll find the Emperor's proof."

"The journal didn't satisfy him. What do you imagine will?"

"Documents concerning the voyage, with Hierem's signature. Even a ship's manifest would do. He is connected to Umbriel—there must be some evidence of it."

She looked skeptical. "Even with the key to his private chambers, I doubt you will find anything like that." She sighed. "I don't believe the Emperor thinks so either."

"Why give me the key, then?"

She brushed his bangs with her fingers. "You're being naive," she said. "It's sweet, but now isn't the time for it."

"Do you really think the Emperor wants me to kill him?"

"Of course. Why else give you the means?"

"Well, I take him at his word. If he wanted the minister dead, why wouldn't he just tell me to do it? Or send a more experienced inspector?"

"When Hierem is dead there will be many questions, and they will all lead to you, a member of the Penitus Oculatus, yes, but operating without permission. You were never assigned to follow me, or spy on Hierem, by any superior. It will be easy to paint you as a rogue because—in fact—you are."

Colin let that settle across his shoulders for a moment. Everything she said made sense; it was all reasonable. He reviewed his conversation with the Emperor and her case grew stronger. Perhaps Titus Mede did mean for him to end Hierem's threat and then absorb the blame, pay the penalty.

What of it, then? He had signed on for this, hadn't he? To serve and protect the Empire, even if that meant doing the nasty, horrible things no one ever sang about in ballads?

Even though he was looking down, he could feel Arese's gaze upon him.

"It may be you're right," he said.

"It won't be easy," she said. "I believe you will need my help. Together we might manage it."

"If it comes to that," he said. "If the Emperor tells me in plain words to kill Hierem, I will. But until then, I do what I've been told to."

"Since when?" she exploded. "We've just been over this. You've been operating on your own for some time now. Why are you suddenly so concerned with permission and commands?"

"I'm not arguing with any of that," Colin said. "But I won't kill Hierem unless I have to."

"I can't stay down here forever," she said softly. "If you won't help me, I'll have to try myself."

"Then this is about your own life."

"That's not fair," she replied. "You know it isn't."

"Look, let me try it my way. If it doesn't work, if I can't find anything to convince the Emperor to move against Hierem, then we'll come back to this conversation again, okay? And I'll at least know more about the layout of his rooms—we won't be going in blind."

She stayed stiff for a moment, but then he saw the cords in her neck soften.

"Okay," she said. "Don't get yourself killed."

"I won't," he said. He hesitated, and then leaned forward to kiss her, but she drew back.

"Not now," she said. "I—just not now."

"That's fine," he said, feeling something twist in his gut.

It was still twisting when he was back out in the sewers. Did she think she'd made a mistake? Did she regret what they had done? If so, he ought to be relieved. It wasn't like they were going to get married, raise children, and live in the country. There was no sort of future for them, and pretending there was would only make them stupid now, when they needed all their wits about them.

But it didn't make him feel any better, and it took him longer than usual to find his way into the darkness that few could see into. But he finally got there, and made his mind as clear as it could be, and moved to the secret door that led into Hierem's private office and quarters. The key fit, turned, and the door opened.

And, as in the house of Delia Huerc, there was something waiting for him.

SEVEN

Attrebus jumped back with an inchoate shout, reaching for his sword, but of course it wasn't there. He realized his hands were up in a defensive position, and left them there.

"Who is it?" he demanded, backing quickly toward the light of his room.

"I—I'm sorry," a woman stammered. "I didn't mean to startle you."

"Well, you did," he said. "Sneaking around in the dark—who are you?"

Her face appeared then, a young woman, probably about his age, with golden hair and a quirky, wide mouth and very blue eyes. He'd seen her before, at dinner.

"My name is Irinja," she said. "I'm just a serving maid."

"What were you doing outside my door?"

"I made up your room," she said, moving a bit more into the light. He saw that she was wearing a heavily quilted robe and thick, knitted footwear. "I was just coming to make sure everything is good for you." She looked up boldly. "Anyway," she went on, "it looked as if you were about to do a bit of sneaking on your own."

"Why didn't you have a lamp, or something?"

"I grew up here, sir. I know these halls like I know my own toes. Besides, I have excellent vision at night. They say I get it from my grandfather."

"Okay," he said, nodding. "Everything is fine. The room is acceptable."

"Good," she said, but continued to stand there.

"That's it, then," he said. "Thanks for your concern."

"Right," she said, nodding. "I'll just be going."

"Good, then."

She started to turn, but then spun back.

"What are you really about, your highness?" she asked. "I won't tell anyone, I swear."

"What?" he managed.

"No one else reads in this bloody castle," she said. "They really don't have a clue who you are. They completely fell for your story. But I've read every adventure about you I could get my hands on."

Attrebus felt a peculiar warmth steal over his face, and realized he was blushing. "Listen," he said, "I think you've mistaken me—"

"Don't you dare!" she said. "You're not really going to lie to me and tell me you're some sort of horker-watcher? I'd know your likeness anywhere."

He sighed, knowing she wasn't going to be convinced. "Very well," he said. "But you really mustn't tell anyone my true identity."

"I knew it," she said. "You're incognito, on some sort of adventure, aren't you?"

"Well, now that you bring it up," Attrebus said, "yes, I am. And it's of a very secret nature."

"Oh, I want to help," she said. "Surely I can be of help."

As he was considering that, he saw a ghostly face appear over her shoulder. The smoldering eyes were those of Sul, and in that instant he felt the girl's life was hanging by a thread. He shook his head violently.

"Oh, please?" she said, mistaking the object of his gesture.

"Come in," he replied. "Shut the door."

"Your highness," she murmured, lowering her eyes, "I hope you don't take me for the sort of girl—"

"No, no," he said. "I just want this conversation to be private."

"Well—okay, then."

She stepped in and closed the door, but even before she did, Sul was no longer visible.

"Irinja, you say?"

"Yes, highness."

"Okay, Irinja. The first thing is you have to stop calling me highness, or prince, or anything like that. I'm Uriel—do you have that?"

"Yes, hi—Uriel."

"Good. The next thing—tell me about this place. You say you grew up here. Tell me about Lord Sathil. I'm puzzled that I haven't met him."

"Well, he's changed," she said. "When I was a little girl, he was always around, always in good cheer. We all went on excursions to the sea, and in the summer played bowling on the lawns. My brother used to hunt with him. It was nice, back then."

"And now?"

"Well—things happened," she said. "He's not the same now. He hardly ever comes out. But he doesn't mistreat us. You shouldn't think that."

"Things happened? What sort of things?"

Irinja looked uncomfortable. "I'm not really supposed to say," she replied. "Nobody talks about it."

"You said you wanted to help me," he reminded her.

"And I do," she replied. "But if this is about Lord Sathil . . ."

"I mean Sathil no harm," Attrebus assured her. "Or anyone here."

"There are just things we don't like to talk about," she said, sighing.

"Okay," he said. "Have a seat. I'm going to explain to you why I'm here, but it will take some time."

"Very well," she said.

And so he told her about Umbriel and its undead army, and Annaïg, and how he and Sul had gone through Oblivion, first to Morrowind and now here. He showed her his scar.

When he was done, she looked down at her knees.

"You've come here for the sword, then," she said. "For Umbra."

"Yes. Because I believe it is the only thing that can stop Umbriel."

"Don't tell anyone else that," she said softly. "Don't ask about the sword at all."

"Why?"

She looked up at him. "I want to help you," she said. "But I have to think."

"Listen," he said. "Every moment we wait, more people die, and the more soldiers the enemy has. Minutes are precious, days are treasures."

"I know," she said. "But I can't just—I have to think."

"Will you come back here, tomorrow night?"

She nodded. "It's probably the only time we wouldn't be noticed and heard."

"Good, then," he said. "I'll see you tomorrow."

She left, and when he was certain she was gone, he went next door to Sul's room.

Sul was waiting for him.

"How much of that did you hear?" he asked the Dunmer.

"Most, I think. Are you sure that was wise, telling her why we came?"

"I had to do something. At least we know that the sword is a hornet's nest, somehow."

"Yes, and that girl is one of the hornets. You've asked her to betray the rest of them, and you don't know why or what's at stake. For all we know, someone will be back here to cut our throats before morning."

"I trust her," Attrebus said. "She might not help us, but she won't do anything to hurt us."

"Hurt you, you mean."

"Look, unless you've had another vision that tells us where the sword is, we've got very little chance of finding it without help. You saw how big this place is. Even if we could move through the castle at will, unobserved, it could take weeks, months. In fact, we don't know it's even here, do we?"

"I'm just wondering how much you thought this through and how much comes from your pike."

"My what?" But then he got it, and felt his face warm. "Now, really—" he began.

"That woman I found you with—the one who kidnapped you. The one I killed. You trusted her, didn't you? Slept with her?"

"Well, yes, but—"

"And this whole chase, this quest of yours—that started with a girl, too—this Annaïg you're so set to rescue."

"Maybe that was part of it, yes, but Umbriel did rather sound like something that needed taking on."

"Your judgment just seems a bit hasty and simple when pretty girls are involved."

"Well, possibly," he admitted. "But it's done now."

"There's still time. Something could happen to her on the way to wherever she's going."

"No," Attrebus snapped. "No, do you hear me? She'll help us or she won't, but I won't have her hurt."

"Well," Sul muttered, "let's hope she feels the same about you."

EIGHT

Glim wasn't aware when silence and darkness claimed him; he didn't know how long they had lasted—it might have been hours or days. But after the quiet came the voices, the gentle murmur of the trees, drawing him into the dream of thought, where past and future were irrelevant illusions and his mind was unhampered by reference to anything at all. And so he remained for a time, until finally the ache of hunger and the pain of his wounds brought him nearer to the world. The voices were still there, leading him through the twisting roots, finally into the light, amidst the great boughs of the Fringe Gyre. He climbed higher, until he could see the buildings above and get his bearings.

None of them looked familiar, which could only mean he was on the wrong side of the rim. Groaning, he began picking his way from tree to tree, hoping his quivering limbs didn't fail him.

It was nightfall before he found the place, and all he could do was collapse and hope he didn't die before Fhena found him.

"I've never seen anyone hurt like this," Fhena murmured,

pressing something that looked like yellow fur against the wound in his side.

He finished swallowing the whatever-it-was she had given him to eat. "That feels good," he said, looking around. They were in some sort of cavity in the tree, irregular in shape. Light came in from around the bend, but he couldn't see sky.

Then her comment registered.

"You've never seen anyone hurt? How do you know what to do?"

"No, of course I've seen injuries. Ixye broke his leg in a fall yesterday. I meant I've never seen someone hurt on purpose."

He coughed out a little laugh. "I don't understand. Murder seems to be the most common pastime in Umbriel."

"Not up here," she said. "Not in the trees. I know below is horrible. I've heard about it. But bad things don't really happen up here."

"Maybe it's the trees themselves," Glim mused. "Their influence. Anyway—I'm sorry to be your first."

"Well, if someone had to be—" she began playfully.

"I can't stay long," he interrupted.

"Right," She agreed. "You need to hurry back down there and get something else stuck in you. I understand."

"They'll look up here for me," he said. "I don't want to get you in trouble."

"They looked up here for you yesterday," she said. "I hid you. They passed by."

"Yesterday? How long have I been up here?"

"Three days, reckoned by this sun," she replied. "I gave you something to help you sleep."

"I— Three days?"

"It's what the trees prescribed," she said.

"The trees?"

"Yes. Our usual medicines didn't help you very much, so I asked the trees what to do and they told me."

"Okay," Glim said, trying to sit up. "Three days? From now on, when the trees tell you to do something, you ask me first."

She frowned. "There wasn't much 'asking you,' " she said. "You weren't really in much of a state to answer. Nor would you be now, if I hadn't done what I did, for that matter."

She turned away from him.

"Look, Fhena—"

"And now you're just going to go right back down there. Stupid!"

"They'll search here again," he said. "Besides, the skraws are counting on me. Who knows what's been going on?"

He saw her head sink a little.

"Wait," he said. "You know. You've heard something."

"Glim, please—"

"What is it, Fhena?"

"They think you're dead," she said. "They've gone crazy, started breaking things all over the place, and the lords have been trying to pacify them."

"Well, then—"

"I'm not listening," Fhena said, covering her ears.

He sat up and scooted next to her, gently taking her hands and pulling them down.

"You have to understand," he said. "I'm responsible for this and I have to deal with it."

She looked at his hands, holding hers.

"Well—how about this?" she asked. "Send them a message. Tell them you're okay and they need to stop. You need a little more time. Please."

Glim blinked, realizing that actually made a lot of sense. "Okay," he said. "We'll see if that works, and if it does, I'll stay up here until things calm down a little. But eventually I have to go back."

She smiled, and then a little tear appeared in the corner of her eye.

"What's wrong?" he asked.

"Nothing. It's just that you listened to me. You really listened to me."

"I did," he replied. "But understand—I can't stay up here forever."

"I understand," she replied, standing up. "But you will for now."

"Yes."

"Okay. I've got to go—more work for us with the sump in such a mess. But I'll find time to send word down."

———

After she was gone, he managed to struggle to his feet and look around. The wooden cave curved a bit, and he saw the hole above where the light was coming through, and a sort of slope going up. He climbed slowly but already felt fatigue when he found the opening. It was covered with a filmlike substance, possibly a large leaf of some kind. Deciding to leave well enough alone, he went back down to his pallet, curled up, and in no time was asleep again.

He woke with something warm nestled next to him. The light was gone, but he recognized Fhena by her smell and realized that she was spooned against his uninjured side, with her head up in the pit of his arm. She snuffled when he moved.

"What?" she murmured.

"It's just me," Glim said.

"Oh." She lifted her head.

He hesitated a moment, then positioned his arm under her, so her cheek rested on his chest. A few moments later her breath evened out again, and he lay there awake. Once again he let his mind simplify, listening to the trees, but after a bit he understood there was something else, something like music, color, and tactile sensation braiding and unbraiding, sometimes together, sometimes breathtakingly separate, but always as recognizable as a scent.

It was Fhena, dreaming next to him, connected to him by the root.

———

"Longer," she begged him two days later. "Stay longer. Things are better down there. They've calmed down."

"Because they're waiting on me to tell them what to do," he said. "If I stay gone too long, they'll start to wonder if I'm really alive."

"The lords will kill you," she said. "They'll be waiting for you."

"They didn't catch me before," he replied. "They won't catch me this time either."

"You weren't this weak before."

"Nonsense," he replied. "I feel fine—you've done a good job healing me."

"Don't go," she said. "I know you want to stay with me."

Glim closed his eyes, wondering what Annaïg was doing, knowing he had to find out, because he had to talk to her. He had never been this confused in his life about anything. Because Fhena was right—he *did* want to stay with her. He didn't feel any sexual attraction toward her—they were too different for that. What he *did* feel was much more compelling and thoroughgoing than lust, and it was weaving knots in his brain.

"I'll come back tonight," he promised. "I'll be back."

"You'd better," she said.

He made his way back down the tree, to his more usual path, and in a few moments was back in the sump. It felt good to have water around him again, and for a while he let himself enjoy the feel of it, marshaling his thoughts. Wert was supposed to meet him near the bottom of the Drop, in a stand of slackweed. But what was he going to tell him? Push forward or give up? If he agreed to give himself up, could he win some concessions for the skraws?

He had even less idea what to tell Annaïg, when and if he managed to see her again.

His toes and fingers were tingling oddly; it had started almost below perception, but now it was beginning to bother him. He touched them and realized that the ends were completely numb; the pain was at the first joint. A moment later it was at the second, and progressing up his limbs at a terrifying pace. He turned and began swimming as fast as he could, back the way he had come, but before he went a hundred yards, he couldn't move his arms or legs anymore, and all he could do was scream as the agony crept into his torso, surrounding his heart. He drifted down, toward the light in the deepest part of the water, toward the ingenium.

He felt his heart stop and icicles grow in his brain. For an instant he felt the trees again, and through them a little echo of Fhena, like a butterfly.

And that was all.

NINE

"Irinja is avoiding me," Attrebus told Sul as he tested his weight on the frozen stream. It was solid as stone. Fruth—one of the hunters assigned to help him with his "research"—gave him a funny look. For a moment he thought the fellow had overheard him, even though he was sure all of Sathil's people were out of earshot. But then he realized the Nord just thought he was an idiot for being so tentative about the stream in such bitter cold.

"Well?" Sul asked.

"I don't know if that's a good sign or a bad sign."

"She's betrayed you," Sul said.

"Maybe not. Maybe she's still thinking."

"Maybe," Sul said. "If that's the case, we might come back from this expedition."

"Why would they take us out into the mountains to kill us?" Attrebus wondered. "I should think it would be easier in the castle—say, while we're asleep."

"No blood to clean up," Sul said.

"Well, there is that," Attrebus said. "But even if murder isn't in their plans, I'm not very happy about this trip."

"You shouldn't have told them you were a naturalist, then," Sul whispered. "They're just doing what you asked them to."

"True enough. But every second we waste here seems like an eternity."

"I have some ideas," Sul said.

"If they involve torturing Irinja, forget it."

"If she knows where the sword is, probably most of them do. But leave that. I tried some minor cantations last night. The sword is in the castle, or very near it."

"Do you know what part?"

"No. But I can try something a little riskier. There are daedra who sense enchantments much as we smell things. I can summon one of them and let it find the sword."

"Why didn't you do that last night?"

"Because if Sathil or anyone else in the castle has any proficiency in the arts, they'll know a conjuring has taken place. Or someone might simply see the daedra. I was hoping we would find it some other way, but as you say, we don't have much time to lose."

"Tonight, then, if Irinja doesn't tell me anything."

"That was my plan."

Attrebus nodded. Up ahead, Fruth beckoned them toward a ridge.

Beyond the rise, a valley spread, and beyond them mountains whose peaks vanished into the oppressively low clouds.

"Ensleth Valley," the guide said, lifting the point of his red beard. "Good hunting here. Elk, deer, muskrey."

"Very good," Attrebus said, scribbling that in his book. "And those mountains?"

"Moesring Mountains," Fruth said. "We don't go there much."

"What makes this valley so good for game?" Attrebus asked. "It looks just like the last one."

"Salt," Fruth replied. "Big salt lick along where the stream comes out. Only one on this side of the mountains. You'll want to see that."

"Sure," Attrebus said. "I suppose so."

As they were about halfway down the slope, Fruth's head jerked up sharply toward the mountains. Attrebus followed his gaze and saw what appeared to be a white cloud rolling down it toward them at impossible speed.

Fruth's gaze darted around, but then he gestured back upslope.

"Hurry!" he shouted.

But they had only gone a few steps before it hit them.

Attrebus had heard of avalanches, huge slides of snow coming down mountains, destroying everything in their paths. He assumed that's what this was, and braced for it, yet what hit him wasn't a wall of snow, but an unbelievably cold mist. Snow came with it, but whirling in the air, biting at his face. He couldn't see anything. He stumbled, then struck his foot against something and went tumbling down the slope, flailing wildly, thankful at least for the layers of fur and leather the servants of Sathil House had given him to wear. Even so, he felt the temperature dropping impossibly fast.

Someone caught hold of him and drew him along with terrific strength, and after what seemed a long time, pulled him down into what felt like a stony grotto.

"Keep close," a voice said—he recognized it as Fruth's by the accent. A moment later something warm and faintly luminous appeared between them. It looked something like flame caught in a ball of glass, and after a few moments it seemed to push the worst of the cold away.

"What was that?" he asked.

"It comes down like that sometimes," Fruth said. "Never seen it come so fast, though. Unnatural, probably Frost Giant."

"Frost Giant?"

"Yah. Unpredictable, this new one, and very strong."

"What about Ozul?" he asked, using Sul's false name. "And the others?"

"We'll find out when this is over," Fruth said. "We go out now, we freeze. Freeze anyway, if this stays too long."

———

Sul managed to scramble far enough up the hill that the wave of freezing air went below him, but it enveloped Attrebus and Fruth, blotting them from view. He started down but was arrested by an eldritch tingle that told him—as his common sense should have—that the event wasn't natural. He spun, fingers clenching on the hilt of his sword, an invocation already begun in the back of his throat.

He faced six well-armed and armored footmen, all of Nordic cast, all wearing the Sathil draugr on their surcoats. A seventh man sat a thick, shaggy horse. He was wrapped in a dark green cloak and cowled in black, but even shadowed it was easy to make out the crimson eyes of one of his countrymen.

"Lord Sathil," he guessed.

"Yes, that's right," the man said. His voice was soft, almost apologetic in tone.

"My companion—"

"Yes, I'm sorry we didn't arrive in time," Sathil said absently. "The new Frost Giant is somewhat feckless. He usually doesn't haunt this side of the Moesrings until midwinter."

"Frost Giant," Sul replied dubiously.

Sathil didn't seem to notice his tone. "You're friend is with Fruth. He should be fine—and if he isn't, there isn't much you can do at the moment."

"I'll take my chances," Sul said, "and do for him what I can."

"Talk to me," Sathil replied. "We'll wait here for the cloud to settle."

Sul got the emphasis and relented.

"What shall we talk about, Lord Sathil?" he asked.

"Oh, so many things," Sathil replied. "Do you have sons, Ozul? Daughters?"

"I do not," he replied.

"Did they perish when Morrowind was destroyed?"

"I never had any children," Sul said.

"I don't know whether to pity you or envy you," Sathil answered.

Sul didn't think that needed any sort of reply. Sathil might have disagreed, for he paused for a long time. Finally he rode his horse nearer.

"Who sent you?" he whispered. "Was it him?"

"No one sent me," Sul replied.

"Ah, if only that made sense," Sathil said. "But many have come here, to this place where no one should come, to where

I try to keep my peace. All sent, in the end, by him. They all admitted it, before it was over."

He leaned forward. "Shall I tell you the story? Do you already know it?"

"I've no idea what you're talking about," Sul said. "Who is the person you keep referring to?"

"Person?" Sathil's teeth showed in either a grimace or a grin. "Person." He jerked his head toward the valley. "Do you think your friend will live?"

"He had better," Sul answered.

Sathil's eyes narrowed and he mumbled something. The air took on a sharp, chlorine smell, and every nerve in Sul's body seemed to hum.

"I will defend myself," Sul warned.

"Stand still," Sathil hissed.

The air snapped like tiny twigs burning in a fire, and Sul felt his lips tighten. He thought to call something, but its name stayed just beyond him.

Then it was over.

Sathil sat back in his saddle. "You are strong," he said. "Stronger than I thought. But you don't have his stench on you. Another prince, I sense, but not the one—not the one. I can't be fooled out here, in the clean air, beneath the righteous sky. You are none of his."

He twitched his reins and the horse began to turn. "Stay as long as you like," he said. "I will not likely see you again. I do not often leave my rooms."

"Lord Sathil, if you have some problem—"

Sathil stopped his horse and looked over his shoulder.

"There was a time I sought help," he said. "I offered rewards. But that time is long past. Things now are as they are, and I live only to curse him."

"Who?"

But Sathil turned again, and without another word he and his entourage rode back toward the castle.

———

Even in the near-boiling water, Attrebus still somehow felt cold. Sul and the Sathil's leech had both assured him he would keep his fingers and toes, but by the gods it didn't feel like it.

The tub was portable, made of some sort of thick, oily hide on a wooden frame, and had been brought into his room. He hadn't seen who poured the water, but a kettle depended from a wooden arm steamed away near the fireplace. Sul sat on the corner of his bed.

"Frost Giant," Attrebus muttered.

"No," Sul said. "Sathil did it himself, I'm sure of it. He wanted to separate us." He handed Attrebus a bottle.

"Drink this. You'll feel better."

"Some sort of remedy?"

"Whiskey," he said.

Attrebus took a swallow. It hurt going down, but left a pleasant glow behind.

"So he wanted us apart. Then why didn't he slough you down into the freezing cold?"

"He wanted to talk to me," Sul replied. "He thought we were working for someone. A daedra prince, from what I could gather. Others have been here before us, it seems."

"Others? Come for the sword?"

"He didn't say anything about the sword. It might be something else entirely."

"That would be a big coincidence."

"Yes."

Attrebus started to say something, but then lowered his voice. "Could they hear us? If Sathil is a wizard——"

"Our privacy is secure, unless Sathil is himself a daedra prince or something equally powerful."

"Okay. I was going to say, if these others he mentioned came for the sword—and if they were sent by a prince of Oblivion—wouldn't Clavicus Vile be the obvious one behind it?"

"Yes."

"Daedra have no true forms, right? They can appear as almost anything."

"Correct."

"What if that wasn't Malacath we met? What if it was Vile?"

"Could have been," Sul said. "Although Sathil seemed convinced we hadn't had any dealings with Vile. It doesn't matter either way. Whether Malacath or Clavicus Vile sent us here, we have to get the sword—and not for either of them. We have to keep it."

"Right," Attrebus said. "But if we're caught up in some plot of Clavicus Vile's——"

"Then we have to keep our brains in our heads," Sul finished. "Same as if he's got nothing to do with us."

"Okay. But if Sathil has the sword, and Vile knows where it is—I mean, how strong could Sathil be?"

"From everything we've heard, Vile is weak. And all daedra

are vulnerable here, in Tamriel. They can't come here unless summoned, and even then their power is curtailed. He could send his followers, but they would be mortal, like us."

"Right. So what now?"

"I'm going to my room to think. I've changed my mind about summoning daedra to explore the castle. From what I saw of Sathil, he would notice that, and I'm pretty sure we won't survive his suspicion a second time."

"Okay. I'm staying in the bath for a while."

"Easy on the whiskey. We may have to fight at any time."

"Sure," Attrebus said, taking a final swallow of the stuff.

Sul left. Between the bath and the whiskey, Attrebus felt pretty human, and after a while the water actually seemed too hot, so he got out and wrapped himself in the heavy robe he'd been provided. He pulled out Coo and opened the little door, but Annaïg wasn't there, so he set the mechanical bird on a table next to the bed.

He was tired, but not sleepy, and sat on the mattress turning the day's events about—and wondering what Sul would do—when he heard a light knock at his door.

He answered it and found an anxious-looking Irinja.

"I heard what happened," she said. "I hope you weren't hurt."

"I'm fine," Attrebus assured her. "But I need to know—did you tell anyone about our conversation? Did you tell anyone that we were looking for the sword?"

"No," she said. "I wouldn't do that."

He studied her face for a moment, searching for signs of disingenuity, remembering the conversation with Sul about his weakness for women.

"Come in," he finally said.

"Your highness isn't dressed for company."

"I'm covered and comfortable," he replied. "Come in."

She did, and he saw the expression on her face, the same as he'd seen on many young women. Not long ago he would have taken advantage of that look in an instant, without thinking. Now he found himself uninterested.

But he needed to know where Umbra was.

"I was having a bit of whiskey," he told her. "Would you care to join me?"

"Highness?"

"None of that, remember? Do you want the Frost Giant to come after me again?"

"Oh, no," she replied. "Yes—a dram of whiskey would be nice."

He gave her the dram and then some. She drank it nervously.

"I want to help you," she said finally, but he could hear what was coming next, and put his hand on hers.

"It's okay," he said. "I've put you in a bad position, I can see that. Just keep me company."

He filled his glass. "I'm going to have a bit more. Join me?"

"I shouldn't," she said, so predictably that he could have mouthed the words along with her.

As predictably, she took the drink.

"I must seem very stupid to you," she said.

"That's not true," he said. "You speak intelligently, you're thoughtful, you don't make important decisions without thinking them through. If I had met you at a ball in the Imperial City, I would have imagined you the educated daughter of Skyrim nobility."

"Rather than a maid," she said bluntly.

"Listen—my father was once just a soldier with ambition. Now he's Emperor. He fought for everything he ever got, and I was born with it. Who should be admired the most?"

Unbelievably, as he said this, something seemed to shift in his chest, and his face became warm.

"What's wrong?" Irinja asked. "Are you—are you crying?"

Attrebus realized a few tears were indeed trickling down his cheek.

He laughed. "Have you ever said something because it seemed like the right thing to say and then realized it was true?"

"I guess."

"When I saw my father last, I said terrible things to him. What I've never told him is what I just told you."

"And now you're afraid you'll never see him again, never get to tell him."

Attrebus paused for a moment. The epiphany was that some part of him had always known he was less than his father but refused to admit it. That's why he'd been so easily convinced of his own greatness, why he had been so blind to all the signs of deception that he should have noticed.

But where her mind had gone was more useful, wasn't it?

"That's right," he said. "He won't flee when Umbriel arrives. He'll stand, and he'll fight, and he'll die. And he will never know how I really feel."

"That's awful," she said, pouring herself another drink and gulping it down. He took another, too.

She wiped his cheeks, and he took her hand, looked into her eyes, let her know that he was going to kiss her, and then did it.

She tilted her head back, eyes closed.

"I want to help you," she said when their lips parted.

"I'm not asking you to," he said, and kissed her again.

This time she kissed back, hard, with lots of enthusiasm and not much technique.

And he felt guilty, which was absurd. He kept seeing the little image of Annaïg's face.

But that was all he had seen, wasn't it? Below the neck, she might be hideous.

And now he felt even guiltier, for such a horrible thought. He pushed Irinja back, gently. "I can't," he said, and sighed.

"I'm not asking you for anything," Irinja said. "I'm not wanting you to marry me or take me away from here or—I just want to be part of your adventure. A part of something important."

He noticed she was shuddering. "May I have another drink, please?"

He gave it to her, and poured himself a large one.

"It's his son," she said softly. "Lord Sathil's son, Elhul."

"What about him?"

"Lord Sathil sent him down to Morrowind, to the ruins of Vivec City. Sent him after that sword, Umbra. But when Elhul picked it up, he went mad and started killing his guards. They had to bind him in chains. They took the sword away from him, and he seemed to get better, but then he found it. He killed his mother, Lady Sathil. He killed his two brothers and half of the guards before they dragged him down again. And then they couldn't make him let go of it."

"What then? What happened?"

"Lord Sathil prepared him chambers, deep in the stone.

That's where he is now, with the sword he can't let go of. He's been there for eight years."

She wrung her hands. "Elhul was so sweet," she said. "He used to play with me, pretend to be my knight, my defender. But when he had the sword, he almost killed me. His eyes—he wasn't there. Nothing was there."

"And you know where this place is? How to get there?"

She nodded, then threw her arms around his neck and began kissing him again. His head was starting to swirl, and he realized that he'd really had too much to drink, but he didn't care about that. The kisses felt good, and why shouldn't they? He had promised Annaïg a lot, but nothing to do with this . . .

Then the world spun, and he was on his back on clean bedding, and flesh was meeting flesh, and for the first time in a long while he gave up worrying, thinking, analyzing, and just was.

TEN

Annaïg was acutely aware of Lord Rhel watching her as she studied Glim's corpse, but she couldn't control the burn of tears in her eyes. They seemed to come from someplace in the middle of her, a place where everything had been seared out. Soon she would be nothing but skin, and fall in a pile on the floor.

"I'm sorry, Glim," she said in their private cant.

"Umbriel is pleased," Rhel said.

"What's going to happen to him?" she asked softly.

"First he'll be shown to the skraws, so they know he's dead. He'll be cut in pieces, and each of the skraw dormitories will get one, to remind them."

"That's barbaric," she said.

"I don't know what that means," Rhel said. "But you've done well for yourself. You should be proud."

"That will take me a bit of time," Annaïg replied.

"Umbriel told me you might show grief. He said you were not to be punished for it, that it would come to you naturally. He also said that it will pass."

"It will," Annaïg agreed. "May I be alone with him for a moment?"

"Why?"

"To tell him goodbye."

"He's already dead. He can't hear you."

"Umbriel would understand," she said.

"Very well," Rhel yielded. "But only a moment."

She waited until she could no longer hear his footsteps before she bent down and hugged Glim's still body. Hoping against hope that no one was watching, she pried open his mouth and took the crystal growing at the base of his tongue. Closing his mouth, she kissed him on the snout. She put the crystal in her pocket, straightened, and wiped her eyes. Then she left to prepare Rhel's evening meal.

Annaïg had endured long nights before, but she had never felt as lost as she did after the work in the kitchen was done that evening. She drank nearly a bottle of wine, remembering drinking with Glim on her father's balcony as the rains came in Lilmoth.

Eventually she opened her locket.

At first she didn't know what she was seeing, but then the tangle of limbs and blankets sorted itself out. Attrebus was in profile, asleep. The woman—whoever she was—was facing Coo.

She snapped the locket shut and sat there a moment as the feeling of betrayal settled over her. On the surface of her mind, she knew she shouldn't feel this way, that Attrebus had never implied that he had romantic feelings for her. And yet, something about the way he spoke to her, as if they had always been friends, as if when this was all over . . .

But no, of course not. He needed her, that was all. To do this thing, destroy this city. He had to keep her on his good side, motivated, willing to do whatever was required, even murder Glim, for the gods' sake. This probably wasn't even the first time, just the first time he'd slipped up and left Coo open.

And who was she anyway? Nobody. A silly girl, worshipping a prince. Probably sillier than the one who lay with him now. What must he actually think of her?

She was really stupid about people, wasn't she? She'd thought that Slyr was her friend. She'd thought that Attrebus might—

Before she could finish the thought, she hurled the locket at the wall, then finished her wine.

ELEVEN

Colin reached into his pocket, but motion brought the thing's attention to him, and it came at him, just as the last one had. He withdrew a small metal box—only an inch on each side—flipped open the lid, and held it out.

For an awful moment he didn't think it would work, that Aronil was either wrong about what he faced or that the Ayleid soul-maze was old beyond functioning, but then the daedra suddenly dwindled, formed a stream that flew into the box, and was gone.

Colin closed the soul-maze and put it back in his pocket, silently thanking Aronil for showing him the book. Then he looked around to see what other wards were waiting to kill him.

What remained was more of the usual sort, and he was able to neutralize them without destroying them. It might take Hierem a while to discover the missing guardian, but if all of his protections were stripped away, the minister would know for certain that someone had been in his rooms.

He knew he should have a few hours—the minister was at

court—but it was hard to resist the urge to hurry.

Hierem's private suite had a bedroom with a dining area, a bath, and a conventional library; Colin noted them and passed on. He also discovered a room that had been converted into a small dungeon with four cells, all currently empty and clean.

More interesting was a spacious room with various workbenches and a large sigil painted on the floor. Avoiding the latter, he looked over the benches, where he found a number of strange objects. Some—like his soul-maze—looked to be of the ancient race of mer known as Ayleids; others appeared more recent and probably of Nibenese origin. He didn't know what any of them were so he didn't touch them. There were shelves of powders, liquids, salts, and such, along with a scattering of alchemical equipment.

What most interested him was a large desk, built with several deep drawers. A few papers lay on it, covered with scrawled notes and a few puzzling drawings, but the language wasn't one he knew. The drawers were locked in both mundane and magical fashion, and it took him a laborious ten minutes or so to deal with that and begin going through them, looking for something—anything—to connect Hierem to the Black Marsh trip or Umbriel. But after a frustrating half hour, he didn't find anything.

He was feeling for hidden panels when he noticed a long tube propped against the side of the desk. One end was open and a large sheet of paper was rolled inside. He spread it on the desk and regarded it.

It seemed to be plans for a device of some sort, but the conventions of the drawing and an unreadable notation left him with no understanding of what it was. He did recognize bits of it from the notes and sketches on the table, however, which suggested that it was something of present concern to Hierem. So he studied it more carefully, and this time saw one word in the notations he understood.

Umbriel.

It could be anything. For all he knew it was a weapon designed to destroy the city, something the Synod had come up with. But he had the feeling that this was somehow key.

If he actually took it, however, Hierem would instantly know something was wrong.

He toyed with the idea of waiting, of murdering Hierem as Letine had suggested.

Instead, he stole some paper from deep in one of the drawers and began copying, as best he could, the things that seemed most important.

———

Letine traced her fingers over the lines of Colin's drawings as he stroked his down her bare spine.

"I've no sense of scale," she said. "It could be the size of a thumb or a siege engine."

"And it might not be anything at all," he said, and sighed. "It certainly isn't the proof the Emperor asked for, at least not in this form. If only I could understand the language."

"Well, it's not a language," she said. "Or not exactly. It looks like Synod encryptions, the sort they use for secret communications. I've intercepted a few of them."

"Can you read it?"

"No, but I recognize some of the symbols," she said. "Obviously, you can see they use the same letters Tamrielic does, but the words are nonsense. Some of the symbols—these small ones after the passages, that look like funny letters themselves—these contain the key to reading the previous passage. I'm told once you have them memorized properly, it's almost as effortless as reading. These others, these large ones—they represent whole ideas—usually spells, artifacts, certain sorts of energies—" She broke off.

"How faithfully did you copy this?" she asked.

"As well as I could," he replied, "without understanding what I was reproducing. The drawing was most difficult—I can't tell even what the parts are, what holds it together. I mean, this seems to be the bottom," he added, pointing, "but that doesn't make sense. It looks like it would just fall over."

"It's not a drawing," Letine said. "Or at least not a blueprint for a device. It's more like a map." He could hear the excitement creeping into her voice. "This, for instance—I've seen this before where it represented a soul gem—or at least the idea of something that can trap a soul. And here, this represents something that flows in only one direction, like a river."

"Then it is a plan, of sorts?" he asked.

"Right. It could be a device, or a spell, or a series of spells involving—well, at least two arcane objects, this one and that one."

Colin drew himself closer. "If that's the case," he said, "this one might represent Umbriel." He leafed through his copies of smaller sketches and notations. "You see? The word 'Umbriel' is in the passage next to it."

"Possibly," Letine allowed. "But if so, what is this one?"

"You know, if you turn it this way," he mused, "it looks familiar to me—I've seen it before, or something really close. Not in Hierem's chambers, but when I was studying to enter the Penitus Oculatus."

"That's a very different context," she warned.

"I know. It was used by necromancers, back before the Mages' Guild schismed. It was used to designate ghosts, but the meaning was more complicated. I think it could also mean 'shadow,' or even 'echo.' "

"I don't see how it can mean that here," she said. "Not knowing any more than we do."

"What, then? Do you know anyone you trust in the Synod?"

"Hierem is a member of the Synod," she said. "Maybe we should just ask him."

"Well, it might come to that," he said.

"I know someone," she said. "But he won't like it if I bring company. You're going to have to let me out of your custody for a little while."

"The Dark Brotherhood is still out there," he said. "They don't give up easily. I would rather you stayed put."

She turned and kissed him. "I'll be careful. I'll avoid anyplace I usually go, and I'll go at night. Your protecting me is all very sweet, but I've been looking out for myself for a long time."

"Things are different now," he reminded her.

"Yes, and I'll take that into account, right?" A flicker of irritation passed over her face. "Look," she said, "just because you saved my life and we've been playing tussle-bug for a few days doesn't mean you own me, Colin. What we have here is a common goal and mutual respect. If we don't have that, then——"

"Easy," he said. "You're right. You have as much right to risk your life as I do mine. I just selfishly don't want you to die. Be that as it may, if you know someone who can tell us if we have something important here or just a recipe for soup, please, go find out."

"I'll be careful," she said again. "What will you do?"

"Well, I still have a job," he said. "Marall will want a report tomorrow. How long will this take?"

"I don't know," she said. "It depends on a few things. A couple of days at most."

"Days?"

"I have to leave the city."

"The city is surrounded," he pointed out.

She smiled. "A girl can't give up all her secrets right away. Meet you back here in a day or two?"

He nodded.

"Right," she said, and started dressing.

"You're going now?"

"It's dark outside," she replied. "And time is of the essence, right?"

"Yes," he admitted. Despite his words, he wanted to grab her, tie her up if necessary. He had a terrible, wrong feeling in his gut, as if he were never going to see her again.

But he didn't stop her when she went through the door. He walked along with her until their paths parted, and she gave him a little kiss on the cheek. Then he returned to his own apartment.

TWELVE

Mazgar gnashed her tusks as Brennus cleaned the cut in her back, but managed not to let any sound escape her.

"You're lucky," he whispered. "Another inch and it would have been your spine."

"Luck is all I'm having lately," she grunted back softly.

"Hey," he said, his voice uncharacteristically serious, "at least we got through. I'm not sure how many of the others did."

"I saw Falcus go down," she said. "And Tosh."

She closed her eyes as he rubbed something in the wound and began to bandage it. She strained her senses at the young night but couldn't make anything out but silence. Too much silence—no night birds, no dogs barking or wolves howling—just the wind and the rustling of leaves as hundreds, maybe thousands of the wormies strode through the forest below the rock shelter they'd found at dusk. Brennus used his sorcery to further hide them, deaden the sound of their voices, their scent, the life force in them. It had exhausted him, and they still hadn't been certain it would be enough, but the wormies had been passing for more than an hour without noticing them.

"At least we got a few decent meals," she said. "And beer! I'd almost forgotten how good it is."

"We'll get another," he said, "when we reach the Imperial City."

"Yah," she agreed. "That's something to look forward to."

"Divines," Brennus breathed.

"Now, don't get silly and start praying," she said.

"No, no," he said. "Look."

She turned, and there it was, a blackness taking up the whole sky. Beneath it, long flickers like lightning reached up from the ground into the shadows, giving the illusion that something huge was walking by on hundreds of tentacles, only a few of which were visible at any given time.

"Each of those is a death," Brennus murmured. "A soul, drawn up to feed that thing's engines."

"Do you think it's caught up to the others?" she asked.

"Not yet," he replied. "Not at that pace. We gave them a good head start. Those must be farmers or hunters who either never got the word or were stubborn, like those who stayed in Cheydinhal."

"Idiots," she muttered. "That's likely them passing us down there right now."

"Right," he murmured. He didn't sound good.

"You're not dying on me, are you?" she asked. "I can't reach back there, and in a few days it's going to be itching."

"There you go," he said. "That's incentive to keep living—the promise of scratching your knobby back."

"Happy to help," she said. "Now get some sleep. I'll let you know if anything changes."

"You're the one with the wound," he said.

"Yes, and it hurts too much to let me sleep, so do as I tell you, okay?"

"Okay," he said. He curled up on the stone floor, and in minutes he was snoring.

Mazgar watched Umbriel pass, running the battle back through her head: the mad charge with the Cheydinhal guard, breaking the wormies' line. That hadn't been so bad. But then they had to set up their own lines on either side of the gate as Cheydinhal evacuated, and that hadn't been so much fun. It took hours, and the wormies didn't rest, didn't retreat or regroup. They just kept coming, wave after wave of them. In the end their line had been rolled up, and Falcus gave the command to fall back and regroup on the Blue Road—just before he took a spear in the throat. She and Brennus had been driven miles from the road, and now here they were.

Suppose they managed to get around the army and rejoin what was left of the Cheydinhal guards and the Imperial company. Suppose they managed to stay ahead of that thing long enough to reach the Imperial City. What then? Another evacuation? Because, by Mauloch, what was going to stop that?

———

As dawn slid red claws up from behind the world, she saw that the wormies had all passed, at least for the time being, so she shook Brennus awake.

"You let me sleep all night," he accused.

"I never got sleepy," she said.

They packed quickly, starting off south and then turning west, alternating between jogging and walking, hoping to flank the main mass of the wormies. It was easy enough to see where they were, at least—Umbriel could be seen from any clear, elevated spot. But that also made it obvious they weren't gaining very quickly on their objective.

Most of the undead army marched together, but they were constantly sending out hunting parties in search of more bodies to steal. Brenn and she avoided two successfully, but were spotted by a third a few hundred yards behind them as they were crossing some fallow fields. They picked up their pace, but Mazgar knew Brennus wouldn't be able to keep it up for long.

She was right; less than an hour later he began to falter, and their pursuers started gaining.

She spotted a farmstead up ahead and steered them toward that. It was abandoned, so they broke in and barricaded the door. There were no windows.

"How many of 'em do you think there are?" Brennus asked as various implements began thudding into the door.

"Fifteen, I guess."

"You can't count any higher than that," he said. "It could be thirty."

"Could be," she said. "Doesn't really matter, does it? They can only get at us one or two at a time."

"Oh, well, I can't dispute that logic," he said.

There was a splintering sound, and daylight and the edge of an ax appeared. Mazgar rested Sister, point down, and took long, deep breaths, watching as the door disintegrated and the leering, rotting faces of the enemy appeared.

"Stand back a bit," Brennus said as the first of them came through.

"You save your strength," she snapped, but it was too late. A sheet of white fire erupted from the earth a few feet on the other side of the door. She saw at least three of the things more or less disintegrated immediately. Half of one fell into the house, but it didn't move again.

She glared at Brennus, but he was sitting against the wall, eyes closed, face pallid.

"All yours now," he said.

So she waited until the eldritch flame began to subside and then placed herself in the frame of the door so Sister could swing freely outside.

But when the spell dissipated, she saw there weren't any wormies left standing. She found herself regarding instead about twenty men in heavy armor, most astride barded horses. Two were dismounted, making certain the wormies weren't going to get up. When they saw her, one of them doffed his helmet, revealing a dark Dunmer face.

"I'm glad we got here in time," he said. "We spied them chasing you from the hilltop a while back, but we had a lot of ground to cross." He bowed his head a little. "I'm Ilver Indarys, and these are the Knights of the Thorn."

"Mazgar gra Yagash," she said, "Imperial scouts."

"You were at Cheydinhal? You can tell us what happened? We were dealing with some of these things in the South—had no idea a whole army of them was coming down on the city.

We found it empty."

"Most evacuated," she told him. "We held them back long enough to give the refugees a head start, and that's when we got cut off."

"Thanks Azura," he murmured. "That's good to know. They're on the Blue Road, then? Ahead of that monstrous thing?"

"Yes, so far as I know," she replied.

"We need to join them, then," he said. "We have extra mounts, if you would like to ride with us."

"I would *love* a horse," Brennus said from behind her.

"Knowing you, you probably would," Mazgar said. "Would you read it poetry first?"

"Whatever it wants to hear," he replied.

"I was implying—" she began.

"Right," he said. "I got it. Can we go now?"

THIRTEEN

When the stonework of the castle gave way to living rock, Irinja stopped.

"It's farther down there," she said. "There's a gate, with a lock. I don't have the key. And I . . . I won't go any farther."

"Why not?" Sul asked suspiciously.

"I don't want to see him. Or hear him," she replied. "They say he wails and curses."

"Who comes down here?" Attrebus asked.

"No one," she replied.

"Someone has to feed him."

She shook her head. "He quit eating after the first year. We kept bringing him food for another year more, but it always went untouched."

"And after he hadn't eaten for a year—he was still wailing and cursing?"

"Yes."

"Thanks, Irinja," Attrebus said. "This will be far enough."

Her face seemed to darken in the light of the lantern and

she looked down. Sul rolled his eyes and stepped a bit away.

When they had a bit of privacy, Attrebus gave her a little kiss. "I hope you're not sorry about last night," he said.

"I'm not," she replied. "It was nice. I just don't want you to think ill of me."

"I couldn't do that, Irinja."

"I know you're a prince. I know I was just a dalliance, and I never expected more. But I don't want you to think I'm like this all the time. That I'm a bad person."

"I think you're an excellent person," he said. "Now—are we straight on that?"

"Yes," she said.

"Just be careful. I don't want you to get into trouble over this."

She shrugged, then kissed him lightly on the lips. "Goodbye," she said, then turned and quickly retreated back up the stairs she had just led them down.

"That wasn't wise, letting her go," Sul said.

"Well, I don't make a habit of punishing people for helping me," Attrebus replied. "Anyway, it's done."

"It certainly is," Sul said.

"Look, we know where the sword is, at least. You can thank me for that."

"I suppose I could thank parts of you, anyway," Sul replied. "Your brain not among them. Never mind—let's go."

The passage was roughly hewn, and continued down into the bedrock the castle stood upon for another sixty feet or so, then opened into what appeared to be a natural cavern. The gate Irinja had mentioned was there, but when Attrebus pushed experimentally on it, it swung open.

He drew his sword and looked around, but on his side of
the gate there was no place to hide.

"I don't like this," Sul said.

"Why? I don't hear any wailing or cursing, do you? He's
dead. He's been dead for years. Probably whoever tried to feed
him last didn't bother to lock the gate."

"I still don't like it," Sul said. "You stay here. I'll go and
find the sword."

"If he really killed all those people—"

"Weren't you just arguing he's dead?" Sul snapped.

"I was, but you don't believe it."

"Just stay here and watch the gate."

"Fine. But if you need help—"

"Right," Sul said, waving him off. "I'll call if I need you."

Attrebus watched him stride off into the darkness, until all
he could see was the lamp he carried, growing smaller. Then
Sul must have passed behind something.

He rubbed his head. The hangover wasn't as bad as it could
have been, and for that he was grateful. Irinja's attitude about
their little tumble together was fortunate, because now that he
was sober, he couldn't shake the nearly unfamiliar feeling that
he had done something wrong. He'd been with a lot of women,
and never had any sense of guilt. That had changed now, and
he knew that against all reason, he felt some sort of loyalty to
Annaïg, a woman he had never seen in the flesh, much less been
with. He was going to have to sort this out, because he didn't
like feeling guilty. But he understood that it couldn't happen
until they were actually together, face-to-face. As it was, the
relationship was too fantastical.

His ruminations were interrupted by the poke of something sharp in his back.

He leapt forward—away from the pressure—and spun, drawing his sword, Flashing.

The gate slammed in his face. On the other side stood Nirai Sathil. She smiled.

"What are you doing?" he demanded.

"I should rather ask what you are doing, sneaking around down here," she replied, wagging her finger at him.

"We were just exploring the castle," Attrebus said, "and we got a bit lost."

"A bit," Nirai replied sarcastically.

"Look, I can explain," Attrebus said. "I'm—"

"Attrebus Mede," she interrupted. "You've come here looking for the sword, Umbra, and you seduced—or think you seduced—our dear little Irinja to find out where it is."

"Irinja isn't to blame," Attrebus began, then stopped. " 'Think' I seduced?"

"I sent her to you, of course," Nirai said. "After she told me what you wanted."

Attrebus closed his eyes, glad that Sul was out of earshot.

"So you know what I want," he said. "What do you want? Your father spoke to Sul yesterday, and he apparently didn't know who I was."

"That's because he doesn't know," Nirai said. "He doesn't know about this either. He's still protecting Elhul. After what he did! And he's determined not to let any servant of Clavicus Vile take the weapon."

"Why?"

"My father made certain pacts with Vile, and in exchange the prince asked him to find a certain sword in Morrowind. What Vile didn't tell my father was what would happen when someone picked the sword up. The rest I think you know."

"I don't serve Clavicus Vile."

"I don't care if you do," she said. "That's my father's obsession, not mine. I want this to be over with, finally. If you can get the sword from Elhul, you can have it, for all I care."

"Then why this game? Why lock us in?"

"It's just tidier this way," she said. "And if one of you ends up picking up the sword and losing your mind, you'll be safely jailed."

"We won't pick it up," Attrebus said.

"Can't count on that," Nirai said. "Sorry. Good luck."

From somewhere in the back of the cave he heard Sul shout, and then an unholy sort of shriek.

"You'd better hurry," Nirai said.

Cursing under his breath, Attrebus turned away from her and, holding his lantern in one hand and Flashing in the other, made his way as quickly as he could over the rough floor in the direction Sul had gone.

The howling continued, a nerve-shivering, inhuman rasp that sometimes broke into what might be words in a language he didn't know.

Another few moments of stumbling brought him to the source.

Sul had dropped—or maybe thrown—his lantern; it had shattered and was now a brightly burning pool of oil. In the ruddy light, Elhul Sathil was hideously revealed.

He had skin but no flesh, and the skin fit him so tightly his bones were all plainly revealed. As he continued his terrible shrieking, Attrebus could see the apple of his throat bobbing, reminding him of a lizard or a frog. There was something strangely childlike in his gestures, the way his almost white eyes darted hesitantly between Sul and Attrebus.

Attrebus almost didn't notice the sword, it was so much a part of Elhul, just an extension of his arm with its tip resting on the floor.

He glanced at Sul long enough to see the dark stain spreading on his arm.

"I told you—" Sul began, but Elhul was suddenly bouncing toward Attrebus with unbelievable speed. There was no attempt at technique; Umbra chopped down toward him like a cleaver. He met the blade with Flashing's flat edge.

The blow drove him to his knees and sent arrows of pain into his shoulder. Gasping, he flung himself forward in an attempt to tackle the apparition—but although Elhul looked as if he only weighed sixty pounds, he felt as if he were made of cast iron.

Elhul boxed his ears, and Attrebus stumbled back, his head ringing exactly like a bell. Elhul came after him. Lightning crackled about him but he didn't miss a stride.

Elhul lifted the black sword to strike again, and Attrebus drove Flashing into his solar plexus. Or tried to; the point didn't break the withered black skin. Still, the impact sent Elhul back a step so that his swing smacked into the cave floor rather than Attrebus's skull. Attrebus cut hard at his foe's head; it felt like hitting a statue. Elhul shook it off as Attrebus backed away. Elhul stopped screaming, and then spoke.

"Take it from him," Elhul said, his voice curiously

high-pitched, but imperiously demanding.

"What?" Attrebus said, trying to gain more ground.

"Take the sword from him, you idiot." He seemed to have a hard time talking. His gaze was full of fury.

Then his eyes changed, and so did his tone.

"Please," he whispered.

Then he flung himself at Attrebus again. Attrebus jumped back and tripped, throwing Flashing's point up in a feeble attempt to ward off the thing that had been Elhul Sathil.

But Elhul stopped in mid-stride, his mouth open as if to scream again, though no sound issued. Instead a smoking green fluid vomited out. He clapped his free hand to his head as the same viscous stuff jetted from his eyes and ears. Holes began to burst in his abdomen, and he crumpled, breaking into pieces. Where the vitriol touched stone, it too began to dissolve.

"Get back," Sul said. "Don't touch it."

"I wasn't considering that, believe it or not," Attrebus said, trying to keep his breakfast down. "That was—" But he didn't have a word strong enough for whatever magic Sul had just used.

"It worked," Sul replied. "I was starting to think nothing would."

"Congratulations. How's your arm?"

Sul glanced at the wound as if he had forgotten it.

"Not bad," he said. "Nothing that won't heal."

Attrebus looked back at the remains—which now consisted of a fuming green puddle—and the sword, which seemed untouched.

"What now?" he asked. "We can't pick it up without becoming like him, as I understand it."

"Probably not," Sul said. "Look around—find something to wrap it in. It's going to be a while before all the acid is gone anyway."

Only then did Attrebus notice the bodies. Most were merely bones, but a few were still fresh enough to smell. The light from his lantern and the dying flame that had been Sul's were enough to reveal half a dozen. He didn't want to know how many lay outside that illumination.

As it turned out, they didn't have to hunt hard or long; in a moldering pile of clothes and bedding they found a sheath. After about twenty minutes, when the floor finally stopped smoking, Sul pushed the scabbard onto Umbra. He stared at the blade for a few minutes, then picked it up by the sheath. His eyes widened and he muttered something under his breath that might have been some sort of incantation.

"Even in its sheath," he said, "stay away from this, Attrebus."

He tore one of the blankets and cut it into strips, first winding them around Umbra's grip—careful not to touch it—then around the scabbard as well, until there were several layers of wool covering the whole weapon.

"Okay," he said. "Let's go."

"Yes," Attrebus said. "About that . . ."

———

Nirai was still there, and when she saw them—and the bundle they carried—she began to weep.

"You did it," she said. "I had begun to believe it was impossible."

"You're going to let us out now," Attrebus said.

She lifted her head. "No," she said, "I'm not. Not unless you leave the sword."

"You know who I am," Attrebus told her. "I'll be missed."

"You're already missed," Nirai said. "But no one knows you came here except a handful of us in this castle—and we keep to ourselves. Besides, from what I've heard, the Empire has more to worry about than a wayward prince."

She glanced at Sul and shook her head. "Don't," she said. "These bars are sorceled to turn spells back on their casters tenfold. Try to harm me, and you will pay the price."

"Wait," Attrebus said. "We can talk about this. I know you don't want us to die."

"I don't," she agreed. "Go back into the cave. Leave the sword there. I will return here with sufficient guards to protect me and set you free, on your honor to never return."

"What you just said about trouble in the Empire—you're talking about Umbriel," Attrebus said. "But that's exactly why I need the sword. We need it to destroy Umbriel."

"For all I know, it already controls you," she said. "I'm not at all certain the sword must be wielded to possess its owner. Proximity might be enough. But even so, at some point someone will put hand to it again, and then the sword will walk its new thrall right back here to kill all of us."

"Why?"

"Don't you know anything about that thing?"

"Some."

"My father sent for every book and manuscript in existence, and some that were believed lost were found."

"Tell us what you know," he said. "Convince me that we should leave Umbra here."

She dithered for a second or two, and he knew in that instant that Nirai wasn't going to let them out no matter what, but was still trying to make herself easier about it, to convince herself there was no other choice.

"The daedra prince Clavicus Vile wished a weapon made," she said. "It was to be an instrument of mischief in Nirn, a source of amusement for him, a weapon that would send him souls. At first, however, he couldn't find a smith who could do the work. He spent months—some sources say years—in frustration, until the witch Naenra Waerr came forth. She made the weapon, but it was unstable, and she told the prince that he would have to imbue it with some of his own power to make it whole and communicate with it on the mortal plane. Vile gave her the power she asked for. But it appears she tricked him, and some even speculate the witch was actually none other than Sheogorath, the Madgod, in disguise."

"Tricked him how?"

"I said appears," Nirai said. "It's unclear whether what happened was part of a plan or merely the result of tampering with daedric forces. The sword is a soul stealer, and over time it comes to possess its owner. But whether by design, or by contact with human souls, or simply because it is in the nature of daedric energies, in time the part of Vile that was in the sword became a thing of its own, a sentient being."

"Yes," Attrebus said. "We know of that. The being of whom you speak has escaped the sword and now empowers the city of Umbriel. We wish to draw him—or his energies, I guess—back into the sword."

"I surmised that the creature Umbra was no longer in the sword," Nirai said. "It still steals souls, but it is unstable, driving its wielder insane almost instantly. I believe this is because it is still in communication with Vile in some way. I have, in fact, come to believe that when Umbra left, Vile himself—or some significant fraction of what comprises him—is now, in turn, trapped in the sword. Whatever the truth is, no mortal mind can long survive the rage and madness in that weapon."

"Then let us make it whole again, and bring down Umbriel."

"But that's what Vile wants," Nirai replied. "And if that is what Vile wants, he shall not have it." Her voice firmed up, became more confident. "And so I'm sorry. You must remain here."

"I thought that was your father's obsession," Attrebus said.

"So did I," she replied.

"What if we agree to leave the sword, as you offered before?"

"I've changed my mind," she replied. "I no longer believe you would honor such a truce. You might have ways of making the sword invisible, or come back for it with others. I cannot release you."

The air quivered and then snapped in sharp report, and a slavering fiend appeared, hurling itself against the gate. Nirai screamed and leapt back, but the monster's cry was ear-splitting. It caught fire and melted in great gobbets.

"You see!" she gasped, then turned and fled.

"You might have summoned it on the other side," Attrebus said to Sul.

"I tried," he replied. "She's right about that gate. There's power at work that I can't undo."

"What then?" Attrebus asked. "I have a feeling she's not just going to let us starve to death now." He brightened. "If she sends guards, they'll have to open the gate to get to us."

"If it were me, I would send down clouds of noxious fumes," Sul said, "or seal the passageway and let us suffocate. Or pour down barrels of oil and set them aflame, if there is no one here with such arcane knowledge."

"If her father made that weather at the valley, I'm sure he can do something pretty nasty to us if we're trapped down here."

"My thought, too," Sul agreed.

"Can you take us into Oblivion?" Attrebus asked.

"I don't sense any weak spots in the walls between the worlds here," he said. "At least not of the usual sort. Even if there were, it could take us anywhere. When we traveled to Morrowind, we were on a trail known to me, one it took me decades to work out. When we escaped Vuhon, we survived only due to the whim of a daedra prince."

"Then—wait, what do you mean, 'of the usual sort'?"

Sul glanced at the wrapped-up weapon in his arms. "I sense something here," he said. "And if what Nirai says is true, we might have a chance at entering Oblivion and escaping this place."

"But wouldn't that take us straight to Clavicus Vile?"

"I think so, yes."

"And didn't you tell me that would be a bad thing?"

"Yes," Sul said, "but now our options have dwindled, and here we're faced with the bad thing and the worst thing."

"Maybe there are options we haven't considered."

"Name them. I will consider them."

"Just let me think."

Sul nodded and sat down.

After thinking for about fifteen minutes, Attrebus heard odd sounds coming from the stairwell.

"Anything?" Sul asked.

Attrebus shook his head. "Nothing. Not a single thought. Except that even if we get through that gate and out of the castle, we'll still never reach Umbriel before it gets to the Imperial City, not unless you have some other little trick I don't know about."

"If we could get back to the ruins of Vivec City, I could take us back onto my track. But getting there will take weeks, probably."

"Assuming we can find a boat that will sail boiling water without cooking us. No, I think we might as well pay Clavicus Vile a visit. Maybe he'll be in a hospitable mood."

Sul took out the ointment he'd made back in Water's Edge, what seemed ages ago, and dabbed some on Attrebus's forehead. Then he stood the sword on its tip; he didn't unwrap it, but instead closed his eyes and put his skull against the wrapping on the hilt.

For a long time nothing happened, except the air began to stink.

Then something like a fist seemed to grab him, yanking him so hard the blood rushed from his head and black spots danced before his eyes. He struck something, hard, and the wind left him.

The air still smelled bad, but it wasn't the same stench that had been building in the cave. And as Sul managed to lift his head, he saw they weren't in the cave any longer, but elsewhere.

PART III

ONE

Annaïg drifted across a floor of rose-colored crystal that gently rose and fell like the frozen swells of an ocean. It met the walls in gradual curves and then lifted into a vast, lucid canopy veined with softly shifting hints of color. Men and women danced on the uncertain floor, stepping, sometimes gliding, often leaving the surface altogether for a time, as weight was less present here than it was elsewhere in Umbriel. Filmy gowns of viridian, azure, hazel, and lemon spun out impossibly wide as they turned, and each garment chimed musical notes that subtly harmonized or clashed with those around them.

"Who are they?" she asked Rhel.

"Why, your peers, of course," he replied.

"There can't be this many chefs in Umbriel."

"Certainly not," he replied. "Only eight chefs stand high enough to join this company. But surely you don't believe cooking is the only art valued by the lords of Umbriel? We love artistry of every sort, and thus value artists of all kinds. These are the most successful of them. Luel, there, he helped create this very

room. Ten days ago it was a dark jungle, an homage to the first
land we saw on coming here—your homeland, as I understand
it. It was wonderful, of course, but a few days and everything
becomes boring. There is no worse taste than stasis, and I won't
be accused of it."

"This is all yours?"

"Rhel Palace," he said. "Greatest of the eight, if I say so
myself."

"How long has it been yours?"

Even with eyes as strange as his, she sensed his puzzlement.

"It has always been mine," he replied. "I built it before
Umbriel ever began its voyaging."

"Oh," she said.

"I am a high lord, Annaïg. We do not move through cycles
as you do. We have always been and we remain. We were here
at the beginning, and if there is an end we will be there, too."

"I didn't know," she replied. "No one ever spoke of it to me."

"I'm sure they assumed you knew, as I did. You mean to say
that the lords in your world are not immortal?"

"For the most part, no," she said. "The world down there
isn't much like this one at all."

"Well, that's a pity," he said. "But you're here now." He
touched her shoulder. "Enjoy yourself—I must attend to Umbriel."

She nodded and, not quite knowing what to do with herself,
walked carefully to the wall and looked out upon the Fringe
Gyre and the landscape of Tamriel beyond. She saw mountains
in the distance, forest and fields nearer, and wondered where
they were now.

"Congratulations," someone said.

She turned and found Phmer towering over her.

"Thank you," she replied, not knowing how else to respond.

"I always knew that Toel's arrogance would be his downfall," Phmer said, following Annaïg's gaze out into the world beyond. "He certainly underestimated you."

"I'm not sure what you mean," she replied.

"Don't insult my intelligence," she said, and sighed. "Toel's body was found in my kitchens. Now—I know that I didn't put him there. I wondered how you could have done it until it became common knowledge that your friend was the leader of the skraws, and now it all comes together. You set us at each other's throats. Perhaps you killed Toel by your own hand; perhaps your friend did it. It was all clever enough, I grant you. But I'm going to give you just this one warning, because there is something I like about you. You were able to accomplish all of this because no one knew just how devious you are—you played the guileless foreigner so well. Toel should have understood his danger when you framed Slyr, but—as I said—his arrogance got in the way. I will never underestimate you again, however. I do not think I am alone in that."

"I'll bear that in mind," Annaïg said.

Phmer smiled, and lifted a finger toward the crystal wall. "Do you miss your world?"

"My world doesn't exist anymore," she said. "I don't even know what country that is down there."

"It is very large," the chef said. "I find the idea of such a large world unappealing. One would always be lost, I should think. One would have trouble finding one's place. Look how quickly you found yours here."

She wanted to protest, but the fact was, it was true. In Lilm-oth her life had been essentially aimless. She might have spent her whole existence without discovering a direction, never learned what a monster lurked beneath her skin, just waiting for an excuse to manifest. But Umbriel had brought it out of her in quite a short time. Maybe this was her destiny. Maybe this was where she belonged. Did she really care what happened to Attrebus and his empire? Hadn't that just been a childish affectation, like everything else about her before coming here?

She noticed that Phmer was walking away, and was glad. She idled another hour, speaking to no one, and then returned to her kitchen.

Yeum looked up when she entered.

"How was it?" she asked.

"Perhaps Rhel will allow me to send you as my proxy," she said. "That way we should probably both be happier."

"Toel enjoyed the company."

"Well, I'm not Toel."

Yeum bent back to her task. "They caught someone sneaking in from the pantry," she said. "Do you want to see her, or shall I just have her killed?"

"Sneaking in to do what?" Annaïg asked.

"She had a knife. She was looking for you."

Annaïg stood still for a moment, feeling as if she were shrinking somehow. How many people wanted to murder her now? How long could she last? Divines, was Yeum even telling the truth, or was this some sort of prank or trap?

"I'll see her," she finally said. "Where is she?"

"In the cell, of course."

"We have a cell?"

"Certainly. Where do you think Toel put his prisoners?"

"I didn't know he had prisoners," Annaïg said. "In any case, where is it?"

"I'll take you," Yeum said.

She led the way, and Annaïg was careful to stay a few steps behind her.

———

The woman glared at Annaïg through the bars. She was young and pretty, and looked like a Dunmer. She wore peach-colored knee britches and a brown top. She didn't look much like a killer.

"Are you her?" the woman blurted. "Annaïg?"

"Yes. Who are you?"

"My name is Fhena."

"Mere-Glim's friend."

"So he told you about me," she said defiantly. "I came down here to kill you. Everyone knows what you did. He thought you were his friend. He loved you. And now his poor body is all cut up."

"I loved him, too," she said.

"So you killed him? That doesn't make any sense." Her eyes were wide and sad, and Annaïg felt just how fragile her anger was, sensed the artless innocence that lay behind the brave facade.

Or was that only how it seemed? Was she just trying to get a chance to strike?

But this Fhena was Glim's friend, and she owed Glim.

"I want to show you something," she told the woman. "If

I let you out of there, will you promise not to try to hurt me?"

"I don't think I could have done it anyway," Fhena said after a moment. "I just don't understand. I have to understand why you would do this to him."

"Then come with me."

She took the woman to her rooms, which had once been Toel's, and led her back to the bath.

"There," she said.

Fhena knelt and stared into the water at the translucent sack and the reptilian figure it contained. She looked up with tears in her eyes.

"It looks like him," she said. "Smaller."

"It doesn't just look like him," Annaïg said. "It *is* Glim."

Fhena's red eyes were huge as she looked back at the embryo.

"Is it?" she breathed.

"If I hadn't killed him, someone else would have," Annaïg explained. "This was the only way, as far as I could see."

"But his body was cut up, parts of it everywhere . . ."

"True. They had to believe he was gone. The drug I put in the water killed him, but it also made his body grow a crystal, a matrix containing his soul, his thoughts, memories—*him*. It's similar to what we call a soul gem—and also, I believe, to your ingenium. I used that to quicken a proform, and here he is."

"How long?" she wondered. "How long does it take?"

"I was able to speed up the process with him," Annaïg said. "He'll have an adult body in a matter of days."

"And he'll know me?"

"He'll remember everything."

Fhena clapped her hands together in delight. "That's wonderful," she said. "He thinks so much of you—I should have known. I should have known it wasn't true."

"I did kill him, Fhena. His body died, and I'm not sure I'll ever be able to forgive myself for that. Or if he will ever forgive me, for that matter."

"But you just said it was the only way to save him."

"It was the only way I could think of," she replied. "But that doesn't clean my hands."

"But he's coming back to us," she said.

Annaïg nodded, not knowing how to respond. She had been forced to delay poisoning the trees until Glim could come out of the water—otherwise he would die with them. But the instant he was conscious, she planned to do it. If it worked, Umbriel would be crippled or destroyed, and there was a small chance that she and Glim might be able to escape. If it didn't work . . .

"Listen to me," she said softly. "There are other Argonian bodies growing in the sump. Only you and I will know this is Glim, do you understand? No one else can know, or he won't be safe."

"I understand that."

"Make *him* understand that," she said.

"Why can't you?" Fhena asked.

"I hope to, but it may not be possible. If anything happens to me, you have to take care of him."

Fhena turned her gaze back to the tub. "I'm not very smart," she said. "I'm not strong at all. But I'll do my best."

She ran her fingers gently over the sack. Annaïg's throat felt tight, so she left Fhena there with him and sat on the balcony, watching the life of Umbriel, wishing for its ruin.

TWO

Attrebus found himself on his back, staring up at what appeared at first to be a few cottony clouds in a perfectly blue sky. But as he garnered his strength to rise, he noted odd unsettling patches, greenish-gray streaks that didn't appear to be clouds but were more like stains on the sky itself.

He pushed himself up and saw Sul doing the same.

They had landed in a field of white clover—a woodland meadow that might have come right out of the paintings of Lythandas of Dar-Ei. But like the sky, a close look revealed withered, twisted foliage and odd melted-looking places that his eyes couldn't focus on. Beneath the perfume of wildflowers, the breeze carried a scent of profound decay, like a wound gone to gangrene.

"That was different," Attrebus said, glancing at Sul. "It never felt like that when we traveled in Oblivion before."

"That's because we didn't travel here," Sul said. "We were summoned."

Attrebus caught a motion from the corner of his eye and

faced it. A small white dog was watching them from the edge of the clearing, where a little path wound off into the woods. It twitched its head toward the trail and wagged its tail excitedly.

"You think he wants us to follow him?"

"I think that's safe to say," Sul said.

"Safe to say, but safer to do," the dog added in a yappy little voice. Attrebus felt he should have been surprised, but somehow he wasn't.

"Do we have a choice?" Attrebus asked, pointing the question at Sul. Unless the dog was really Clavicus Vile—which, given his experience with Malacath, wasn't impossible—they didn't seem to be in any immediate danger.

The Dunmer shook his head in the negative. "Follow the dog," he said.

The dog led them from the clearing along the little trail, where the vegetation seemed to grow progressively sicklier. They crossed a brook on a fallen log, and he saw fish floating on the surface, their gills working desperately. Something fluttered by in the trees, which he at first perceived to be a bird, then a butterfly the size of a hawk, and finally a caterpillar with wings.

They wound along a spiral trail up a hill, where they found a table large enough to seat thirty or so, with whimsically slim legs that terminated in hooves. Now and then one of the hooves would lift and stamp, rattling the empty plates and cups on the table. Beyond the hill, the colors of the world seemed to melt and flow before the sky gave way completely to shimmering chaos. From this height, Attrebus could see that the trees and grass only extended a mile or so in any direction before similarly dissolving at the edges.

Seated at the head of the table, on a large wooden throne, was what appeared to be a boy of perhaps thirteen or fourteen years, although his lack of shirt displayed a paunch that would have been more at home on a middle-aged beer glutton. He had what appeared to be a goat horn growing from above his right eyebrow, but over the left there was a festering sore. He had his bare feet up on the table crossed at the ankles, and a mean little smile showed on his face. His eyes were most peculiar; Attrebus somehow could not focus on them, but his impression was contradictory: They seemed empty, but empty in a way that nevertheless held limitless meaning.

When the boy saw Sul and Attrebus, he laughed. It was an eerie laugh, almost like the imitation of one, although there seemed to be a tinge of genuine madness there as well.

The dog hopped up on the table. "I give you Prince Clavicus Vile," it announced, and then fell over and began licking itself.

The boyish figure inclined his head slightly in acknowledgment. Then he pointed a finger.

"You, Sul. Bring me that thing."

"We bring it in good faith," Sul said. "We wish to discuss a compact."

"A compact," Vile said, exaggerating Sul's Dunmer accent. "Oh, do you? Oh, very well. Why don't *you* sit here, and be the daedra prince, and I'll just stand down where you are and be the stupid mortal who doesn't know exactly how close he is to being a turnip. Or a boil on a turnip." He turned to the dog. "Do turnips get boils?"

"Galls, I think," the dog replied. "Not boils."

"Whatever," Vile said. He turned back to Sul. "I don't have

to ask nicely, you know. It's mine."

Something happened, but it was too fast for Attrebus to see. Sul grunted and dropped to his knees, and Vile—still in his chair—had Umbra.

"Don't think I'm weak," Vile said. "Everyone who comes here now thinks I'm weak, just because a wee bit of my stuff has been stolen. The trick is, if you've got less to work with, you just don't spread it so thin. My realm may be a little smaller than in happier times, but in it I'm just as strong as I ever was."

"Well," the dog said, "I wouldn't go that far."

"Hush, Barbas, before I feed you to my hounds."

"Which would be me, sir," the dog said.

"If you're after making a point, I really don't take it," Vile said as he unwrapped the blade. When he touched it, a shudder went through him, and he cast it on the table.

"Well, it's no good to me like that," he said. "Sul, don't you at least know better than to bring it to me like *that*?"

Sul was having trouble answering, however. He was still on his hands and knees.

"What are you doing to him?" Attrebus demanded.

"What?" the daedra asked, and then blinked. "Oh, right."

Sul suddenly heaved a deep breath. He sat back on his heels, gasping.

"Haven't I always done my best by you people?" Vile asked. "Haven't I always tried to provide instruction and opportunities for you to improve yourselves? I've treated you with good humor, like equals, really. And where is the respect I'm due? Really, I'm just tired of it now." He sat back. "Just tired. Really."

"We know what happened to Umbra," Attrebus said. "We

know where he is. That's why we've been looking for the sword in the first place."

"First of all," Vile said, "let's not go calling anyone 'Umbra.' There is no Umbra. This—thing—that suffers from the delusion that it is its own—person—is actually nothing of the kind, do you understand? No more than a stone rolling down a hill is capable of real self-locomotion. Or an abacus of doing math by itself. What was in this sword was me, plain and simple. If someone cut your leg off and the leg starting calling itself 'Umbra,' it would still be your leg, wouldn't it? You wouldn't humor it, would you? Help it out with its delusions of grandeur?"

"No, certainly not," Attrebus said.

"There you go," Vile said. "That's just what I've been saying. Not nearly so dumb as you look." His strange eyes narrowed and he put on a boyish smile.

"But go on. You were telling me where the rest of me is."

"In Tamriel, in a city known as Umbriel."

"Again," Vile snarled, "the name of the city isn't Umbriel. I created it, me. Its real name is—" He scratched his chin. "Well, I don't remember. But it isn't Umbriel. More, with the putting on airs." Vile swung his feet from the table and leaned forward, bracing his hands against the table.

"So it's in Tamriel now? I've caught glimpses of it, now and then, but how could he possibly have gotten into Nirn?"

"We're not sure of that ourselves," Attrebus said. "But we're determined to stop Um—ah, your city."

"By returning what was stolen to the sword," Vile said thoughtfully.

"Yes."

"And then you were just going to bring the sword back to me, weren't you?" Vile said.

"Ah—of course," Attrebus agreed.

"You most certainly were not," Vile said. "But that's fine, things have changed. You've come to me for a reason."

Attrebus looked at Sul, who gave him a warning glance.

"The city of which we speak is destroying Tamriel," Attrebus said. "It's on its way to the Imperial City."

"Is it?" Vile said. Attrebus thought the daedra's ears actually twitched. "Ah, I see. And you found the sword in Solstheim. So you don't have time to get there. This is really funny."

"I don't see how," Attrebus said. "I should think you would want us to reach it."

"I want what was stolen from me," the daedra admitted. "That means someone has to stab this nonentity that calls itself Umbra with that sword. Given the circumstances of the city's existence, I can take it from there. But it doesn't matter to me if that happens sooner or later, does it?"

"But if you wait until my country—my people—are destroyed, why would I help you then?"

"It needn't be you; I have mortal followers, lots of them."

"I don't understand, then," Attrebus said. "What do you want from us?"

"What he wants is a deal," Sul said. "A contract."

"Now, there you go," Vile said. "A man who knows the ways of the world. Or worlds, as it were."

"What sort of deal?" Attrebus asked.

"Well—one of your souls will do."

"That's outrageous," Attrebus said.

"Very well," Vile said. "I'll just send you on your way, then. Without the sword."

"If it's a soul you want—" Sul began.

"Stop!" Attrebus commanded.

And Sul actually did, his lips in mid-syllable.

"The pup is barking," Barbas said.

Sul and Vile both turned withering gazes on him, but he held himself straight.

"Vuhon is taking Umbriel to the Imperial City for a reason," Attrebus said. "It has to do with the White-Gold Tower. I don't know what he's up to, but I think you do. I think if he gets to the White-Gold Tower, you lose, which means you need us, now—not some followers who might or might not do the job in the future. You're just trying to trick us, get a little extra out of it. So there is only one deal here, Prince Clavicus Vile—you get us as close to Umbriel as possible, and you do it immediately. We get your missing power back, we're rid of Umbriel. No conditions."

Vile hunched forward, his face wrinkling in a sneer.

"Do you honestly think you can talk to me like that? That after that little bit of impertinence I'll just let you alone?"

"You don't have a choice, unless you plan for this dreary little realm to be all you have for the rest of time," Attrebus rejoined.

Vile smiled and leaned back. "Right then," he sighed. "But that doesn't mean I'll let you alone. There are costs, whether a bargain is struck or not. You're clever, but you don't think toward the long term, and you will regret it eventually. But here we are. Fine. Take the sword, but be careful not to wield it until it's time to thrust it in, yes? And I'll put you close. I can't put you in my city because he's made it so I can't see it, but if it's going to the Imperial City, why don't I just send you there?"

"That sounds good to me," Attrebus replied.

"Well, what are we waiting for?" the daedra asked, his tone brightening. "Good meeting you fellows. Best of luck to us all, eh? At least for now."

He gestured for Sul to pick up the sword. The Dark Elf rewrapped it and slung it on his back.

Then Clavicus Vile waved them away with his hand, and they were gone.

———

Attrebus had come to expect surprises moving to and from Oblivion, but that didn't stop him from yelping when he appeared ten feet off the ground. He waved his arms desperately, striking a tree, which overbalanced him. He landed on his heels going back, and his butt took a lot of the force before his spine slapped into the pine needles and the all-too-solid earth they covered.

He kept his wind, and almost felt like laughing. Had Vile dropped them on purpose? Or was the daedra prince even weaker than he let on, and not in good control of his powers?

Sul would know.

Attrebus stood up and brushed off, then looked around for his companion, but didn't see him in the immediate vicinity. What he did see was a large stone statue of Clavicus Vile with a dog at his side, albeit a much larger animal than the one they'd just encountered. A clearing surrounded the statue, but gave way to forest pretty quickly in every direction.

He had heard rumors that there was a shrine to Vile some-where west of the Imperial City, not far from the Ring Road. If this was it—and that made a certain amount of sense—then they didn't have too far to go.

He looked around again, this time more carefully. Dark things were supposed to happen at places like this, and even though the daedra himself had sent them here, that didn't mean they were safe from his followers.

Closer inspection didn't reveal anyone else, but he did notice Sul's boot sticking out from behind the shrine.

"Sul?" he cried, running across the clearing.

Sul was breathing, but his eyes were closed and he was bleed-ing from a nasty gash in his head. He must have fallen, too, but hadn't been as lucky as Attrebus.

"Hey, Sul!" Attrebus patted him on the cheek, but that didn't draw a response. He poured some water from his skin and washed the wound. He couldn't see any bone, and the skull didn't seem dented. He stripped off the heavy coat he wore and cut strips of the lining, then tied the bandage around Sul's head. Through all of that, the Dunmer showed no signs of waking up.

Attrebus sat there for a moment, trying to decide what to do. He felt very alone, and it began to sink in exactly how much he relied on the old man for strength, knowledge—even occa-sional encouragement. What if the wound was more serious than it looked? What if Sul was dying? Would he have any chance of finishing this? A chance, maybe, but a much bleaker one than if he had the sorcerer at his side.

He couldn't just sit here, could he? But on the other hand,

sometimes those who were injured ought not to be moved. Maybe he should go for help.

But the nearest village could be hours away—even if he knew which way to go—and that would give wild animals far too much time to find a fine, easy meal.

He cut up more of the horker hide coat and chopped off some willow branches, which he then spent an hour or so fashioning into a travois. A few moments later he was dragging Sul through the forest, worried, but feeling a sense of accomplishment. He was pretty sure he knew which direction the Ring Road was, and from there he could find almost anything.

It was slow going in the woods, and he had to stop frequently to reposition the makeshift harness or to rest. He was sure there was a better way to design a travois, but he'd never had occasion to build one before, and although he had seen them, he hadn't studied their structure.

He dithered a bit about where he ought to go. If they were west, the Imperial City was close, but so was his hunting lodge in Ione. Should he go there first, get Sul tended to, acquire some guards? Or go straight for the Imperial City?

Attrebus reached the road more quickly than he thought he would, an hour or so before sundown. Lake Rumare was the most beautiful thing he had seen in a long time, its familiar waters turning coral as the evening deepened. The familiar cries of curlews and coots were music to him. And then there was the Imperial City itself, standing proud and strong on its island, the White-Gold Tower at its center like a pillar holding up the heavens—as some claimed it actually did.

For Attrebus, however, it was proof that his quest had been

worth it, that he wasn't too late. His father would listen to him now. With or without Sul, they would invade Umbriel somehow and return Umbra to his sword.

It still wasn't dark when he saw a small fishing settlement, built on an old stonework that probably dated back to Ayleid times. He was vacillating about checking to see if they had any sort of healer when he thought he heard something odd behind him. Turning, he saw them.

For an instant his heart took wing at the sight of a military formation; to run into a patrol at this point would be excellent luck. But he'd apparently had his allotment of that today, because a few seconds of watching them approach resolved the truth. They wore no uniforms and carried a motley assortment of weapons. These were Umbriel's unholy warriors.

He turned off the road, picking up his pace, dragging Sul toward the village. It seemed like a long way, but frequent glances back didn't show pursuit, so maybe they hadn't seen him.

Hiding behind a house built of driftwood, he watched the hideous procession pass, reckoning their number at about twenty.

The sun was gone by then, but Masser stood bright in the sky as he searched the village. It had been abandoned, he couldn't tell how long ago.

At the little floating dock, however, he found a small boat, complete with oars.

He glanced at the silhouette of the Imperial City.

He hadn't seen Umbriel in the sky; he thought he should if it were here. That meant the walking corpses could go far from their city, which surprised him a bit, although given what Annaïg had told him, there wasn't any reason why they shouldn't be able to do that.

He didn't have any idea how many were here, but it was a good bet that if they were moving freely on the Ring Road, there were a lot of them. Possibly the city was under siege.

Either way, the boat looked better than the road at the moment. Sul needed help sooner rather than later, he was starving, and he didn't think there would be food or medicine in the abandoned village.

So without further deliberation, he got Sul off his traveling frame and into the boat, then began rowing toward the distant lights of the Waterfront District.

THREE

———

Around midnight Sul began to moan in his sleep. His arms jerked and fingers twitched, and Attrebus hoped he wasn't trying to conjure something or set fire to an imaginary foe.

He took it as a good sign, although he knew that didn't come from any medical knowledge, but rather from the feeling that when it came to a man who was unconscious, it seemed better if he was doing something rather than nothing. It suggested his soul was still bound up with his heart.

That there was no obvious pursuit he did not take as any sign at all, although it gave him plenty to think about. He knew from experience that Umbriel's creatures didn't need boats or anything of the sort; he'd seen them emerge from the boiling waters that surrounded the shattered remnants of Vivec City. If any of them were following him, he wouldn't see them. Still, those on the road seemed not to have spotted him, or at least not to have cared if they did. That didn't fit his previous experience with them or Annaïg's testimony. Their pattern was to kill everything they came across—or at least everything with a soul of the sort Umbriel preferred, which seemed to be those of sentient beings. But then again, Annaïg had said that the souls of the dead were drawn up into the city by crystalline threads, and so only those killed directly beneath the city fed it. The ones he'd just seen weren't beneath Vuhon's city, and by the way they marched, he imagined they were on task—either looking for Imperial patrols to slaughter or, more likely, heading to the causeway to put it under siege, or to join one already in progress. In that case they well might ignore the stray traveler.

Another thing occurred to him as well: The last time he had met these creatures, they had somehow known who he—or at least Sul—was. Would they know him if they saw him here? Or was he even making the right assumption? After all, Vuhon might have ordered them to capture anyone at the site where the sword was supposed to be and only recognized Sul later.

Maybe Annaïg would know more, and since his arms felt like they were about to fall off from rowing, he withdrew Coo from his battered haversack and opened the locket door.

At first there wasn't anything, but then her face appeared. He felt a grin start on his face, but then saw hers wasn't nearly as welcoming.

"What is it?" he asked. "Are you able to talk now?"

"I am," she said. "I'm so happy I can accommodate you."

"Something's the matter," he said. "What's happened?"

She appeared to be in a bedchamber illuminated by several glowing orbs. There wasn't anything furtive about the way she acted, not like usual. No, she actually seemed to be mad at him. As if she knew about Irinja, which hardly seemed possible . . .

But then he felt a guilty little burn in his belly-pit. He

remembered taking Coo off the table that morning. Had the door been open? Had she seen . . .

"Look—" he began.

She waved him off. "You don't owe me any explanations, Prince," she said. "I'm not as foolish as you might think. It's just that things here are very—complicated."

"How so?"

"I'd rather not say right now," she said. "I'm still working it out. I've a list of things you might like to know, however, if you have a moment."

"A few," he said, starting to feel a little angry himself. "Things are a little tough here, too, you know. Sul is hurt—he may be dying. I've just had to face down another Oblivion prince, and I'm trying to paddle across Lake Rumare, which on a pleasant day with a picnic basket might be nice but at the moment is rather a lot, considering. I'm sorry if your feelings were hurt somehow. I can only tell you that anything I did was to further our cause, not to—"

"For our cause?" she half shouted, her eyebrows lifting high. But then she closed her eyes, and her forehead smoothed until she just looked tired.

"What is our cause, Prince?" she asked softly, looking at him again. "I'm not sure what my cause is anymore."

"Look—"

"No," she said, cutting him off. "You don't understand. And it's my fault, because I don't want to tell you. Not right now. I just don't want to talk about it. You think it's about that girl, but it's not, you see? It's about who I am. I'm not who I thought I was. The person I believed I was could never—" She stopped and passed her hands over her eyes.

"I can't argue now," she said. "I don't have the strength for it. I'm going to try something in a few days. It might work and it might not. If it doesn't, I want someone else to know what I've learned since we last spoke. That's all I want of you, Attrebus. That's all I need you for."

"Listen," he said. "I'm almost to the Imperial City, Annaïg. You just have to hang on a little while longer. But I understand you. Tell me what you've learned, and know we'll put it to good use."

She nodded, and then spoke of strange trees and stranger births and poisons that might bring it all down—but nothing about herself.

"Have I ever told you how brave you are?" he asked. "How strong? Stronger than me. I know something about making unpleasant discoveries about yourself. But I know that whatever you may have done, you had to do it, and it was for the best."

"How?" she murmured. "How can you?"

"Because I've listened to you," he said. "I've heard you. And I believe in you."

Something flickered a little in her eyes, and her mouth quirked to the side.

"Those are fine words," she said. "I have to go now."

"Wait," he said. "May I contact you tomorrow?"

"If I'm still alive," she replied. Then she closed her locket.

He sat there for a moment, watching Sul breathe, and then put his back into rowing.

———

When Secundus rose, he could see the waterfront not far ahead.

It was on an island, separated from the city, with the harbor facing inward. The old stone buildings formed a semicircle enclosing the harbor, and he was coming up from behind. In the pale light he could see the hundreds of shacks, shanties, and lean-tos that crowded between the wall and the water, and in fact many were built raised up from the water. He smelled the stink of it already, the various stenches of human waste, rotting fish and offal, cheap beer. He thought about going around, but it was a long way and he was tired of rowing, so he passed as noiselessly as possible through the stilts and ladders of the outer houses.

He'd been to the shantytown before, when he was fifteen, curious to see the poorest and most dangerous part of the city and attracted by its reputed vices. He didn't remember it being this silent—even at night there was usually drunken singing, screams, fighting. Now it was as still as the village he'd taken the boat from. Had the people here also fled Umbriel's hosts?

He slowed his approach, squinting to make out if anyone was on the shore.

The boat rocked, gently, then more forcefully. He looked back to see what he'd bumped and saw a hand gripping the hull. For an instant he just stared at it, but then it was joined by another, and another, as decaying limbs rose from the water and gripped the gunnels. With a shout he drew his sword and began chopping at them. They came off easily, but he felt the boat rise and realized there were more of them—many more—beneath, lifting the vessel. He leaned over and tried to cut at them, but he couldn't get a good angle, and the boat continued to ascend as its bearers took it ashore. Desperate, he tried to get Sul on his back, planning to fight through them. If he could get around to the harbor, it might still be manned by Imperial guards.

But then the boat tipped and dumped them both unceremoniously into the stinking, muddy shallows. He swatted blindly for a few seconds before they had him disarmed and held tight.

And as before, they didn't kill him. Instead they dragged him farther inland, to one of the nicer cabins, and milled about it for a while. They didn't appear to care if he called for help, so he did, with sinking hopes that it would do any good.

After a time, however, the door opened and he saw a lantern.

The face revealed in the light appeared human and alive. He was probably on the other side of forty, with a large bald spot in his reddish hair. He had a notch in his left ear.

"Well, now," he said. "What's this?"

"Came from the water," one of the things gripping Attrebus rasped. "Can we have him?"

The fellow held the lamp closer to Attrebus, and his eyes widened. "I don't think so, fellows," he said, shaking his head. "Who would have thought it? Well, I guess he did, and by Malacath, it weren't a waste of time at all."

"I warn you," Attrebus began, chilled by the man's casual oath. "If you don't release me—"

The man laughed. "That's him all right. Don't worry, prince-me-boy. I'll not be keeping you. I'm sending you right along."

"To where?"

"Someplace—nicer." He looked over Attrebus's shoulder. "Umbriel?"

"Naw, not there. You're going to the palace, boy-o."

"Then tell these things to let me go. I can walk there."

"I trust you could, but I've been told not to let you exert yourself."

"By whom?"

"Patience, m'lad."

"My friend is hurt—"

"Yes, well, that's not up to me," the man said. He went back into the cabin and came out followed by a sleepy-looking Khajiit and a Bosmer woman. One of them put a bag over his head. He tried to shout, but after a few breaths of something with a funny smell, his senses dimmed and were replaced by strange, vividly colored dreams.

———

He woke up to the smell of cinnamon tea and a face with eyebrows like fuzzy caterpillars perched over calm blue eyes. It was a very familiar face.

"Hierem!" he exclaimed. He looked around. They were in a sort of parlor, decorated in odd alchemical devices and Ayleid curiosities. Attrebus was in an armchair. He tried to stand up but found he couldn't; his body seemed immensely heavy.

"What is this?" he demanded.

"Let's be honest," Hierem purred. "There's no love lost between you and I. We've never much liked each other, that is to say."

"Release me, now," Attrebus snapped. "When my father finds out—"

"But your father isn't going to find out," Hierem said.

"Not unless I choose to inform him."

"Do you plan to kill me, then?"

"Eventually," Hierem nodded, "when I'm certain I have no use for you—when this whole business is over." He smiled. "Really thought you were going to play the hero again, didn't you?"

Attrebus gritted his teeth. "What about Sul?"

"He's better, for the moment. His wounds have been doctored, but I've kept him asleep. He's far too dangerous otherwise, from what I can tell." He settled back into his chair. "Odd weapon he was carrying."

Attrebus felt a little thrill of hope. Did Hierem not know what Umbra was?

"Is it?" he asked.

"Yes. Lielle, one of the ones who brought you here, drew it and went mad. I had to kill her. Would you like to tell me why you have such a thing?"

"It's an heirloom of Sul's," Attrebus said. "He's trying to find the grave of his father or something so he can bury it there."

"I see," Hierem said. "It has nothing to do with Umbriel?"

"No," Attrebus said, desperate to deflect attention from the weapon. "But you do, don't you? You're in league with Vuhon."

"Vuhon?" Hierem chuckled. "He doesn't call himself that anymore, but then again he isn't exactly himself, is he? You met him, I believe. And escaped him, I gather, although not through any art of yours."

He lifted a small porcelain cup and sipped from it. "I thought you might eventually come here, so I convinced Umbriel— which is the name Vuhon does affect—to lend me some of his ground troops to sweep up anyone entering the city. No one is entering, you see—they're either staying put or leaving, which makes people like you rather easy to spot."

"But why?" Attrebus demanded.

"Well, because Umbriel wants you, very badly. Sul primarily, but you as well."

"So you're going to give us to him."

"You know," Hierem said, "I think you really ought to be called 'Attrebus the Clever.' That's how you should go down in history. 'Attrebus the Clever,' the prince who thought he was a hero. My idea, do you know that? Talked your father into it. 'The people need a young hero,' I told him." He laughed. "He may have thought I was right. He may have just been trying to placate me, but he went along with it. It worked, too. The people love you." He took another sip, then directed his gaze back at Attrebus.

"No, you idiot, I'm not giving you over to Umbriel—at least not right away. There weren't any taskers in the bunch who found you, so he doesn't know I have you. What I want to know is, why is he afraid of you? What do you have over him?"

"Nothing," Attrebus said. "He's not afraid of us—he and Sul have a lot of bad blood between them. I think he just wants to torture Sul to death."

"No," Hierem contradicted, "he's afraid of something. He took his city up to Morrowind, in completely the wrong direction. Umbriel has an irrational side, but that made no sense at all—unless he was looking for something. And what did he find there? You two. Imagine my surprise—you were supposed to be dead. Then you turn up alive in Water's Edge. But a few days later you're in Morrowind." He shook his head.

"These are things we need to discuss."

"You can forget that," Attrebus said.

"We haven't started yet, don't worry," Hierem replied. "That's all still to come. I just wanted to welcome you home."

"Why are you doing this?" Attrebus asked. "Do you want my father's throne? If Umbriel reaches the Imperial City, there won't be anyone to rule over! They'll all be dead."

"It's not going to be like that, actually," Hierem replied. "I'm going to save the city your father couldn't. You're going to die a traitor, a conspirator against the state—at least in the current version of my plan."

"And Vuhon—or Umbriel—will just go on his merry way? He can't—his city needs souls to keep flying."

Something quickened a bit in Hierem's eyes. "Yes, your published letters said as much. But how did you know that?"

"I—" He stopped. They didn't know about Annaïg. They couldn't. "Sul told me."

"Ah. And how did he know?"

"He worked with Vuhon before, in Morrowind. They used souls to keep a building aloft."

"The ingenium of the Ministry of Truth. I suppose that makes sense. Perhaps he's worried Sul knows how to wreck the ingenium in Umbriel."

"You don't trust him, then," Attrebus said. "Whatever deal you two made, you're worried he won't honor his terms."

"There is that," Hierem replied. "But on the other hand, I'm not so keen to honor mine either."

"How could my father have trusted such a despicable traitor?" Attrebus wondered aloud.

"To his credit, Titus has never trusted me. He's kept me around because he doesn't have a choice." Hierem smiled again. "Trust me; you are your father's son only in name. Titus may be an ill-mannered, badly bred Colovian upstart, but he at least has brains in his head."

He lifted the cup again, looked in it, and set it down.

"I don't want to wear you out," he said. "Umbriel—the city—is nearing arrival, and I have a lot to do, and preparations to make before our next conversation. Until then I've had quarters prepared for you. I hope you find them comfortable."

FOUR

"Mazgar!" a familiar voice shouted, and suddenly Goblin was there, leaping at her from the mass of refugees. If her instincts had kicked in, she would have probably killed the kid, but somehow they didn't, and the girl was clinging to her like a leech.

"Okay, okay," she said. "I missed you, too. No need to get crazy about it."

"What happened? Where have you been?"

"Brenn and I got cut off when we stormed out of Cheydinhal," she said. "It took us a while to catch up with the rest of you."

"Well, I'm glad you're alive," Goblin said. "I thought maybe you weren't." She looked around. "Where's Brenn?"

"He's taking a rest on the wagon, there," she said.

"How long have you been back with us?"

"Two days," Mazgar said.

"And you didn't come looking for me?"

"Captain Arges put us in charge of this bunch," she said. "I haven't had a chance to do much else but shepherd them."

"Well, I'm glad we ended up on the same side of the split,"

Goblin said.

"Right," Mazgar agreed.

It was clear that they weren't going to reach the Imperial City before Umbriel overtook them. Arges, the ranking officer, had decided their best bet was to split into two groups, one north and one south of the Blue Road, and hope the main army of wormies didn't come after both of them.

It had worked, at least so far; it seemed that Umbriel was trying to get to the Imperial City, and they just happened to be in the way. They were still harassed by groups like the one that had attacked Brennus and Mazgar, but no large groups had detached.

Mazgar wondered why they didn't just make a big circle and march back to Cheydinhal, and a lot of the refugees were starting to say the same thing, rather loudly. After all, the Knights of the Thorn hadn't found an occupying force in the city. Behind Umbriel seemed to be the safest place to be.

Arges, however, was focused on getting to the Imperial City, and without soldiers to protect them, most people weren't willing to chance running into hunting parties. Not yet anyway. She had a feeling that wouldn't last much longer.

They were walking on, with Goblin chattering away, when a rider came alongside them.

"Imperial troops up ahead," he shouted. "Stand by for orders."

"There we go," Mazgar said, rubbing Goblin's head. "Things are looking up."

———

"Who's in charge here?" the young commander shouted in

a strong Colovian accent.

"That's me, sir," Mazgar replied.

"Name?"

"Mazgar gra Yagash, Imperial scouts."

"Scouts? How did you end up here?"

She explained, and when she was done he nodded.

"I knew Falcus," he said. "He was a good man."

"Yes, sir."

"I'm Commander Prossos, and I'm in charge of this wing of refugees now," he said. "Given your experience, I'm giving you a field promotion to captain, and you'll act as my second in command."

"Thank you, sir."

"Our orders are to go north immediately. General Takar is going to meet the enemy a few miles west of here, and we don't want the civilians in the dust-up. Frankly, I'm not sure why you all were still anywhere near that thing's path."

"I just follow orders, sir."

He laughed. "I like that. You know Arges is an idiot, but you don't want to say so. Well, if you think I'm being an idiot, you'll speak up. In private, of course. And that's an order."

"Yes, sir."

"Okay. Take a party and make sure that hill south of here is free of the enemy. If it is, send us a messenger and wait. We'll be along."

"Yes, sir."

She'd heard of General Takar. He was from Hammerfell. He'd fought against the Empire, before Titus Mede won him over—supposedly through personal combat. It made a good story, but she doubted it somehow.

Whatever the truth was, Takar was now one of Mede's most trusted generals.

The hill wasn't occupied, so she sent a runner down with the news and settled in.

Takar had about five thousand men with him, mostly mounted infantry and mages. She could see them formed up in a huge field, along with some eight large wagons that might be siege engines of some sort.

"I wish I was down there," she told Brennus. "I'm deadly sick of running."

"Well, at least we'll get to watch," Brennus said.

———

Brennus was right. Less than an hour later the legion met its counterpart as the shadow of Umbriel moved toward them. For whatever reason, the wormies had constricted their range, marching more tightly beneath the flying mountain than they had in the countryside.

Mazgar heard the distant shock as the front lines met a few seconds after it actually happened, and for a while that was the last time she watched the ground battle—because the air war had begun. Half of the legion suddenly left the ground, along with the wagons, and flew toward the city.

"Oh, yeah!" Brennus whooped, so loudly it startled her almost as much as watching an army fly.

When they got near Umbriel, she saw something coming to meet them. She had seen them before; they looked like birds, at least from a distance. They would drop down and then appear to dissolve, turning into trails of smoke. Brennus told her that they were the spirits that took over the bodies of the newly dead, and lost corporeal form when they passed through the rim of the bubble of Oblivion the city traveled in.

But the Imperials were now apparently inside that bubble, and the bird-things were smashing into them in swarms. Lightning and flame seemed to fill the sky, and the soldiers with her cheered. But their cheers dropped away when it became clear that most—if not all—of the bodies dropping wore Imperial colors.

It was over in less than an hour; one of the wagons made it as far as the rim, but none of the others even got close, at least not that she saw.

Below, the wail of horns went up. Takar was in retreat, and Umbriel moved on, undeterred.

———

They continued to march the civilians out of harm's way that night and the following day, with no sign of the wormies, not even raiding parties anymore.

"Whoever is running things up there has tightened their focus on the Imperial City," Prossos said to Mazgar. "Command thinks the refugees will be okay with a skeleton guard. A lot of the civilians have been slipping off back to Cheydinhal, and we're letting them go. We can't feed them forever anyway." He stood a little taller. "I'm leaving you in charge, Captain. Take care of these people—use your own judgment."

"Where are you going, sir?"

"To reinforce the city," he said.

"I'd like to go with you, sir."

"I'm doing you a favor," he replied softly. "You've already seen a lot of action."

"No, sir, you aren't. If you order me to do this, I will, but my place is fighting, not nursemaiding. My mother went down in battle—what would she think of me if I didn't? Please, sir. There are others here who can get these sheep to pasture."

He studied her for a moment. "Very well," he said, and sighed.

Brennus cleared his throat and spoke up.

"She's under orders to watch out for me," he said. She turned—she hadn't known he was anywhere near.

"Is this true?" Prossos asked.

"Under Falcus, sure," she admitted. "Each of the mages had a bodyguard assigned."

"That came from the Imperial war office, directly," Brennus said. "It can't be countermanded in the field."

"That mission is over, Brenn," she said.

Prossos shook his head. "He's right. If what he says is true, you have to stay here with him."

"Not at all," Brennus said. "All it means is that I have to come along, too."

FIVE

―――――――

"It looks calm," Intendant Marall said.

"It does," Colin agreed. Viewed from atop the walls, the vast
waters of Lake Rumare were perfectly turquoise, the Heartlands
beyond verdant with field and forest. Only at the farthest edge
of sight was the vista blemished, and then because he knew that
what appeared to be a distant storm cloud wasn't.

"How long before it arrives?" he asked Marall.

"Two days," the Intendant replied.

"And then what?"

"The Emperor can't be convinced to evacuate, if that's even
possible now. General Takar made a preliminary strike—he
took a legion. The Synod managed to spell almost three thousand
of them airborne, but some sort of flying daedra killed them
all in short order. Other magicks were tried—I'm told over a
hundred—with no result. As if they knew in advance what we
were going to do and were prepared for it. So now we know a
lot about what doesn't work."

"Not much time left to find out what does," Colin said.

"Do you have any ideas?"

Colin hesitated, and Marall caught it.

"You've been missing a lot," the Intendant observed, "and distracted when you're around. I told you when you began this job that your job wasn't to think, but we both know the truth is more complicated than that. Sometimes I believe it's my job to not notice when one of my inspectors takes his own head. I don't know what you've been into, but if you know anything that will help us, tell me now. Or, if you think it best not to tell me—then you should act."

"Yes, sir," Colin said. "I'll think about that."

"Do so. And here is another thing that might interest you."

"What is that, sir?"

"I've a report from a source that is sometimes reliable that Prince Attrebus was seen at the waterfront."

"Since it's been overrun by the enemy?"

"Yes. My source did not see this himself. The story is that Attrebus was abducted, taken away with a bag on his head." He clasped his hands behind his back. "I know Vel took you off the Attrebus case. I just thought you might be interested."

"When did this supposedly happen, sir?"

"In the past few days. My source wasn't clear on it."

"Thank you, sir."

———

Attrebus paced, he tested the bars, the walls, the floor of the tiny cell. He tried to get Sul—unconscious in the cell across from him—to wake up. He wasn't sure how long he had been doing this.

Finally, exhausted, he sat on the floor and turned the situation over and over in his head.

When he heard footsteps, he lay on the floor and pretended to sleep, but kept his eyes cracked open a bit.

It was Hierem, who didn't even look in his direction. He walked across the room and into the next. Through the open door, Attrebus saw him stop. Then something flickered, like a spinning, full-length mirror, and he was gone.

Where? Obviously, magic was involved. He'd heard stories about teleportation, but never met anyone who had actually done or seen it. Or he didn't think he had. It might have been an illusion of some sort—but why would Hierem bother, if he was the only witness?

"Umbriel," he muttered.

Of course. Obviously Hierem and Vuhon/Umbriel were in contact. He'd assumed it was through some device like Coo, but what if they were simply meeting face-to-face this whole time?

He stood to get a better look; he could make out a red sigil on the floor.

He kept watching, but exhaustion caught up with him. He was on the verge of sleep when a movement caught his eye. Then he saw it was only a rat, sniffing about on the red spot. It cocked its tiny head up, then crouched low to the ground, as if frightened of something above.

Perhaps half an hour more passed, and Attrebus was again having trouble keeping his eyes open, when the light turned again, and Hierem stood there.

But now the rat had vanished. It hadn't scurried away or

been stepped on—he had been watching. It was just gone, as Hierem had been earlier.

He hoped the minister would just pass through, but he didn't—he stopped at Sul's cage and touched the bars, which glowed briefly. Then he stepped back and seemed to examine the unconscious man for a few moments.

Sul stirred and then screamed.

"Stop it!" Attrebus said.

Hierem turned and lifted an eyebrow.

"That's not my doing," Hierem said. "I'm just waking him up, now that I've had some time to secure things. I find it easier to question people in pairs, if you understand me. No, whatever that was about, it's in his head. But don't worry, I'll find some other reasons for him to scream."

"Hierem," Attrebus said, "listen to me. There's still time to change your mind. Whatever bargain you made with Umbriel—"

"If you're going to keep moving that mouth of yours," Hierem said, moving toward his cage, "it had best be to tell me something useful. I'll make it easy on you—I'll ask a specific question, and you tell me the answer. How's that?"

"I'm not telling you anything," Attrebus said.

"Really? Not even your name?"

"What do you mean? I'm Attrebus Mede."

"Good," Hierem said, making an odd gesture with his hand.

Attrebus felt as if something had touched him lightly in the forehead, and then his knees gave way as the most absolute pleasure he'd ever felt rushed through his body. He wept in ecstasy and moaned involuntarily, overcome.

Then it stopped, and he realized he was quivering on the floor, aching to feel again what he'd just felt.

"That's what you get for a right answer," Hierem said. "Do you want another sample of it?"

Yes! he thought, but he pressed his lips together and didn't reply.

But it happened again, this time longer. He tried to hold on to his anger and purpose, but it was useless, and he soon surrendered completely, hoping it would never end.

But it did, of course, and he wanted to die.

"Stop it," he heard someone croak. "His mind can't take much more of that. You'll destroy him."

It was Sul. The Dunmer was on his feet, leaning against his bars.

"We can discuss that, Sul," Hierem said.

"I remember you," Sul said. "You were an ambassador to Morrowind."

"Indeed I was. You have a good memory—let's put it to use. Why is Umbriel afraid of you?"

"Because I'm going to kill him," Sul replied.

"Yes, but you tried that already," Hierem said. "It didn't work out very well for you. And yet despite that fact, Umbriel is worried by you. Why is that?"

"You don't know him as well as you think you do," Sul said.

"No, I don't," Hierem replied. "And of course, that concerns me. Everything is aligning—the moment I've waited for for many years is coming near. I don't want any surprises, not from him."

"Life is full of surprises," Sul said.

Then he shrieked, and not at all in pleasure—it sounded

as though scalding water was being poured on him, except Attrebus couldn't imagine even that drawing such an agonized
response from Sul.

Hierem turned back to Attrebus. "That's what happens
when I don't get an answer, or get one that doesn't make
sense," he said.

Attrebus slammed into the bars, reaching with both arms
for the minister, but he was too far away.

"Let's keep it simple," Hierem said. "It's not just Sul he's
afraid of, is it?"

Attrebus stood there, panting. Hierem had already guessed
that, hadn't he? That wouldn't be telling him anything he didn't
know. And if he kept quiet, he would hurt Sul again.

"No," he murmured, and knew he had done the right thing,
as delight once more filled every pore in his body.

"Is it the sword, then? Does he fear the sword?"

Attrebus laughed with joy, but then the sensation was gone,
and Sul screamed.

"Yes!" he shouted. Happiness returned, briefly, but then
Hierem asked him something else, which he didn't understand.
He wanted—desperately—to have the feeling back, to please
Hierem in any way he could, to just have it keep going . . .

But he couldn't focus enough to understand the minister's
words. All he could think about was the memory of the feeling,
the devastating loss of it. He ground his face against the stone
floor, weeping.

It seemed that hours passed before he could form a thought,
maybe days. For the first time in his life he honestly wished he could
die. The world was a horrible, ugly place, and he wanted no part of it.

"Attrebus," Sul said. "Attrebus, listen to me."

He forced his eyes open but couldn't find the energy to sit up.

"What?" he muttered.

"You'll get over it. It doesn't feel like it, but you will."

"No. He'll come back. He'll get me to tell him the rest, and then he'll kill me."

"He won't," Sul said. "He won't come back because I told him."

"Ah, damn you!" Attrebus howled, climbing to his feet, yanking at the bars. "I'll kill you! That was the only thing, the only way he might—" He broke off in a paroxysm of fury, slamming arms and elbows against the walls, punching them until his knuckles were bloody.

"That was the only thing I had to look forward to!" he finally got out.

"I know," Sul nodded.

"Why did you tell him?"

"Because he would have kept asking you, and it would have destroyed you. As it is, you're still able to get angry. That's a good sign."

"But now Hierem— You told him about the sword? What it will do?"

"Yes."

Attrebus sank, trembling, back to the floor. "Then why are we still alive?"

"In case, I think," Sul replied.

"What do you mean?"

"If things don't go Hierem's way, he said he would give us the sword and send us up to Umbriel."

Attrebus wiped his tears with the bloody back of his hand.

"We might still have a chance?"

"We might. He just teleported somewhere, and he didn't take the sword with him. But you have to pull it together, do you hear? In case."

"I don't think I can," Attrebus said.

"I know you can," Sul replied. "I'm telling you that you can. So do it."

————

Colin returned, as he did each evening, to the room beneath the city. Letine had been gone for five days, and he was starting to believe she wasn't coming back, so when he saw someone waiting there, his hand went to his knife.

"It's me," she said.

He didn't know what to do. Should he rush over, hold her, kiss her?

"Are you okay?" he asked instead.

"I'm fine. It just took longer than I thought. The countryside was crawling with those things."

"Did you find anything out?"

"Nice to see you, too," she said.

"I—I was worried about you," he said. "I starting thinking—"

"It's okay," she said. "Come here."

————

"I didn't find out anything about the diagram," she told him later. "I'm sorry."

"It's probably nothing," he said. "Just a stupid distraction."

"What now?"

"I'm going back," he said. "Back to Hierem's quarters."

"Why?"

"I think he may have Attrebus captive," he said. "It's a long shot, but if he does—"

"That would certainly be enough for the Emperor to act on."

"I think I'm past needing to convince the Emperor of anything anymore," he said. "Umbriel's nearly here. I've got to do something."

"That's good," she said. "That's great."

"Okay," he said. "I've got a few things to get together. If I don't come back—"

"Then I'll know why. This time, I'm going with you."

"Letine—"

"If you're going to do more than sneak around, you'll need me, I promise you. No arguments."

He saw her resolve, and knew in that instant he wouldn't have it any other way.

"Okay," he said. "Are you ready?"

"I think I'll get dressed first," she demurred.

———

Attrebus never heard a sound, but suddenly they were there, gazing down at him, a man and a woman in dark clothing. The woman was a pretty blonde, the man rather nondescript, with brown hair and green eyes.

"Prince Attrebus?" the man whispered.

Attrebus just stared at him, wondering what Hierem was up to now. Had the minister changed his mind?

"Are you here to kill me?" he asked.

"No," the man answered. "Is Hierem here?"

"He's not," Sul answered. "But he could return at any moment."

"Right," the man said. "Listen—we work for the Emperor. We've come to get you out."

"There are more than locks here," Sul informed them.

"I can see that," the man replied. "Just give me a few moments of quiet."

The man studied Attrebus's cell. He closed his eyes, concentrating on something. Attrebus felt the hairs stand up on his neck. After a few moments the man seemed satisfied and touched the lock. It clicked, and the door swung open.

"Who are you?" Attrebus asked.

"I'm Colin Vineben," the man replied. "If you'll just come with me, highness—"

"Sul. Get Sul out."

Colin studied Sul's cell. "That will be harder," he said. "That will require time."

"Take it, then," Attrebus said.

"If Hierem returns—" the woman began.

"We think he's on Umbriel," Attrebus interrupted. "He steps on the sigil in the next room and vanishes. He returns in the same spot. If you wait in there you might be able to surprise him."

"That's a good idea," Colin said. "Letine?"

"I've got it," she replied, padding into the next room.

"Hierem must have really been worried about you," Colin

remarked almost half an hour later, as the last of the wards finally succumbed.

"Not worried enough, apparently," Sul said. "How did you know we were here?"

"I've been watching Hierem for a while," Colin said. "There was rumor that the prince had been seen abducted, and I thought it was worth looking here."

"Now what?" Letine asked.

"Now you get the prince back to his father," Colin said. "I'll stay here and deal with Hierem."

"He'll kill you, Colin," Letine asserted.

"I'll get him as soon as he appears."

"No," Attrebus croaked. He'd been sitting despondently outside of his cell, but now he stood up.

"Your highness—"

But Attrebus was talking to the Dunmer. "We can get up there, Sul," he said. "Up to Umbriel, just as Hierem did."

"He's got some sort of object with him," Sul replied. "I think it activates the portal. We'll have to get it from him."

"No, we won't," Attrebus said. "I think if we stand in the middle of the sign, we'll go up when he comes back. I saw a rat vanish once, when he appeared."

"Wait," Colin said. "Listen to me. If we return you to your father, he can send a hundred men through the portal—soldiers, battlemages—there's no point in you going, Prince."

"What if the portal only works for Hierem? What if he's the only one who knows the magic word, or whatever? We can't take that risk. Sul, we have to find the sword before Hierem returns."

"What sword? What's this about?" Colin demanded, but Sul was already out the door. Attrebus started after him.

"I'll explain if we have time," the prince said.

"What if he doesn't return?" Colin pressed, walking with him. "What if he just stays on Umbriel until this city falls?"

"I don't know," Attrebus said. "But I think he'll be back. You stay here in case it's sooner rather than later."

"I think he's right," Letine said after they were gone. "I think Hierem will be here when Umbriel reaches the city."

"Why?"

"Just a feeling in my gut," she replied. "The prince is determined—let him do whatever it is he wants to do—we'll wait here for Hierem."

"The prince is delusional," Colin whispered.

"You can't make him go."

"Sure I can. His father will thank me."

He heard them returning. Sul was carrying something wrapped up in cloth. It was the size and shape of a sword.

Sul and Attrebus moved to the sigil. Nothing happened when they stepped on it.

"Can you open it, Sul?" Attrebus asked.

The dark elf shook his head. "It's not an Oblivion gate or trace. It's beyond me."

"We'll wait, then."

"Highness," Colin said, hoping one more try would do the trick, "my charge is to get you to safety, not watch you jump into the midst of the enemy."

"I know what you probably think of me," Attrebus said, "To be honest, right now most of me just wants to go back to my villa and lay down on my bed, if only to die there. But I can't. I'll never be the man the books talk about. But I started something, and I'm going to finish it. I won't argue about this anymore, and as your prince I forbid you to bring it up again."

Colin drew a deep breath and nodded. "As you say, my prince."

———

Attrebus and Sul took positions on the sigil. The inspector—Vineben, the prince recalled—and the woman, Letine, stood behind it. Sul unwrapped Umbra and replaced his usual weapon with it.

"What's the plan?" Attrebus asked.

Sul's gaze seemed even more intense than usual as he turned it on Attrebus.

"If we're lucky, Hierem is meeting with Vuhon, and we'll appear right in front of him. If that happens, I'll stab him. If we're right about all of this, the sword should reclaim Vile's energies. That should allow me to kill Vuhon."

"And then what?"

Sul cocked his head, as if studying some strange creature speaking an even stranger language.

"Then he'll be dead." He said it quietly, like a note plucked softly on the tightest wire in the world.

"But what about Umbriel? Without Vile's power to run the ingenium, will it just fall out of the sky, or—"

"Vile said he would take it from there," Sul said shortly. "Remember?"

"Right, but—" Then he understood. "You don't care about anything but killing Vuhon."

"When did I ever say otherwise?" Sul snapped.

"Well—never. But I just thought—"

"Don't try to think for me," Sul said. "And don't act surprised. I kill Vuhon—anything else is up to you. You know what's going to happen when I draw Umbra—you remember Elhul. Best get away from me when that happens, find that girl or do whatever strikes your fancy."

"Then why do you want me along at all?"

"Because if Vuhon isn't there when we appear, we'll have to find him—and you're the one with the magic bird and the friends in high places. So I might still need you. And speaking of birds . . ."

"Right," Attrebus said, reaching into his bag.

SIX

He swam in black water, probing through the rotting leaves, lifting his eyes now and then above the surface to search the shallows and shore for movement. Larger things in the depths of the swamp couldn't reach him here, amidst the twisting cypress roots; here the danger usually came from land.

Something in the mud moved, and he snapped at it with webbed paws and lifted a feathery-gilled wriggler into view. He ate it happily and searched for more, but in a short time his belly was full and he felt like basking. He swam lazily back to the gathering hole.

The old ones had already claimed the choicest perches, so he crawled onto a log already crowded with his siblings and wriggled down among them until he felt the rough bark against his belly. When his brothers and sisters gave up their sleepy, halfhearted complaints at his added company, he felt the sun on his skin and began to dream his life; swimming, basking, killing, avoiding death, the sun and moons, all mystery, all terrifying, all beautiful. Each day the same day, each year the same year.

Until the root came, and the taste of sap. Some changes were slow, others came quickly, and he—they—flowed together, found the stream of time. His old body wasn't forgotten, but it changed, became more like things the root remembered from otherwhere; his hind legs lengthened and his spine stood up. Small thoughts in his head put out branches, and those branched also, until what had before been warmth, light, shadow, movement, fear, contentment, anger, and lust became categories instead of simple facts. The world was the same, but it seemed more, bigger, stranger than ever.

Death followed life and life death, but it all flowed through the root, each life different, each the same.

Until that, too, ended, and the root was ripped away, and he was alone. The gathering place was empty except for him—no elders, no siblings. He swam in black water, forgetting everything. Losing his form, melting away.

But in that dissolution, the illusion was also dissolved. He was many, and he was one. He sang, a plaintive tune, a remembrance, a prayer. All of his voices took it up, trembling it out through every branch and root, through heart and blood and bone.

I want to go home, he sang. *I want to go home.*

———

Glim woke gasping, spitting water from his mouth, remembering the ache closing in on his chest. He smelled his own terror, and remembered more—his heart stopping, the cold, nothingness.

. And Fhena. Then he understood that he wasn't just thinking of her—she was looking down at him anxiously.

"What?" he managed.

"You're talking!" she said.

"Where am I?"

"You're safe," Fhena said. "Just know you're safe."

"I don't understand," he grunted. His skin felt tight, itchy, and he was shivering. His mind was full of shifting images and half thoughts, as if he were back home, touching the root of the City Tree but stronger, stranger, freer.

"What happened to me?" he said. "I'm not the same. The trees—"

"You hear them now," she said. "Like I do." She touched him, and her face changed to an expression of purest wonder. "No," she said, "not like me. Better—more—it's like you're one of them, Glim."

"I'm not," he said. "I'm me. I'm me."

He fought back the thoughts invading his head.

"What happened?" he demanded. "I thought I died. I was sure I died." He felt at his side, then his face. "Where are my wounds?" There weren't even any scars.

"She did it to save you," Fhena told him. "To keep you safe."

"Did what?" Glim asked, starting to feel hysterical.

"I killed you," another familiar voice said. "I killed you."

The face was Annaïg's, but the words made no sense juxtaposed with it.

"She did it to save you," Fhena murmured, laying her hand on his shoulder.

"Neither of you is making any sense," he snarled.

"Be calm, Glim," Annaïg said in their private cant. "Just be still and let me explain."

———

Annaïg watched Glim's face as he listened to her, as she tried to explain to him that he was still Glim, still the friend she had grown up with, that she had rescued him, not murdered him.

But his face wasn't exactly the same. It looked younger, which made sense, but there was also a little something different about the shape of it; the same for his coloring, which had more rust in it now. If she had seen this body a few months ago, she would have thought it one of Glim's brothers, but she wouldn't have mistaken it for him.

But inside, he had to be the same. He had to. Sure, he seemed somehow more distracted than the old Glim, seemed to have a hard time focusing on what she was saying, but surely that was a side effect of the incubation process. To go from a worm to an adult with eighteen years' worth of memories in a few days had to be a shock.

But Glim didn't come to that conclusion.

"You're saying I'm not me anymore," he said, in as strange a tone as she had ever heard him use. "I'm a copy."

"No," Annaïg said. "You have the same soul, Glim. The poison I made caught it before Umbriel could take it away."

Glim scratched at his flesh. "But this isn't my body. It isn't even a Saxhleel body. It's grown from a proform. I'm not—" He jerked to his feet.

"This is all I've ever been to you, an experimental subject!

'Drink this, Glim, you'll turn invisible, this will let you fly, this will *kill* you and bring you back to life,' but not quite right, never quite right!"

Annaïg felt as if layers of cloth were wrapped around her, muffling everything, hiding what Glim ought to be able to see, trapping anything she could say that might help in dense warp and weft.

"I'm sorry, Glim, it's all I could think of," was the best she could do, and she saw now that it wasn't good enough, might never be good enough.

"Listen," she said, reaching to soothe his spines, "I know this is a lot right now. I know you may hate me. But I need to tell you a few things, about what I'm planning—"

"No," Glim said, jerking away from her touch. "I've had it with your plans, with doing things your way. I'm finished with it."

"Glim, listen," she said, but he turned and stamped from the room. She went after him, but his wet footprints led to the balcony and ended there. She stood looking down at the spreading ripples far below, while Fhena came and stood by her.

"Go back to the Fringe Gyre," she told Fhena. "I'm sure he'll find you there, if he doesn't get killed again immediately. Maybe you can talk some sense into him."

Fhena nodded and padded silently away, leaving Annaïg staring out at the wonder and madness that was Umbriel.

Her locket chimed.

She held it up and stared at it for a moment, then flipped it open.

Attrebus looked like he hadn't slept in a month.

"Hello," he said. "How are you?"

"As best as can be expected," she replied.

"Look," he said, "I may not have long. Sul and I think we've found a way to get up there. I'm not sure exactly when it will happen or where we'll be."

"What's going on?" she asked.

"Hierem, my father's minister—he's in league with Umbriel. We think he's been traveling up there and back using a magical portal. We're hoping when he comes down, we'll go back up."

The threads about her seemed to tighten.

"What can I do?"

"We're going to try to use the sword, as we discussed earlier," he said. "I'm not exactly sure what will happen then, even if we manage it. But I thought you should know, so you can be ready if—if any chance for escape comes."

"What about you?"

"When it's all over, Sul may be able to take us into Oblivion again."

To her ear, it almost sounded like he didn't care if he survived.

"Attrebus," she said, "I'm sorry if I seemed angry before—"

"It's okay. I think . . . I think maybe you had a right to be. I think we might have to talk about that someday."

"Right," she said. "Someday."

"I'm going to put Coo up now—I need to be ready to fight whenever this happens. I just wanted you to know what was going on. If I have a chance to contact you after we get there, I'll try."

"Do that," she said.

The locket went dark.

She took one last look at the vista beyond the balcony and then began striding purposefully toward her kitchen.

———

Hours passed, and Attrebus began to fear that perhaps Vineben was right, and Hierem had no intention of returning to the Imperial City. The wait did provide the time for a fuller exchange of information, but beyond that it was sheer torture. His mind kept trying to return to the feelings Hierem had violated him with, and he feared if he let that happen he would be useless in any confrontation, and so pressed for more conversation when he could.

"Arese?"

"Yes, Prince Attrebus?"

"You say you worked for my father."

She glanced at her companion, but he didn't give any sort of reaction. She pulled her shoulders back.

"I was at one time in his small circle, majesty."

"You have the brand?"

She nodded and reached to show him, but he shook his head.

"That's okay. I believe you." He took a deep breath. "So you knew, then? About me?"

"I'm not quite sure what you mean, Prince—"

"I'm sure you know exactly what I mean," he said.

She made a little grimace, and then acknowledged with a tilt of her head.

"Can you tell me why?" he asked.

"Your father—he's a brilliant general, a cunning emperor.

I've never known a man so strong. But when it came to you, he always had something of a weak spot."

"Weak spot? My father doesn't have a sentimental bone in his body."

"I don't mean that way," she said. "I mean he had no idea what to do with you. When Hierem suggested you be groomed as a sort of boy hero, I think he was relieved to have some sort of direction. It was a way to keep an eye on you and keep you entertained at the same time."

"Yes, when I was ten, I might see that," Attrebus said. "But when I was fifteen? Nineteen?"

"Sometimes when something like that gets started, it takes on a life of its own. No one saw how far it was going to go, how locked into the role you would be. It's been ten years since I could talk freely with the Emperor, but I'm sure he was hoping to draw you out of it gradually, marry you, settle you down, prepare you to rule."

Attrebus absorbed that, remembering Gulan saying something about marriage not long before . . .

"I got them all killed," he murmured. "And I should have known better. I should have seen it myself, but I didn't want to. And for that, everyone who rode with me—"

"Hierem did that, not you," Vineben cut in.

"He's right," Sul said tersely. "This is no time for this sort of thing." His voice softened a little. "Maybe you should do what he suggests—go to your father. If I can't kill Vuhon by myself . . ." He trailed off.

"Then me being there won't help?" Attrebus finished. "What about all of that about needing Coo?"

"I'll find him," Sul replied.

"I'm not the warrior you are," Attrebus admitted. "I've got

no arcane arts. But if I hadn't been with you in the cave, Elhul would have killed you."

"Maybe," Sul admitted.

"You need me."

Sul was taking a breath to say something else when Attrebus heard a thud loud enough to leave his ears ringing and his stomach threatening to rush up and out of his mouth. He swayed, trying not to lose his footing. It was dark, and someone was standing right in front of him.

"Vuhon!" Sul snarled.

The Dunmer's eyes arched in surprise and his mouth opened, but before he had a chance to say anything, Sul had already stabbed him with Umbra; the blade went in deep.

Vuhon vented an odd little gasp as Sul yanked the sword out and cut at his head, but the Dark Elf caught the blade with his hand, which burned with a steely blue light.

Attrebus swung Flashing at the joint of Vuhon's leg; the blade struck, but it felt as if he'd hit iron. Vuhon ignored him in favor of striking Sul with his other hand, sending the sorcerer staggering back.

Attrebus was making another cut when Vuhon's eye flicked to him, and suddenly he felt unbelievable cold spike through his body. He lost the timing of his attack, and Vuhon easily sidestepped the blow and caught him by the collar.

Then a bellowing Sul smashed into Vuhon, stabbing him again, and they all went out into space.

Animal terror passed through Attrebus as the world, the starry sky, and dark Umbriel spun nightmarishly around him. The fall seemed to go on much too long, but in reality he knew he'd only drawn one good breath for screaming before they struck a strangely yielding surface. Fire flashed and he was buffeted away as if by an enormous burning hand. He flailed to get up, but the surface he'd landed on shifted crazily.

Then he understood where he was—on top of the glass forest.

It was the best name he had for it; it was where Sul and he had arrived on their last visit here. Far below, a great web of flexible, glasslike cables anchored to various buildings along the rim formed a large web suspended over the valley and sump below. From the web, hundreds of smaller tubes grew skyward, branching, and those branches dividing until they at last became a virtual cloud of translucent twigs no bigger around than a little finger—and it was this upper layer they had fallen on.

He managed to get to his knees and heard Sul screaming. He'd heard Sul cry out in his sleep, but this was different; it was hysterical, insane in temper. It reminded him of Elhul.

Sul struck at Vuhon again, but glass coils sprouted up below the lord of Umbriel and raised him above the reach of the weapon. The crystalline forest suddenly pulsed with blue-white light, and Vuhon's eyes shone with the same radiance. Attrebus felt tendrils grip at his feet, pulling him down, and Sul as well.

"You dare to bring that here? You think I'm afraid of *that*?" Vuhon roared so loudly that the sound shocked against Attrebus's face.

Sul's only answer was an incoherent screech and a slash at the tubules supporting Vuhon. They shattered, much to Attrebus's surprise.

It appeared to surprise Vuhon, too, as those supporting him collapsed in shards. Attrebus felt a strange hum—it seemed, almost, to be in his teeth—and then most of the cables suddenly darkened. Only those that plucked Vuhon away from Sul's next attack—and those that held Sul—still shone with unabated light.

Vuhon shouted something, and a darkness smote Sul, sending him tumbling back and Umbra flying from his hands. More of the tubules went dark or shone with a sickly violet color.

Attrebus, now completely free, struggled toward Vuhon, who seemed drained by his attack on Sul.

He got within five unsteady strides before Vuhon seemed to notice him. Attrebus swung hard at his neck, nothing fancy. The sword struck, and this time bit a little. Not much, but it cut the artery. Vuhon slapped his hand over the sudden spurt of blood.

Then a glowing cable caught Attrebus by the ankle and another wrapped around his neck. He slashed as best he could at it, but in an instant his sword arm was immobilized as well. The cables passed him away from Vuhon, then began drawing him slowly down into them.

Sul was back up. Attrebus saw him glance at Umbra, which lay between him and Vuhon, then back at him. Even from ten yards away, Attrebus could see his companion shaking as if with palsy.

"What have you done to me?" Vuhon exploded. "Tell me, or he dies immediately."

Sul took another step toward the sword.

"I cut him, Sul," Attrebus yelled. "He's weaker. Something's wrong with him—"

The cable tightened on his neck and he couldn't breathe.

Sul took another step. More of the cables pulsed darkly, and Vuhon began backing away. Attrebus saw the fear on his face, because Vuhon knew what he himself knew—that nothing would stop Sul now.

Then the cables pulled him down and he couldn't see anything. All he had to concentrate on was how much he wanted to

breathe, and how he couldn't, would never again. He strained
every fiber of his being against the coils that held him, but they
still glowed brightly. Above, broken into rainbows by hundreds
of strange prisms, he saw what must be Vuhon's radiant perch.

Kill him, Sul, he thought as his muscles began to finally loosen.

But then everything around him seemed to shatter and Sul
was there. They were falling again.

This time they hit water, but if it had killed him, he would
never have known it wasn't stone.

When Mere-Glim reached the weak end of the bough, he
stopped and stared down. He saw the moons both above and
below, and for a moment he didn't care to wonder why or
how—it just made sense. Then he reluctantly sorted out that
they were over water, a vast body of water. The sea?

But no, ahead he saw a great tower in the moonlight, and
the vast circle of a city, and he knew—from all of Annaïg's
ramblings—it could only be one place.

"What is it?" Fhena asked from behind him.

"The Imperial City," he replied.

"It's huge."

"Yes," he replied. But he was having a hard time concentrating on the city.

Because the trees were loud now—as strong in his mind as
the Hist had ever been, except they weren't telling him what to
do; they were singing, a deep and melancholy song.

"Can you hear that?" he asked. "The trees?"

"Yes," she said.

"Have they always sounded like this?"

"Yes and no. Their song changed a few days ago."

"A few days ago? Before or after I died?"

"After, I think."

"I dreamed this," he said. "When I was—before waking, just now."

"You weren't waking," she said. "You were being born."

"Annaïg brought me back," he murmured. "But the trees . . ." He examined his limbs again, which looked and did not look like those he remembered, and he realized his heart was beating more softly.

"She loves you," Fhena said. "She thought she was doing what was best for you."

Glim knelt and then lay against the bark, closing his eyes, feeling it all turning under him.

"It's okay," he said. "I didn't realize before. I shouldn't have been angry."

Fhena sat down on her heels. "What is it, Glim?"

"They shaped me," he murmured. "Like the Hist. They shaped me to do something."

"What?"

He started to tell her, but then felt it, like a sickness in his bones.

"No," he gasped. "Oh, Annaïg, no!"

"What is it?"

"I've got to go," he said. "I've got to stop her."

"I'm coming with you, then."

"It's dangerous," he said. "It's no place for you."

"I know where my place is," she said quietly. "And you need to realize it."

Her gaze caught him and turned something inside of him.

"Okay," he said. "Follow me."

SEVEN

Hierem appeared and Colin struck from behind, cupping his left palm to the minister's forehead and thrusting his knife toward the base of his skull.

"No!" Hierem shouted. He sounded exactly like the man on the bridge, before Colin had stabbed him.

Colin flinched. He dropped the knife and shifted his grip to a choke hold.

"What are you doing?" Letine yelled, lifting her own dagger.

"No, don't kill him," Colin said. "We still don't know what he was up to. We need to—"

"You don't understand," Letine said, stepping up to deliver the blow.

It never landed. The blade hit something an inch from Hierem's throat and exploded in a blinding flash of light. Letine shrieked and fell back. Colin tried to tighten his grip, but suddenly Hierem was as slippery as an oiled snake, slithering free of his grasp as if from a child.

"You really don't understand," Hierem said.

Colin dropped and got his knife, but as soon as he touched it, he again remembered the man he'd murdered, and all those corpses by the road, like broken dolls. He took a deep, shuddering breath, but he knew it was pointless. It didn't matter what happened here today. It didn't matter what happened anywhere, ever, because in the end there was nothing. He looked at the knife and felt a sob heave up from his chest. Then he slumped down to the floor.

"I can't imagine what you think you're up to, Arese," Hierem said, stepping toward the woman. Her eyes looked blind, unfocused.

"Colin?" she shouted.

"He's not much use to you, I'm afraid," Hierem said. "He's a bit glum right now."

A sharp report rang from the walls in the room, and suddenly something appeared, something shaped a bit like a man but covered in black scales, with three scythelike fingers on each hand. It hopped, birdlike, toward Hierem, and Colin noticed it had sickles on its feet, too—one on each foot.

Hierem jabbed his fist at it, and although he didn't hit it, the thing went flying back into the wall. It bounced up and came back at the mage.

"He's done something to you, Colin," Letine shouted. "Overcome it!"

That was probably true, Colin thought, but it didn't matter. There was no redemption. His hands were never going to be clean.

The daedra attacked again, but this time Hierem failed to deflect it completely; it skittered by, and one of its foreclaws caught the minister across the chest. His robe ripped with an oddly metallic sound, and Colin saw he had on some sort of mail beneath. That had torn, as well, and the mage started to bleed.

Snarling, Hierem turned, struck the daedra with his hand, and it collapsed. It wasn't dead, but didn't seem to be able to move, as if it suddenly weighed a few extra tons.

"Colin!" Letine shouted as something like lightning jagged from her hand and struck Hierem. It shivered about the minister and then seemed to reverse itself, knocking Letine to the floor.

All Colin could hear now was Hierem's harsh breathing. The minister examined his wound and shrugged.

"So much for assassins," he muttered. "I should ask why and who sent you, but it doesn't matter, or won't soon enough. What concerns me more is where the prince and his companion have got off too."

"Oblivion take you, and your plans," Letine gasped, trying to rise.

"Ah!" he sighed. "Arese! I am so disappointed in you—or should I say proud of you? You found out what I was up to, didn't you? I thought someone had been in my things."

"It's the tower," she said, pushing herself away from him with her hands, trying to get her legs to work. "It's the key. I didn't get it until Colin remembered one of the symbols meant 'echo.' The White-Gold Tower is an echo of the ur-tower, the first object of our reality the gods created. It's one of the axes of creation."

Hierem smiled. "Umbriel thinks it can emancipate him from Clavicus Vile, make him free of the prince forever. Possibly it would if I gave him the chance. But I see you know I've found another use for it."

He reached into a pocket and produced a cylinder about an inch in diameter and six inches long. He gave it a little shake and it telescoped out to about three feet. It seemed to be a dull reddish black with glowing, scarlet daedric script all over it.

Some things matter, Colin told himself. They matter.

Hierem pointed the tube at Letine. Colin felt the moment slow down, understanding that when it was over the woman he'd kissed, touched, made love to, was going to be dead.

He got the knife, raised it to throw.

Hierem must have seen, because he swung the weapon toward him. Colin's knife went over the minister's shoulder and spanged into the wall.

"You've got more spirit than I imagined," Hierem said.

Colin tried to keep his face neutral, but he knew the sorcerer must have seen something in his eyes, because he started to turn as the daedra came on him from behind. Hierem screamed then, as the great curved claws butchered him, but he didn't scream for long.

Feeling a little lighter, Colin slowly came to his feet as the daedra savaged the minister's body and then vanished. He walked toward Letine, who was coming unsteadily to her feet. He caught her by the shoulder and helped her stand.

"Thanks," she said. She was shaking.

"What was he talking about?" Colin asked. "I thought you didn't find out anything about the—"

The knife slipping in under his ribs cut him off. Letine stepped back, leaving him to stare at the hilt protruding from his torso.

"What?" he asked, dropping to his knees.

Her eyes were wide, her mouth formed an O, and she looked stricken. She reached for the hilt of the knife, as if she thought she could somehow undo what she had done.

"Colin . . ." she said. Then her expression grew harder.

"I'm sorry, Colin," she said. "Ten years. *Ten years!*" Fury strained her voice to the breaking point. "I'm owed something. Hierem owes me. And I'm going to collect." She picked up the rod Hierem had dropped and went through his clothing. Colin didn't see if she took anything. He kept looking at the knife in him.

She paused at the doorway—he couldn't tell if she was trying to decide whether to finish him off or wanted to tell him something.

She did neither—she simply left.

He realized he was having a hard time breathing. She had probably hit his lung.

———

Annaïg watched as the poison began to flow from the tree-wine, knowing there was no going back at this point. Whether it worked or not, Umbriel was going to know, and probably sooner than later.

Which meant it was time to leave the kitchens. She picked up her bag and threw it across her shoulders, hoping she hadn't left anything she needed, but not willing to stop and think about it. She wondered if Attrebus and Sul were on Umbriel yet, but that, too, would wait until she was someplace else.

She wished she knew where Glim had gone.

She was almost to the pantry when she heard the commotion, and when she entered the corridor, she saw Glim in the pantry shaking workers off and trying to reach the corridor, where Yeum and six cooks were lined up, fully armed.

"Xhuth," she muttered. She fumbled in her bag until she found a glass vial and tossed it to shatter on the floor, just behind Yeum. The chef turned, but the yellow cloud had already engulfed her and the rest. As they collapsed, unconscious, Annaïg held her breath and jumped over them.

"Glim," she said, "what in the world are you doing?"

"You have to stop it, Annaïg," he said. He sounded urgent, but there wasn't any anger in his voice. "Stop poisoning the trees."

"Glim—there is no stopping it. It's done. I'm sorry, I know how you feel—"

"You don't know anything," he said. "They just want to go home."

"This isn't making any sense to me," she said. "This is it, Glim. We're out of time. All we can do now is try to escape."

"But—"

"We have to get out of here now! If you have something to tell me, tell me while we're leaving."

She got onto the lift that brought things to and from the Fringe Gyre and activated it, and they began to rise.

"The trees," Glim said. "I understand them now. They changed me so I could help them."

"Help them do what?"

"Go home."

"And where is that?" she demanded.

"I don't know—somewhere else. Not Tamriel. Isn't that what we want?"

"What I want is for all of this to die, Glim."

"I can feel it, too," Fhena said. "Don't you understand? If it kills the trees, it will kill all of us—including Glim."

The lift reached the top.

"We'd better hide," Annaïg said. "They'll be after us soon."

"Aren't you listening?"

But Annaïg's head was whirling. It was too much, wasn't it? Could she really be expected to listen to all of this, put up with it?

"Just—one thing at a time," she said.

Her locket was begging for attention.

———

In the gray, unnatural mist, Mazgar bent to her oars, feeling the longboat glide through the water. She felt Brenn huddled close behind her, crowded there by the five other soldiers stuffed into the small craft. As unnatural as the concealing mist was the silence. The lack of chatter and even of breathing left her feeling unsettled. Even the water of the great lake bore their passage without so much as a single lap of oar in water.

But that could work both ways. When the arrows started falling, she didn't hear them either, or the screams of those they hit. Her first clue was when a man in the boat ahead of her clutched at a shaft in the side of his neck; only then did she notice the cloud of fletched death swooping down on them.

Fortunately, Ram and Dextra were ahead of her, hefting their shields to catch most of the darts coming their way.

But while all eyes were turned up, Mazgar felt something seize her oar. She jerked at it, and then the boat heaved up on one side.

The wormies were in the water.

Ahead, the mist was suddenly incandescent with bursts of orange and azure.

So much for surprise, she thought.

The boat started to flip, so she jumped clear into the water. To fight the panic being submerged always brought on, she concentrated instead on finding the bottom with her feet, as all around her the upper bodies of wormies appeared, water draining from the cavities in their faces and chests.

She set her footing in the muddy bottom and boxed away the nearest before drawing her close-work dagger. Ram, Dextra, Martin, and a Redguard whose name she didn't know formed a diamond formation around Brennus and started pushing toward shore. She went for their hands first; grab with her left, sever at the wrist with her knife, cut the side of the neck, move on. She was slower in the water, but so—thank Mauloch—were they.

She saw Ram had one on his back and cut its arm off at the elbow, ruining its grip, but then another hail of arrows dropped into the water and Ram went down anyway, screaming soundlessly and gripping at a shaft in his sternum.

Mazgar felt a pleasant shock, and then the wormies fell away from them, moving off to other targets. She was relieved—because that meant Brenn was alive—but turned to confirm it anyway. He nodded at her.

By the time they reached the shore, the survivors of the first two waves of boats had formed a double line, one to face the enemy coming from the sea, the other looking landward. Sound came back—battle cries, screams of pain, terse orders passed up and down the lines. She found Prossos and he put her in the front line, which suited her fine. She drew Sister, which was more suited to this sort of work.

And work it was going to be.

She had started the day with five hundred soldiers. Their job was to cross Lake Rumare from the north, there to join with a massive push toward the northwest side of the city. That's where the enemy was massed most deeply, and lately had begun actively trying to break through the gate that led to the Imperial prison. It was also where Umbriel would arrive, if it continued on the course it was presently following.

Now she stood with something between two and three hundred comrades. They looked to be lined up against three times that.

Still, they gained ground steadily. The land was pretty flat here, and the archers who had plagued them earlier either seemed to have been dealt with or more likely couldn't make decent shots with ranks so close. As they pushed forward, their line formed a wedge, to prevent the wormies from outflanking them with their numbers and rolling them up. After that, they settled into a bloody pace. Someone off to her left starting bellowing "General Slaughter's Comely Daughter" a little off-key, and a few heartbeats later the whole cohort was shouting the response, and it started to feel like a party.

A blond man to her right dropped with a leaf-shaped spear pushed all the way through him. She felt a tap on her shoulder and nodded, dragging the wounded man back as an orc half again her size filled the gap.

In the empty center of the phalanx, she yelled for a healer, but it was clear Blondie wasn't going to make it.

He knew it, too.

"It's okay," he managed. "Just be quick."

She nodded and closed his eyes. Then she took off his head with a single blow, followed by both hands and feet. Sometimes they came back, even without heads.

She took her ten-minute rest and had a long drink of water while watching the huge bulk of Umbriel draw ever nearer.

Brennus fell in with her.

"I know that's hard," he said. "I'm sorry you had to do it."

"Orders are orders," she said. "Especially when they make sense."

"I know," he said. "That doesn't make it easy."

"How long before it gets to the walls, you think?" she asked, jabbing her tusks toward the flying city.

"Hours," he said, "unless the Emperor has some tricks to try still."

"I heard from that rat-face, Solein, that they made two more tries to invade by air."

"We're not supposed to spread it around, but yes, both just as unsuccessful as that first one. But the wall might be a different matter; the Synod and the College of Whispers will give it all they've got, you can be sure of that. And they've had a long while to prepare defenses."

Mazgar handed him the skin. "I'll let them worry about that," she said. "I've got my own job to think about."

She clapped him on the shoulder and went back to take her place on the line.

EIGHT

"Attrebus."

He opened his eyes at the sound of the voice and found Sul's crimson gaze only inches away.

He felt stone beneath his back and was soaking wet. Behind Sul he saw a rough, faintly luminescent wall.

"Where are we?" he asked.

"We fell in the lake in the center of Umbriel," Sul replied. "This is some sort of cave above the waterline."

Attrebus remembered then.

"Did you do it? Did you kill him?"

"No," he said. "Do you think you can walk?"

"What happened?" He pushed, shaking water from his ear. "You had him."

Sul didn't answer, but instead stood and reached an arm down. Attrebus took it and let him half pull him to his feet.

"You know more about this place than I do," Sul said. "Where do you think we are?"

Attrebus felt his face flush as he finally understood.

"You came after me instead," he said. "You saved my life."

"I failed," Sul said. "After all this time—" He broke off. "You were right—something is wrong with him, and it's no doing of ours. The sword didn't hurt him much, if at all. It certainly didn't reclaim anything of Vile's."

"Annaïg's poison, then," Attrebus guessed. "That must be it."

"It seems likely, and that means Vuhon will be trying to stop her, to reverse whatever she's done."

He turned, and Attrebus saw Umbra was sheathed again.

"Wait," he said. "How were you able to put it away?"

"I almost wasn't," Sul admitted. "Next time—"

"There's no reason for a 'next time,' " Attrebus argued. "If it doesn't work, why take the risk?"

"I have a feeling about it," Sul said. "Leave it at that and talk to the girl—we're wasting time."

Attrebus nodded, pulled Coo out, and flipped open the little door. A moment later Annaïg's face appeared.

"Attrebus," she said. "Where are you?"

"We fought Vuhon. The sword didn't work, but something's wrong with him."

"I may have distracted him," she replied.

"Your venom is working?"

"It's doing something. Where are you?"

"We fell in the lake in the middle of this place, and now we're in some sort of cavern just above the waterline."

"You're in the skraw caves, then."

"If you say so."

"Stay where you are," she said. "Keep Coo open."

She closed the locket and then turned to Glim.

"The sword didn't work," she said. "Our only hope is my poison. When the trees start to die, we may get a chance to escape. Fhena can come with us."

"It doesn't have to be this way," Glim insisted.

She closed her eyes, tired of his persistence. "I need you to go down to the skraw caves and bring Attrebus up here," she said.

Glim's pupils dilated wide and his fighting musk filled the air. She inched back a little.

"No," he said.

"They deserve a chance, too. You need to hurry."

"I said no," the Argonian said, in a quiet but firm voice. "Not unless you save the trees."

"I've told you, that isn't possible. Most of the poison is in now—"

"If you know how to make the poison, you know how to make the antidote," he said.

She stared at him for a moment, then reached into her pocket and produced a long, stoppered tube.

"This is the antidote," she said. "This is for *us,* when we're affected, if we are. It's not nearly enough to counteract what I've pumped into the roots."

"They're already fighting it," he said. "If they taste that, they'll know what to do—they can produce enough antitoxin to save themselves."

"And the lords, and Umbriel," Annaïg said. "Then the Imperial City is destroyed, and we don't escape."

"No," Glim replied, his voice measured. "I'll help the trees go home and take the city with them."

"You really believe you can do that?" Annaïg asked.

"Yes."

She rubbed her forehead. "Go get Attrebus and Sul. Then I'll give you this."

"I could take it from you," Glim said very softly.

"I'll throw it, if you try."

"It may be too late by the time I find Attrebus. Give it to me now, and I promise I'll do as you ask."

"Glim—"

"No, it's me."

"Right," she said. "Weren't you just threatening to use force on me?"

"I'm sorry," he said. "If you could feel them, like I do . . . Nn, our whole lives, it's always been you, your desires, your needs. And despite my protestations, I've been happy to be at your side. But this time you have to stand with me. You have to trust me."

She closed her eyes, trying to remember what he was talking about, to a time when everything hadn't been about suspicion and betrayal and heartsickness, but nothing came, nothing—until, finally, an image. The face of a five-year-old girl with long, curling black hair, and that of a young Saxhleel about the same age, reflecting up from water twenty feet below. She saw their feet, too, perched on the crumbling wall of an ancient, sunken structure.

"Let's jump," the girl said.

"That's too far down," the boy replied.

"Ah, come on. Let's do it together."

"Well . . . fine," he grumbled.

And they jumped.

———

Annaïg opened her eyes, and Glim suddenly remembered her

when she was a little girl, how full of everything her eyes seemed to have been in those days.

She didn't say anything. She just handed him the bottle.

"Thanks," he said. He turned to Fhena. "Take her to the hiding place. I'll be back."

"I've heard that before," Fhena said.

Glim slipped the antidote into his belt-pouch and bounded down the trunk, feeling the sickness invade it deeper. He wondered how to do it—if he could simply empty the contents where the roots would find it, or use one of the nutrient injectors the fringe workers used. In their pain, the trees had become unfocused, distilled to need and demand, and it was all he could do to keep his mind singular enough to be Glim, and not just a part of the hurt and panic. But Annaïg trusted him, and he had to be worthy of that trust now. He would find the prince and his companion, and hopefully by then he would figure it out.

The sump felt sick and oily, and he nearly retched when he pulled in his first breath. He surprised a school of bladefish, but they hardly reacted, and instead continued along, unsteadily, as if they had lost half of their senses.

He found shattered crystal tubes in the shallows and followed them to their greatest concentration, and then began searching the caves. He discovered them in the third one he tried. The Dunmer saw him first, reaching for his sword before Glim was even out of the water. Then the Imperial turned.

"Wait," he said. "That's an Argonian. Mere-Glim?"

"Yes, Prince," he replied, making a little bow.

"Do you know these people?" the prince asked.

Glim noticed a number of skraws on the other side of the

cavern. Several of them were armed. As Glim approached, Wert pushed through.

"I know them," Glim replied.

"Who are they, Glim?" Wert asked. He looked tired, more jaundiced than usual.

"You can leave them alone. What's wrong?"

"I don't know," Wert replied. "Hiner and Skrahan dropped dead. The rest of us—it's like everything is getting sick, all at once."

He coughed, and for a moment Glim thought he would fall.

"What should we do?"

Glim took several deep breaths, looking at the skraws. His skraws, and in an instant he felt not just the trees anymore, but all of it, everyone, and he knew what to do.

He took out the antidote, removed the stopper, and drank it all.

———

Annaïg paced back and forth in the wooden cavity, wishing she had something to do, something to cook with. One minute she'd been in control of everything, and suddenly she didn't know what was happening anymore.

"Glim can do what he says," Fhena said. "I believe him."

"Of course you do," Annaïg said. "And maybe he can. But maybe—have you thought of this?—maybe he's gone crazy."

"No. I can feel it. The trees made him different, and now somehow they've changed, too. As if they got something from him as well. They have a purpose for him. Anyway—you gave him the antidote. You must believe."

"No," she said. "That's not why I gave it to him."

"I don't understand. I—"

Fhena was interrupted by an odd coughing sound. Annaïg saw the other woman's eyes dart past her and turned.

Umbriel stood there. "It had to be you," he said. "As soon as I felt your venom, I knew your scent on it."

"Lord Umbriel . . ."

"The trees are fighting hard," Umbriel said. "They've shunted the poison through the ingenium, poisoning the rest of the city while they try to synthesize an antidote. It will cycle back around to them in time, but by then most of the damage will be done. I don't know if you meant it to work that way, but it was brilliant; it's attacking the head first—which means me. I had to absorb Rhel and three other lords just to keep going on in this body, to find the venom's mother."

"So much for Rhel's illusion of immortality."

"His illusion was that he was any less a part of me than everything here. It's an illusion you share. The poison will kill you, too."

"If that's what it takes to stop you, I'm willing," she replied.

"I see. And yet you have an antidote."

"I don't," Annaïg said.

"I'm weak," Umbriel said, his voice beginning to change. "I'm not deaf."

"I don't have it. I gave it to someone else."

"Possibly," Umbriel replied, moving toward her. "But you still have it, right there behind your eyes."

"Stay back," Annaïg said. "Keep away from me."

"We're almost there," Umbriel snarled, revealing sharp, yellowed teeth. "All we have to do is reach the White-Gold Tower, and we're free of him forever."

"I don't care," Annaïg said.

He lunged at her, and she whipped out the invisible blade, slicing three of his fingers off.

He barked a harsh sort of laugh and made a fist. He didn't hit her, but something did, hurling her against the wall and knocking the wind out of her.

He held up his hand, and the fingers grew back. His spine seemed to straighten; the lines of his face filled in.

"What's this?" he murmured. "Incredible. They did it." He looked down at her, his lips curling up in a malicious grin. "It was a nice try," he said.

"Get away from her," someone else said.

At first the voice didn't sound right to Annaïg—it was too full, somehow, too large. But then she recognized Attrebus striding toward Umbriel, sword in hand. Glim and an ancient-looking Dunmer came with him.

"No," she shouted as Umbriel's words sorted themselves into sense and she understood. "Attrebus—the sump. The sword didn't work because his soul isn't in him—there wasn't anything to reclaim. Glim! His soul is in the ingenium—"

But then Umbriel's eyes stabbed green fire at her, and every muscle in her body went rigid with pain.

———

Sul snarled in agony, and something erupted into existence between them and Vuhon, something with huge bat wings and claws, but in the shape of a woman.

Then Sul turned and ran back toward the way out, grabbing Mere-Glim by the arm.

"Wait!" Attrebus said.

"You heard her!" Sul shouted.

Sul's monster and Vuhon slammed together. Attrebus could see a dark elf woman dragging the fallen Annaïg away from the confrontation. He stood there, paralyzed. He'd come here to rescue her, hadn't he? She was so near . . .

But if he died here, rescuing her, what of the Imperial City? His father? His people?

He knew then, in that moment, that he was ready to die trying to save Annaïg—but didn't have that luxury.

So he turned and ran after Sul.

He emerged from the trunk of the tree and saw the old man and Glim bounding down a branch. It took him a few seconds to catch up, but the three of them hadn't gone another thirty steps before they saw figures boiling up the tree toward them. Some seemed human or elven—others were stranger. There were a lot of them.

Glim hesitated only an instant before changing direction, climbing from branch to branch with dexterity that was difficult to match.

"Don't we want to go down?" Attrebus asked him as he clambered over one rough bough and reached for another.

"Everything takes you down eventually," the reptile replied. "This is just the long way."

Their exertions eventually brought them to another huge trunk, and as they scrambled up on it, despite everything, Attrebus was struck momentarily still by wonder.

They were at the top of the fringe, with the whole mad forest sweeping down and away from them, a massive bent fan.

And below that, the Imperial City from high above—as he had never seen it, and indeed he saw only part of it now, because Umbriel's shadow must already be over the wall. Before them loomed the White-Gold Tower. Whatever Umbriel hoped to do, he was about to do it.

"We're out of time," Attrebus said. He turned to the Argonian. "You said you could use the trees to take Umbriel out of Tamriel."

Mere-Glim nodded tersely.

"Do it now."

"You'll be trapped here," the reptile-man said.

"If that's the way it is, then so be it," Attrebus replied.

Mere-Glim nodded, and after a slight pause, knelt and put his face against the bark.

———

Glim could feel the poison dissipating; the trees could hear him again. He felt his self soften and flow around the edges as everything that was Umbriel opened itself to him. He heard the call of return, and with an easy bending of his mind gave it greater voice.

Or tried to, but then a spear of pain seemed to drive through him, an absolute command that he acquiesce and fling himself, to break on the lower boughs before falling and vanishing from this world and every other. He rose and took the first step before pushing back against the command, and for an instant he thought he could beat it, push through.

But it was ancient, and the trees bent to it from long habit.

Annaïg had been right to doubt him. He'd been so sure, it hadn't occurred to him that the Umbriel could countermand him.

Now all he could do was escape with his life.

———

For a moment it looked as if Mere-Glim would jump into the open air, then he stopped, the stippled lids uncovering his eyes.

"I can't," he said.

"We're wasting time, then," Sul said.

The three of them sprinted up the bough to where its roots grappled with the stone of the rim, and after a short climb, stood on the edge, in a gap between two strange, delicate buildings of glass and wire. A long cable went from the base of one all the way across the valley; several small buildings hung suspended from it, like lanterns at a festival. From the first of those a second cable ran down to the water's edge.

"There," Sul said, gesturing at the cable. "That's the quickest way. It would take forever to climb down there."

"I'll have to go with you," Glim said. "You won't make it to the bottom of the sump without me."

The cable was five feet in diameter, but the footing was still pretty tricky. They were a few yards short of the hanging building when Sul shouted and pointed. Vuhon and several other figures were flying toward them.

Sul ran three long steps and jumped; Glim went after him

with only an instant's hesitation. Attrebus followed, wondering how many times he was going to have to fall into the damned thing.

———

Glim smiled as he fell, remembering a long-ago day when Annaïg had dared him to jump with her into the ruins of an old villa. He hit the water feetfirst and let his body relax—become the air, the water, the very shock that tried to slap the soul from his skin. He plunged deep, pulling a train of bubbles behind him that trailed to the broken mirror of the surface above.

As their descent slowed, he caught Attrebus and Sul by their wrists and kicked fiercely down, toward the little star he'd always been told to avoid. Now he felt it, the pulsing heart and mind of Umbriel, the core that was the true lord of souls. All other light diminished until at last they reached it.

———

Attrebus felt the pressure against his lungs mount and knew they would never make it back to the surface. He watched the light grow as Mere-Glim pulled them down.

When they reached it, he realized that Sul was unconscious, so he did the only thing he could—he drew Umbra from the sheath on the Dunmer's back and stabbed it into the light. Even as he did so, he felt a rush of absolute rage. He became the blade, the edge, as Umbra drank him utterly in. He was steel and something more than steel, infinitely worse than steel. The thing waving it around and screaming was no longer Attrebus, and soon he wouldn't be either.

The light seemed to explode about them, but he didn't care anymore. Everyone and everything was to blame. The pleasure in Hierem's cell, the lack of it after, the little pains of moving through any day, anywhere were too much to bear anymore. But he knew he couldn't die yet—only when everything else was dead would he know any peace.

The light cleared, and he was lying on the floor, shuddering. Umbra lay a few feet away, as did Sul and the Argonian.

They had fallen into a vast nest of polished stone and shining crystal. The air was filled with delicate tones and fleeting incomprehensible whispers, as if motes of dust were excited to speech when light struck them. In the center of the great cavity a translucent pylon rose and met the gently rippling water above and kissed it with light pulsing up from a platform ten feet below, where a thousand glowing strands tied themselves into a coruscating sphere.

Sul was sitting up groggily; Glim was staring up at the water suspended over their heads.

And through the water, Vuhon came, lightning crackling from his eyes.

Sul leapt up to meet him. Blue flame erupted from his open palms and engulfed Vuhon, clinging to him like burning oil. Vuhon staggered back a step, then made a peculiar shaking motion and the fire vanished, replaced by gray smoke. Glim leapt forward, claws raking at Vuhon's chest. The Dunmer replied with a vicious backhand blow that sent the reptile hurling to the floor. Then he did something that stopped Sul mid-stride;

Attrebus didn't see anything but could feel a crackling on his skin, and the air smelled like hot iron.

Sul strained to take another step, then collapsed.

"So much for your pointless revenge," Vuhon muttered.

Attrebus looked toward where Umbra lay, trying to drive the terror from his mind, to do what he had to do.

"Stop!" Vuhon shouted.

Attrebus screamed in despair as he dove for the sword. He picked it up, and as he was drawn into it again, into anguish and horror that would never end, he aimed himself down, at the sphere. Vuhon came after him, quick as lightning.

Almost quick enough.

Then Umbra struck into the heart of Umbriel, and everything was changed.

NINE

When Attrebus plunged Umbra into the ingenium, Sul heard the Universe scream. The tortured cry rang from every surface, from the air itself, from Vuhon's gaping mouth. A tongue of white blaze licked out from the ingenium and struck his old enemy, and his body twisted, deformed, grew blacker, hunched, feral.

"Umbra," Sul said.

"Umbriel," the creature snarled, slumping toward him. The flame had thinned, but remained, like a tether. "Why?"

"This has nothing to do with you. It was about Vuhon."

"I can cleanse myself of him. I can make you powerful, more powerful than we were. We can still escape Vile."

"No," Sul replied. "I'm done with this."

"You are not," the thing snapped, leaping forward. Sul felt fingers as hard as steel close on his windpipe. He struck into Umbriel's throat, but the creature only squeezed harder.

But then Umbra vented one last howl, and the grip softened. The flame snaked back away from his body and into the ingenium as the body went limp.

Sul pushed it off him, coughing, sucking air into his lungs.

Below, Attrebus was starting to glow and was beginning to distort. Sul glanced at his enemy, which looked like Vuhon again. His chest was still rising and falling. Sul's hand went to his knife, but he didn't draw it. Instead he jumped down to join Attrebus.

"It's working," Attrebus said. But it wasn't his voice, and the eyes staring out at Sul were the strange eyes of Clavicus Vile.

"Let him go," Sul snapped. "You're destroying him."

"He made the sacrifice," Vile said. "You, I think, knew what the price would be."

"It wasn't supposed to be him."

"Well, things don't always work out as we plan," the daedra said. "In coming here, I lifted the restraints around this place. A deal is a deal—you're free to go."

Sul balled his fist and swung, but Attrebus—or the thing wearing him—was fast. It whipped Umbra out of the ingenium and stabbed him, just under the sternum. It knocked all the wind out of him, and his legs and arms went loose, so he just hung on the blade.

Sul turned into himself then, searching for the fury that had driven him for forty years, remembering Ilzheven, the ruins of Morrowind, years of torture and hardship.

He felt his heart stop, and opened his eyes, staring at his killer, at Attrebus. It was then that he found what he needed, and it wasn't anger, or hatred.

As if in a dream, he reached out and grabbed the hilt of Umbra and pulled himself up the blade, and with everything left in him he struck Attrebus in the jaw.

Attrebus fell back, releasing the weapon. Sul saw his gaze return to puzzled normalcy.

"It's okay," he told the boy. Then he took one step, fell against the glowing orb, and let go of everything. Light filled him, and coarse, mocking laughter—but then he was gone.

———

For Attrebus, it was like waking from one nightmare into another. Sul slumped against the sphere, and he and the sword seemed to melt together into a dark smoke with a heart of lightning.

"Sul!"

"You can't help him now," a weary voice said.

He looked up and saw Vuhon gazing down at him. With a cry of fury, Attrebus clambered up the wall of cable and wire and stood over him.

"I can kill you, though," Attrebus said. He reached for Flashing.

"You might," Vuhon said. "And you might not. It would be a wasted effort. Vile will have me now no matter what. I can fight him—I had power before I met Umbra, and that he can't take back—but I won't last long. But maybe long enough."

"Long enough for what?"

"For your friend there to save something of Umbriel," Vuhon replied.

"I don't understand."

"Clavicus Vile will have the city now. Is that really what you want? He'll probably just drain it and let it fall on the Imperial City, but knowing him, he may just play in your world for a while." He nodded at Mere-Glim, who was standing up, wiping blood from his nose.

"The Argonian is a part of this place now. He has the power

to remove it from this plane."

"That's what he said. He tried it and it didn't work."

"Because I became aware of him and stopped him. After all, I have been master of this place for decades." He looked at Mere-Glim. "Do you feel it now?"

The Argonian nodded.

"Go, then," Vuhon said. "The membrane will allow you to pass from this side as well."

Then he turned to face the cloud, which was now twenty feet high and beginning to take on something like a human shape again. His face, so like Sul's, was set in an expression of quiet determination.

"He's right," Glim said. "But we have to hurry."

———

Annaïg felt Umbriel shudder beneath her, and then she was suddenly falling. It lasted only an instant, but it was a terrifying one.

"What's happening?" Fhena asked.

"I don't know," she replied. "Maybe they made it to the ingenium."

"You mean maybe they've destroyed it? What does that mean?"

"Well, if the ingenium stops working, I imagine we'll fall," Annaïg said.

"But then we'll die."

Annaïg reached into her pocket and produced a small vial.

"There is a chance," she said to Fhena. "If you drink this, you should be able to fly. We might dissolve into smoke, but it's worth a try."

"But what about Glim? And your other friends?"

"We'll wait as long as we can," Annaïg said.

"But what about everyone else?" Fhena demanded.

"I don't care about everyone else," she replied. "Come on; let's get above, so we can see what's going on."

They climbed up to where they could see Tamriel spread before them. She could see a lake, but the Imperial City wasn't visible, so it must be beneath them.

Umbriel shuddered again.

They sat and waited, while Fhena wept.

———

Umbriel was trembling constantly by the time Attrebus and Mere-Glim reached the hiding place. They found the women outside, clinging to branches. Fhena rushed to Glim, sobbing, as a deeper convulsion quaked the tree. Attrebus found himself staring at Annaïg, wondering what he was supposed to do. He felt as if he was watching everything through Coo now—the fight, Sul's death, this meeting—all seen from a great distance. He didn't seem to feel anything at all about any of it.

But Annaïg strode purposefully across the shivering branch.

"Drink this," she said. "At least we'll have a chance."

He took the vial numbly, glad he didn't have to respond to anything more—emotional.

———

When Annaïg reached Glim, he threw his arms around her and enveloped her in his familiar musk. Something burst in her then, and tears trickled on her cheeks as he stroked the back of her head.

"I'm so sorry, Glim," she said. "About all of it."

"It's fine," he said. "You know I love you."

"Still?"

"Always." He held her for a few more heartbeats and then pushed her gently back. "Vile lifted his striction. You'll be able to leave this time."

Annaïg felt her heart pause.

"You mean we," she corrected.

He shook his head. "I'm taking the trees home," he said. "I'm going with them."

"You can't," she said. "What will I . . ." She broke off and put her forehead against his scaly chest.

"What will *I*," she repeated. "*I*. But this is about you, isn't it?"

"Finally, after all of these years, yes," he replied. "I have people who need me. I have a place that wants me."

"I understand," she said. "I don't like it, but I understand."

"I'm glad," he replied. "It makes it easier. Now, go. I have to do it now."

She wiped her eyes and glanced over at Fhena.

"Take care of him," she said. Then she drank the contents of her vial and turned to Attrebus.

"Let's go," she said.

"What do I do?" he asked.

She lifted her arm toward him and spread her fingers.

"Just hold my hand," she said.

———

Colin thought of Anvil, where he had been born, of the docks

and the autumn evenings, when the sun painted the sky red
and gold and the waves seemed to murmur in a melancholy
but somehow contented way.

He remembered the fingers of a five-year-old boy, fiddling
with a little boat made of reeds. He'd put a lot of care into it,
because he knew it had a long journey to make. He glanced
down at the stream that wound through the willows toward
the sea, but he knew the boat wasn't ready yet, so he brushed
the cracks with pine resin.

He remembered his grandmother placing those same little
hands on the altar of the great chapel of Dibella.

"The gods are good," she told him. "They came from an
infinite place, but for us they limited themselves and became this
world. They are everything we see and touch, everything we feel.
And of them all, Dibella is most kind." And she smiled so beau-
tifully that he wondered if it was really his grandmother at all.

He woke on stairs, sticky with blood, laboring to breathe.
He wasn't sure how long he'd been unconscious; he hoped not
long, because he didn't have that much time left.

Doggedly, he dragged himself to his feet, leaned against the
wall, and put one foot in front of the other. He felt oddly stronger,
as if the prayer to Dibella had actually been answered in some
small way, although he'd never had that talent.

But he knew soon enough he was either going to bleed to
death or drown in his own blood.

Letine must have known or guessed where the stairs
were—they hadn't been on his map. He doubted it was a coincidence that the steps began at a hidden door in Hierem's chambers; the minister must have been thinking about this moment

for a long time. Colin guessed the secret stairway was hidden just below the much broader, higher staircase that led up from the Emperor's quarters to the summit of the White-Gold Tower.

He moved slower now, but knew he couldn't stop again.

He heard her before he saw her, or in fact saw any light at all. She was talking to herself, but he couldn't make out the words. Presently he encountered a flat surface, and after a little searching found the catch that opened it.

He'd expected to be on the summit of the tower, but instead saw a large, low-ceilinged room. Signs and sigils were painted all over the floor, familiar to him from the diagram he'd seen in Hierem's chambers. Fires of strange colors flickered on some, while arcane objects of various size were on others. Letine stood in the center of the room, what was probably the very axis of the tower. Beyond her, a long, broad window showed him a little sky but mostly a vast rocky surface that resembled a mountain—except it was moving, steadily growing in size.

"Come here," she was saying.

"You mean to steal its power," Colin said, on his knees on the floor.

Letine spun to face him, surprise evident on her face.

"I don't believe it," she said. "I knew I should have . . ." She started to walk toward him, but seemed to think better of it.

"Should have finished me off," he replied.

She shrugged. "I'm usually more efficient. I think I must have let my emotions cloud my judgment this time."

"So you *do* love me," Colin said with a rueful chuckle.

She took him seriously. "I might have," she said, "under other conditions. But I know you would have tried to stop me."

"Hierem tricked Umbriel, didn't he? He planned to use all of this to siphon off the souls the city collects. And you used me to get it."

"I didn't know exactly what he was up to," she said. "Not until a few days ago. Hierem imagined it would make him a god. I don't know about that. But I do know I'll have enough power to never be afraid again, to take what I want from this life, this world." She looked out the window.

"It's almost here, Colin. Once it happens, there is no need for you to die. I can fix your body."

"Maybe," he said, crawling forward on his hands and knees. "But the things I need fixed, you can't do a thing about."

"Don't come any closer," she warned.

"If you're not right in the middle, it won't work, will it?" he asked. "What if this isn't right here?" He reached to move a crystal sphere with silvery wire wound about it.

Her eyes rolled back as she started to summon something.

He yanked the knife from his chest; blood from his wound gouted onto the floor. He sat back on his heels, cocked his arm, and threw.

Letine looked up at the ceiling and took a step back. He thought he'd missed, at first, but then she toppled back and he saw the hilt of the dagger standing from her eye.

He sat there, watching her for a moment. The air crackled, and rainbow colors flickered about the construct she lay in. He heard what might have been voices, calling from far away.

Outside, the rock face was so near he could almost touch it—then it seemed to turn sideways, before it vanished, leaving behind a boom like a thousand thunders at once.

"Attrebus," he murmured. "Good for you."

He managed to get to the window. It was solid, thick as stone, but transparent. He wondered idly if it was transparent from the other side as well, or if it appeared as stone.

He looked out across the city and Lake Rumare, to the green valley beyond, and watched it as his eyes dimmed.

He felt the breeze on his face, heard it sigh through the willows. He put his little boat in the stream and watched it carried away, and wondered where it would go, wishing he could be with it, share its adventures. He dipped his hands in the stream and took a breath that went on and on, filling him, at last, with peace.

———

They met up with what was left of the Twelfth Legion a few hours from sundown and pushed the wormies into the wall. They cleared the gate and set up positions to defend it from another siege.

Mazgar and Brennus found themselves on the western flank of the action, where little or no fighting was going on.

Umbriel was closer than Mazgar had ever seen it, blocking most of the sky, casting a shadow east that she couldn't see the end of, the strange light of its soul-stealing filaments dominating her field of view. What would it feel like when she was beneath it? If she grabbed one of the things, would it pull her up? Had that been tried?

She heard a commotion off to the west, and Brennus swore. She started to ask what the matter was but then saw.

Wormies—thousands of them—were swarming from the west, pushing what remained of the cavalry before them. That wasn't enough for the gods, apparently—more were pouring from the lake and from the east, as if every single one of them had been called to this one place on the wall.

"Why?" she grunted as they hastily tightened ranks.

"This is where Umbriel is crossing over," Brennus said.

"So? There's no gate here to breach."

"Not yet," Brennus said.

Mazgar growled, raised Blondie's shield, and locked it with her companions on the left and right.

The wormies came at a dead-on run, in nothing resembling ranks. They reminded Mazgar of ants, converging on a bit of offal.

The first shock slid them back two yards, leaving a pile of the enemy like a low wall before them. But that didn't deter the foe in the slightest; they scrambled up over each other and tried to run over the line, using the soldiers' heads and shoulders as stepping-stones. They needed spearmen, but those were mostly at the gate, where the main assault had been until moments ago.

Mazgar roared her battle cry and sent Sister chopping over her shield. Maggots and putrefaction spattered on her face; she could taste them on her tongue, and like a tide coming in, more and more of them rolled out of the water.

"The wall," she heard Brennus gasp.

She had a second a moment later to spare a glance to see what he meant. Their left flank had collapsed, but instead of rolling up the line, the wormies were throwing themselves on the wall, building ladders with their bodies. Above, the sky was bright with eruptions and incandescences, making a strange semblance of daylight that revealed the rotting faces leering at her, making colored jewels of their filmed eyes.

Another wave of wormies hit, and they were pushed back almost to the wall itself, and more of them were ignoring her completely now as they tried to join their comrades in their insane climb.

The man on her right fell, and as four wormies poured into the gap, she felt a bright and terrible pain in her side. Howling, she swung her shield and decapitated one as she slung it off, then took Sister two-handed to slay other wormies.

Above, Umbriel passed over the wall, undeterred.

Brennus cried out and fell against her from behind. With a grunt she swept one arm back, found him, and retreated until his spine was against the wall. A semicircle of blue flame arced out around them, and she braced for the wormies to come through, but they didn't. More likely they were just going around.

It was over.

Brennus lay against the stone, heaving ragged breaths. She saw his wound, and felt her heart go cold.

"It's bad, isn't it?" he asked.

"I've seen worse," she replied.

"Right," he coughed. "But I'll bet this is good enough."

"Brenn—"

"I know," he said. "I know what you have to do."

"Don't worry," she said. "I'll be right behind you."

"It's been an honor," he said. "I may have said some things . . ."

"You were right," she said.

The look of surprise on his face almost made her laugh. "About what?"

"Children. I would have liked to have done that."

"I hope you know it wasn't a proposition," he replied weakly.

"Yeah," she said. The fire was starting to die. "I've gotta do it now."

He nodded.

She raised Sister, fixed her gaze on Brenn's throat.

Then the sky seemed to crack, and her ears popped before a wind from above slapped her to her knees.

Ears ringing, she fought back to her feet. Something had changed. She looked out over the ebbing flames and didn't see any motion. Wormies were everywhere, piled against the wall as if blown there. But not a damn one of them was even so much as twitching.

She lowered her sword.

"What do you think happened?" she asked Brennus.

He didn't answer, and when she realized he wasn't ever going to, she slid down next to him and wept, unashamed, until the sun came up.

EPILOGUE

Attrebus tapped his fingers on the sill of a high, narrow window in time to the jubilant music drifting up from below. The streets were filled with color and life, the air with delicious scents of roasted meat, fried fish, and pastry. In the wake of the vacance of Umbriel, his father had thrown open the storehouses, flooding the city with food and wine. Across town the arena hosted spectacle after spectacle, and tonight everything would culminate in the Emperor's appearance and the presentation of the heroes.

"There you are, Attrebus," a strong voice behind him said.

"Hello, Father," he said, turning. The elder Mede hadn't yet changed into his formal costume, but wore a simple robe over shirt and breeches. He seemed distracted by something, a bit unsure of himself, and that, to Attrebus, was a very strange thing.

"I apologize for not seeing you alone earlier," his father said.

"You're the Emperor, father," Attrebus said. "I know you have many burdens."

"That's true. But . . . I am a father, also. I forget that sometimes."

Attrebus nodded, uncertain how to answer. His father looked away, then took four quick strides and, to his astonishment, took him in his arms and wrapped him in a bear hug.

"I thought you were dead," he said. "I was sure of it. And my entire fault, for encouraging—allowing—the situation to develop as it did. I never meant you any harm, son. Quite the contrary."

"I know that, Father," Attrebus assured him.

"And look at you now," the Emperor said, stepping back. "A man. A hero."

"I'm not a hero," Attrebus said. "Whatever all of this has taught me, it's that I'm not that. Sul was a hero, and Annaïg, and Mere-Glim, and the countless soldiers who died outside of these walls. I was frightened, I made mistakes, at times I wasn't even sure what I was doing or why I was doing it."

"And yet you did it anyway," his father said. "What in the world do you think a hero is if not someone who does just that?"

"I'm not the man in the songs."

Titus Mede rolled his eyes. "Of course you aren't. Neither am I. We're both better than those guys."

"You were the real thing," Attrebus said.

"In a way, perhaps. But you saved the Imperial City, perhaps all of Tamriel."

"You really believe me, then? About what happened?"

"You were never the dishonest one, Attrebus," his father said. "The lies never came from you. It has always been in your character to tell the truth. And in this case, the story is really too fantastical to have been made up. Besides, there were witnesses to the flight of you and the girl from the city. Never fear, tonight you will be given your due. The people will know their prince was their salvation."

"But I thought—"

"I've had time to think," the Emperor said. "I've changed my mind. The Synod and the College of Whispers may wish to claim credit for this victory, but I will not let them, not at your expense. Our people will know the truth."

"They shouldn't," Attrebus said.

His father gave him a curious look. "What do you mean?" he asked.

"I've never been very interested in politics, Father, but I've been catching up these past few days. With Hierem dead, you have a dangerous situation on your hands. You need the support of the council, and to have that you must have the support of the Synod and the College of Whispers. Besides which, those two groups have been at each other's throats for years—here, they are claiming to have worked together. Perhaps it can be a start to their reconciliation."

"Are you saying I *should* give them credit?"

"Yes," Attrebus said. "Gods know I've gotten the credit for so many things I shouldn't have—I can stand to relinquish what little I may be due here, if it's what's best for the Empire."

His father stared at him for a moment, and Attrebus swore he saw a bit of moisture film his eyes.

"You really have returned a man," the Emperor said. "More than that—a prince."

"Maybe not yet," Attrebus said. "But it's time I started trying to fill that role the way it should be—don't you agree?"

"Very much," his father replied.

————

Annaïg twitched the reins of her dappled gray mare and enjoyed the play of light and shadow in the forest around her. Attrebus rode a few feet away. It was strange to be with him, to see him, and to be silent; when they had known each other through Coo and the magic locket, every moment of contact had been filled with words.

The silence went on a bit longer, but inevitably Attrebus broke it.

"How are you feeling now?" he asked.

"I hardly know," she replied. "It's all very strange, isn't it? To be so afraid."

"Afraid?" he said, sounding puzzled. "I—well, I'm hurt. I grieve for Sul. But I don't think I'm afraid."

"You are. You're afraid of talking to me, as I am to you. Strange, isn't it, after all that time we strove to keep each other's company, to have a single word between us. And now . . ." She shrugged.

He stroked the mane of his horse. "Things happened to me," he said. "Things I don't want to talk about. I thought at first I was broken in a way that could never heal, that the best thing I could do was die. That's how I felt when we finally met. I didn't have anything to say to you because I didn't have anything to say to anyone. And I know you had experiences that—"

"Yes," she said, cutting him off.

"And now . . ." he began, but did not finish.

She felt a sort of heaviness in her heart.

"Now what?" she said.

"I've begun to see that one day I will feel human again. I may never be the same, but I will have something to offer—ah, to someone—if they could be patient with me."

"Someone?"

He nodded. "You, of course," he said softly. "I've never

learned anyone the way I learned you. I'm not sure what I thought love was before. I'm not sure I can define what I think it is now. But I cannot imagine life without you. I want to know you better and better as the years go by. I just need—patience."

She felt a little smile trying to lift the corners of her mouth, and perhaps it did, a very little.

"I'm not a patient girl by nature," she said. "I tend to rush into things or fall off of them. But if you can be patient with me, I can be patient with you."

And so they fell silent again, and let the music of the forest entertain them.

———

Far away, another man and woman listened to a deeper, stranger music and watched the luminescent films they had named wisperills do their slow, colorful aerial dances, as if welcoming them. The trees hummed and murmured, not as before, but with the strength of the millions that spread out and away in the strange land, whose great boughs supported the island when it could no longer fly and helped settle it deep in boggy ground.

Fhena leaned back against Glim and exhaled deeply. "This is a nice place," she said. "I like it."

"So do I," he said. "What I've seen of it."

"What do you mean by that?"

"Only that I don't know where we are. At first I imagined that we would be returned to Clavicus Vile's realm, but although I've never been there, I don't think this can be that place."

"Of course not," she said. "This is where the *trees* are from, not Umbriel."

"But where is it?"

"Home," she said softly.

"Well," he said. "Now."

"Always."

He smiled, and surrendered for a moment to contentment—after all, it surrounded him. Everyone wasn't content, of course. Down below, with the lords gone, the chefs and others who considered themselves elevated were doing their best to kill each other. But the skraws and fringe workers were free, and many of them had already left the city to find their livings in the lush world around them.

"What do you think that is?" he asked, pointing to a sort of spire near the horizon.

"I don't know," Fhena said. "A rock? An old building? What about it?"

"Tomorrow I think I'll walk over and find out," he said.

"Fine," she replied. "But tomorrow." And she nestled deeper in his arms, and they watched the wisperills dance.

About the Author

Born in Meridian, Mississippi, in 1963, Greg Keyes spent his early years roaming the forests of his native state and the red rock cliffs of the Navajo Indian reservation in Arizona. He earned his B.A. in anthropology from Mississippi State University and a master's degree from the University of Georgia, where he did course work for a Ph.D. He lives in Savannah, Georgia, where, in addition to full-time writing, he practices ethnic cooking—particularly Central American, Szechuan, Malaysian, and Turkish cuisines—and Kapucha Toli, a Choctaw game involving heavy sticks and no rules. While researching the Age of Unreason series, he took up fencing, and now competes nationally. Greg is the author of *The Waterborn, The Blackgod,* the *Babylon 5* Psi Corps trilogy, the Age of Unreason tetrology (for which he won the prestigious Le Grand Prix de l'Imaginaire award), and three *New York Times* best-selling *Star Wars* novels in the New Jedi Order series.

About the Type

This book was set in Granjon, a modern recutting of a typeface produced under the direction of George W. Jones, who based Granjon's design upon the letter forms of Claude Garamond (1480–1561). The name was given to the typeface as a tribute to the typographic designer Robert Granjon.

For more fantastic fiction from Titan Books check out our website: **www.titanbooks.com** where you'll find details of all our exciting titles, including:

BioShock: Rapture by John Shirley

Crysis: Legion by Peter Watts

Dead Space: Martyr by B. K. Evenson

Deus Ex: Icarus Effect by James Swallow

Dragon Age: The Stolen Throne by David Gaider
Dragon Age: The Calling by David Gaider
Dragon Age: Asunder by David Gaider (Dec 2011)

God of War by Matthew Stover and Robert E. Vardeman

Homefront: The Voice of Freedom by John Milius
and Raymond Benson

The Infernal City: An Elder Scrolls Novel by Greg Keyes

RuneScape: Betrayal at Falador by T.S. Church
RuneScape: Return to Canifis by T.S. Church

Star Wars: The Force Unleashed by Sean Williams
Star Wars: The Force Unleashed II by Sean Williams

Star Wars: The Old Republic: Fatal Alliance by Sean Williams
Star Wars: The Old Republic: Deceived by Paul S. Kemp
Star Wars: The Old Republic: Revan by Drew Karpyshyn

Uncharted: The Fourth Labyrinth by Christopher Golden

WWW.TITANBOOKS.COM

The Elder Scrolls® V

SKYRIM™

"AN INCREDIBLE GAME - BEAUTIFUL AND VAST"
- CVG